the girl in the painting

max monroe

The Girl in the Painting
Published by Max Monroe LLC © 2019, Max Monroe

ISBN-13: 9781797721323

This is a work of fiction. Names, characters, places, brands, media, and incidents are either the product of the author's imagination or are used fictitiously. The author acknowledges the trademarked status and trademark owners of various products referenced in this work of fiction, which have been used without permission. The publication/use of these trademarks is not authorized, associated with, or sponsored by the trademark owners.

Editing by Silently Correcting Your Grammar
Formatting by Champagne Book Design
Cover Design by Peter Alderweireld

dedication

To those who "can't even": Guess what? You totally can.

To Carl, the dog Monroe met at the airport: You are the goodest boy. We hope you've conquered your fear of escalators.

To Love: You are, well…sometimes, you're a bit of a bitch. Sorry, but it's true…
Brad Pitt and Jennifer Aniston ring any bells?
How you could *ever* let them break up *still* boggles our minds.
And don't even get us started on Channing Tatum and Jenna Dewan…like, *seriously?*
What were you *thinking?*
But, despite all of that, we can't deny you're pretty damn amazing.
You do, in fact, make the world go round.
So, thank you for being so prevalent in our lives.
And thank you for being the foundation of this book.

author's note

The Girl in the Painting is a full-length stand-alone novel.
At the end, we've included an excerpt from **The Day I Stopped Falling for Jerks**, one of our best-selling romantic comedy and sports romance novels.
The Girl in the Painting concludes at around 90%.
Prior to beginning your reading adventure, please prepare yourself to read a story that is unlike anything you've read before.
Prepare to fall in love with love all over again.
And get ready to fall in love with this story.
Fast. Hard. Deep. *Insane* kind of love.

Happy Reading!
All our love,
Max & Monroe

soundtrack

"Do you think the universe fights for souls to be together? Some things are too strange and strong to be coincidences."
—Unknown

Blue Madonna—Børns
Dust it Off—The Dø
What Is And What Should Never Be—Led Zeppelin
Tip of My Tongue—The Civil Wars
Comptine d'un autre été: L'après-midi—Yann Tiersen
Four Seasons—Vivaldi
Sail Away—David Gray
Unsteady—X Ambassadors
Real Love—Tom Odell
Brindo—Devendra Banhart
Sweet Love—Ghinzu

intro

Ansel Bray, an artist known around the world for his tragic hiatus from the canvas.
Ansel Bray, a broody, handsome man not known by me, at all.
Long dark hair, blue eyes, and dimpled cheeks. I've never met her, but her image is imprinted in my mind. An angel muse who inspires me to paint again.

There is something about him. Something that spurs a need to be as close to him as possible. A need to find out why.
There is something about her. Something that draws me in. Something that urges me to find out what her presence means.

Why does the girl in his painting look so much like me?
Who is this girl, and why can I see her so vividly?

I shouldn't fall in love with him.
I shouldn't fall in love at all.

But fate plays her hand.
But fate has other plans.

The lines of my life will blur.
The needs of my heart will change.

What a beautiful mess we've made.

chapter one

Ansel

I watch the way the brush swipes across the canvas, and it's like my mind is directing my hand without me as my fingers move in soft, fluid strokes.

Slowly and with precision, I add blues and purples and etch grayish hues into the color palette. Instinctively, my hand moves to the right spot, building a new picture that's locked inside my mind, a visual that's only released through brushstrokes and paint and silent poetry. It is a reflection of my own mind, the way I think and feel and see the world around me.

This, painting—*creating*—is my home.

My passion and my life.

I look away from my work and move my eyes around my studio, taking in the order and chaos, the blank canvases, the finished paintings, anything and everything I can swallow up hungrily.

God, it doesn't get any better than this...

This is *living*.

But when I move my gaze back to the canvas, the brush disappears from my hands, and the colors of the painting fade away in a pixelated breeze.

A gasping breath escapes my lungs and encourages my heart to follow its lead. It races inside my chest and vibrates its erratic rhythm against my rib cage.

It was just a dream, Ansel.

I blink my eyes open and, instead of the light of day filtering in through my pupils, darkness replaces everything.

Fuck.

Waking up is harsh when your dreams are better than reality.

Sometimes, my dreams are so vivid I find myself forgetting my sight is gone. I'll open my eyes and expect to see my bedroom, expect to see the sun peeking in through the windows, expect to find crumpled blankets over my body and the paintings on my walls.

And then I *remember.*

I remember the physical pain and the actual trauma of the accident, but mostly, I remember the moment I woke up to the heightened sounds of a dark abyss. The moment I knew my future would be bleak and empty.

Every single fucking day, I wake up and choke on the grief of it all.

I'm blind. And I have to come to terms with the fact that I'm a painter who can't paint. An artist who can't create. A man who can't even see his own fucking dick hanging between his legs.

It's been nearly a year since I lost my sight, and a part of me wonders if, eventually, even my dreams will change to the unsatisfyingly bottomless pit of monochrome shadows.

It would be both a blessing and a nightmare.

Because it's the dreams that keep me going.

Yet, it's also the dreams that tear me apart.

Each foray into the unattainable makes the process of mourning start all over again. Truly, you don't know what you're missing until it's gone.

It's a tortured process, but eventually, my grief becomes less acute, and I ease myself out of my bed, using only memory and sense of touch.

The bathroom I can remember, but no longer see, sits just off my bedroom—a convenience I never fully understood until after the accident.

While I piss, wash my hands and face, and brush my teeth, I

visualize the stone tiles beneath my feet and remember the soft white hues of the walls. I picture the porcelain fixtures and the small gold-framed abstract painting that reflects itself in the mirror.

And I visualize myself.

My face, my hair, my jaw, *my eyes*. I know what they looked like a year ago, but that's where it ends. Time has worn the lines and muddied the details of my features in ways I'll never witness.

I slip on reflective aviators over what's left of my eyes, and by the time I make it into the kitchen, the sounds of the front door clicking open and my brother's voice bellowing out from the entryway reach my ears.

"Ansel!" he calls out. "You up, bro?"

"In the kitchen," I grumble as I attempt to make coffee without it turning into a disaster.

The sink is two steps from the coffeepot.

Ten seconds of the faucet running equals four cups of water, which equals two scoops of coffee.

The can of Folger's is one-hand's width away from the coffeepot.

At least, it *should be* Folger's. Fuck if I know what the label actually says. I am the epitome of a blind taste tester.

I follow the specific directions I've memorized and set the coffee-maker to brew by tapping the third button on the right.

The sound of Bram's footsteps gets louder as he approaches, changing subtly as he transitions from the wood of the front hall to the tiles of the kitchen. "Looks like you're off to a good start this morning."

If I had eyes that worked, I'd sure as shit be rolling them at him.

Don't get me wrong, I love my brother Bram.

Hell, *everyone* loves Bram. He's the fun-loving rock star with a killer voice and enough charming swagger to sell out stadiums.

It's the whole *being blind* thing I despise.

"I told you you'd get this down."

Being blind *and* his holier-than-thou chipper attitude, that is.

"Oh yeah, what used to take two minutes now only takes thirty," I grumble. "At this rate, I think a decade or so from now, I might be able to make a fucking cup of coffee in under fifteen minutes."

My brother chuckles. Good God, he must be on uppers.

The rustling of paper ends what could have been one hell of a bitter inner diatribe.

"Did you get groceries?"

"Just a few things I figured you needed."

Shit like this—other people helping me—is *exactly* what makes me feel pathetic.

While I've learned how to do basic things for myself over the past twelve months, I still have to rely on people like Bram to get my fucking groceries. Every Tuesday, I give him a list, and he fulfills it. A list of things *I* deem necessary. What I don't need are his overachieving assumptions about what I *need*.

No way in hell my brother with his perfect life and perfect sight really knows what I need.

"Eggs sound good?" he asks, and the urge to swipe my hand across the kitchen counter and hear everything crash to the ground is strong.

"I don't want any fucking eggs, Bram."

"Okay," he responds, an emotional flatline. My mood has officially soured the sweetness out of his. "What about toast? Oatmeal?"

He's unwaveringly patient with me, and it only fuels my frustration.

"Bram," I say through clenched teeth, slamming my fists down onto the counter. "I can handle it. I might be fucking blind, but I'm not an invalid. There is shit I can do for myself."

"Fine," he mutters. "Eat breakfast. Don't eat breakfast. Burn the whole fucking place down for all I care."

His unexpected words spur a laugh from my throat. In the entirety of my suffering, I don't think my sullen attitude has ever broken him. Unfortunately for Bram and everyone else in my life, the only satisfaction I get these days tends to stem from sarcastic verbal judo. His breakthrough serves solely as an opening for the start of this match. "If you keep acting like a mother hen, I might consider it."

"Get over yourself, you cranky fuck," he says through a soft, mostly annoyed chuckle. "I'm just trying to help you out."

Help. Fuck, I hate that word.

"That's the thing, Bram." I spit out my frustration. "I don't need your goddamn help."

It's a lie, we both know it, but that does nothing to soften the conviction with which I wish it weren't.

He sighs but, smartly, keeps his mouth shut. We've had our fair share of heated spats over the past year, and experience tells him there's only enough room for one antagonist in this kitchen. As the owner in residence, I call dibs.

"So, all issues with breakfast aside, are you planning on going into your studio this week?"

What's the point? It's not like I'm going to paint...

"I don't know." I shrug. "Why?"

"Lucy's been fielding quite a few calls from interested buyers, and I'm sure she'd love to discuss them with you."

She'd love to discuss them with me? Pretty sure he means my assistant would love to stop answering so many goddamn calls. Honestly, I'm surprised she's even answering the phones without me there. Lucy Miller is about as prone to doing her job as my eyes are to see my fucking feet.

Before the accident, I was in the studio every day. Now, it's all I can do to force myself to go once a month. Clearly, going weeks on end without checking in on her has only impugned what little work ethic she had.

Ironically, ever since the world found out I would never paint again, the value of my paintings has shot up exponentially. *Morbid fascination at its finest.*

Last month, one of my paintings sold at auction for two million dollars.

Created when I was twenty-one, it was one of the first paintings I ever leaned into with my entire soul. Full of movement and passion, the young boy and his bubbles embodied everything I felt at the time. I sold it to what I'd believed to be an impassioned buyer. Turns out, the only impassioned fool was me.

The thought of someone selling one of my purest creations for monetary gain left a sour fucking taste in my mouth, and as a result, I'm starting to despise every single potential buyer. Do they love art? Or do they see an investment piece that, when turned over, will buy them a house they don't need or a fucking Lamborghini they won't drive?

Art is meant to affect your heart, your mind, your goddamn soul.

Not serve as a conduit for a bigger bank account.

Bunch of greedy fucking bastards…

"Who's interested?"

"Well…" Bram clears his throat. "Lyle Jacobs."

An NBA basketball player who wouldn't know real art from his asshole.

"Carly May."

A reality TV star who probably thinks Mona Lisa is a pop singer.

"Jeff Simmons."

A pretentious billionaire who has more money than any one human being needs. He's flashy and ostentatious, and he wouldn't know true art if it smacked him across the fucking face.

"Not interested."

"They're offering a lot of money—"

"It's not about the money," I mutter. "They and their money can go fuck themselves."

Bram sighs and laughs at the same time. "God, Ans, could you be any more of a dick?"

"If I tried hard enough?" I shrug. "Probably."

Thankfully, Bram gets wise and drops the subject altogether.

"Are you taking me to my appointment today?" I ask as I carefully pour myself a cup of coffee.

Another pointless appointment where the doctor confirms what I already know all too fucking well. *Yeah, Doc, I get it. I can't see.*

"Yeah."

"You do realize it's not until four, right?"

"Also yes," he says, stepping into my body, grabbing my hand, and directing the pot of coffee back to the machine I would have missed on my own. "But don't worry, I have to leave to meet my band for a few hours, and then I'll be back to get you around three."

"When are you going on tour again, Mom?" I tease halfheartedly. It's either that or cry. Fucking hell, I hate what my life has become.

"Not until summer, you ornery prick."

"I'll start counting down the days."

"You're an asshole."

I am, I know. I really know.

After a long commute across town, both Bram and I reach Dr. Smith's Manhattan office right on time.

A world-renowned eye surgeon, he's one of the physicians who has been following my case since I lost my sight.

The instant we step inside, the receptionist ushers us into a room and tells us the doctor is finishing up with a patient and will be in shortly.

So, we sit and wait.

And wait.

And I quickly remember that a doctor's version of *shortly* isn't the same as the rest of us.

It's been no less than thirty minutes by the time he makes his grand entrance into the room.

Well, I'm assuming it's grand, but I have to assume a lot of things these days.

"Ansel," Dr. Smith greets, and the sound of a door clicking shut echoes off the walls. "It's good to see you again."

"I'd say the same, but we all know I can't see."

"Jesus," Bram mutters. He probably meant for it to be under his breath, but it's really true what they say. Losing one sense heightens the others.

"Still heavy with the sarcasm, I see," the doc says through a chuckle, after which the room grows quiet for a moment. No sarcastic remarks from my brother and no sounds of movement from the doctor as he's obviously settled behind his desk.

Quiet stretches like this make me uncomfortable. Without sound to guide me, the black behind my lids seems endless.

"Dark humor at my eyes' expense is about the only thing that gets me through these days," I admit to cut off the silence.

It has just the effect I desired. Bram swallows loudly and shuffles his foot on the rug, and Dr. Smith starts typing something on his laptop. At least, I assume that's what the clacking sound I hear is.

I let out the breath I didn't realize I was holding and mentally picture what his notes might look like.

Thirty-year-old patient is still blind, sarcastic, and a dick.

I nearly laugh.

"Is there a specific reason you wanted to see Ansel today?" my brother asks, and the doctor clears his throat.

"Well, I have some news," he says. "After eight long months, we've received approval."

"Approval?" I ask.

"For a bilateral transplant," he answers.

"I'm sorry, what?" I can barely keep my voice steady. I'm surprised and, worse yet, hopeful. Somehow, I push the question past the clog in my throat anyway. "Are you talking about an eye transplant?"

"I am," he confirms.

"But I thought that wasn't possible?" Bram chimes in.

"It wasn't a year ago, but it is now," he explains. "Ansel would be one of the first in the country."

"Are you fucking with me right now, Doc?" My breathing is erratic and forced and so loud, I'm almost certain I'm not the only one in the room who can hear it.

"No," he says and then adds, "Ansel, we can make you see again."

chapter two

Ansel

"Ansel!" Bram calls toward me. "Shit! Slow down!"

I keep moving, tapping my cane fast and furious on the ground in front of me, out of Dr. Smith's office building and onto the pavement. I never move this quickly anymore, and I barely know this area of town, so I have a feeling the exercise is just for show. If there's anything in my path, the crash landing is going to be hard.

But I can't stop my feet from moving.

Fucking hell. He thinks he can make me see *again.*

He wants me to trust him and his team to perform an intense, extremely difficult surgery that's barely even been performed before, let alone established a solid success rate.

Coma.

Death.

Permanent brain damage.

When Dr. Smith started reading through the long list of risks, I had to get out of there.

My heart races, and the sounds of cars rolling by on the street guide me to stay on the far side of the sidewalk.

One of the first eye transplants in the country...

My boots move over the concrete as fast as I can manage, and it's not until I accidentally bump into someone that I stop.

"Shit, sorry," I mutter after a soft female voice squeaks out her surprise. "Are you okay?" I ask and, out of reflex, I reach out my hand, but I know my blind ass isn't going to be able to do a damn thing to help her.

I can hardly help my fucking self.

"I'm fine," she says, pity lacing the edge of her words. "It's fine."

Fuck. I want to scream, pound on my chest, and break shit like a fucking lunatic, but I rein in my frustration. It won't do me any good.

Believe me, I've tried.

All it's ever given me is a scratchy throat and a renewed sense of self-loathing.

It doesn't take long before Bram's footsteps catch up with me.

"You okay?"

Not even fucking close. "Yeah."

"You sure?"

"Yeah," I say through clenched teeth. "I'm fine."

I inhale a deep breath and prepare myself for the onslaught of his questions and concerns *and fucking hopes* that have most likely been created from Dr. Smith's big news.

But they never come.

Instead, he wraps his arm around my shoulder. "You hungry?"

"No." I shake my head. Anything I eat right now will come back up.

"Thirsty?"

I shrug. "I guess that depends."

"On what?"

"If you're talking about grabbing a coffee, count me out. But if we're talking whiskey, then yeah, I'm fucking thirsty."

"Whiskey it is." Bram's chuckle fills my ears. "I know just the place."

<hr />

Three hours and four whiskeys later and I'm blessedly numb.

I don't make a point to drown my issues in alcohol because if I did, I'd be dead from cirrhosis of the liver by now. But every once in a while, it's needed. And today…definitely qualifies.

Dr. Smith's news was meant to be some kind of godsend.

Some answered prayer. *A fucking miracle.*

But that's not what I felt when the words came out of his mouth.

Instead, the acidic sting of hope replaced the blood in my veins, and it did it easily.

So easily, it terrifies me.

The past year has been the worst year of my life.

After the accident, I was desperate to find some sort of loophole. Something, *anything,* that would let me see again. But it wasn't a wound that would mend or an illness that could be cured. My eyes were destroyed by the glass of the windshield, and there was no going back.

I hate it. Of course, I fucking despise it. But I've been working toward closure. Toward finding some sort of internal peace that will fill this dark void inside of me.

But now, Dr. Smith is trying to tell me there's a possibility I could see again.

It's downright unbelievable. Preposterous.

Unreal.

If I start to hope for it, and in the end, I'm still the blind artist who can't paint…I won't be able to handle it.

I'll officially become a lost cause, and all of my effort—all of Bram's effort—will have been for nothing.

Fuck, just drink your whiskey and stop thinking about it…

"Hello… Are you…uh…Bram Bray?" a timid female voice pulls me from my thoughts. Despite the mood that got us here—the mood that still clouds my every nuance—I can practically hear my brother's smile.

This is the fifth or sixth woman who's found her way into our VIP section at this bar, and every one of them wants the same thing.

A chance at Bram Bray.

My brother the rock star, ladies and gentlemen.

"I am," Bram responds with his familiar cocky confidence.

"Oh my god," she all but squeals. "I can't believe this! I can't believe I'm meeting the lead singer of New Rules! Oh my god! Oh my god!" she rambles, tripping all over her words—and likely her tongue as it lolls out of her mouth—before finally asking, "Can I…uh…take a picture with you?"

"Of course."

Of course, I mock silently. Always so doting to his adoring fans.

The whiskey burns as I take too healthy of a pull.

"Wait…if you're Bram Bray, then are you Ansel Bray?"

Ah, hell. I bite back the urge to sigh and consider pretending to be deaf too, but my bastard brother answers for me.

"He is, in fact, Ansel Bray."

I don't even have to say anything. All it takes is his confirmation to make her start to freak out again.

"Oh my god! I can't believe… I don't know… Oh my god… My name is Laura, and I'm such a huge fan…such a huge, huge fan."

"Well, thank you," I say sarcastically, and because of the whiskey, it sounds like I actually mean it. "It's *so* nice to meet you, Laura."

Bram reads the bitterness in my voice and punches me in the leg under the table.

"I'm an art major, and you are my biggest inspiration…*were my biggest inspiration…*" I hear the nervous titter of her throat over the music pounding from the speakers of the bar. "God, I just…I just can't believe what happened to you. It's devastating."

And there it is. The *sympathy.*

The mood around us takes a nose dive into the place I've been swimming all night, and I can practically hear my brother tensing up in anticipation of what I might say. In his defense, though, I have a bit of a track record when it comes to pity.

"Something happened to me?" I ask from behind my aviators.

"Uh…the accident," she stutters over her words, "…the one that made you go blind…"

"I'm blind?" I question, feigning shock and dismay. "Bram? *I'm fucking blind?*"

I can't see her, but I can feel the discomfort vibrating off her body in waves. Staccato breaths and fidgeting heels, the poor woman doesn't know what to do with herself.

"He's just kidding," my brother says on a sigh. "But it was great meeting you," he adds in an attempt to move her on her merry way. Probably before I get another opportunity to make her uncomfortable.

"Uh…thanks," she mutters, my sick sense of humor officially knocking the wind out of her fangirl sails. The sound of her heels fades away and takes my brother's easygoing nature with it.

"Do you have to be such an asshole?" he asks. "She was just try-ing to be nice, Ans."

I shrug. "Maybe I'm just a little tired of all the sympathy."

"You'd think, *with whiskey on your side*, you could manage to, you know, smile and act friendly or something."

I lift my glass and shake it, the ice clanking around inside. "I think I need a few more of these for that to happen."

A half-amused, mostly frustrated laugh rings from his lips. "God, you're *such* a dick."

Bingo. I shrug and move the glass to my mouth for another drink.

"I'm curious…" he says, a new lilt challenging the usually genial nature of his voice, and pauses long enough for me to take the bait.

"About what?"

"When's the last time you got laid?"

It's on the tip of my tongue to tell him to fuck off, but suddenly, the fight leaves my lungs in a sigh. "A while."

Since before the accident, specifically.

"Be honest," he says. "Who was the last woman?"

"Naomi Phillips."

"That model?"

"Yeah." An extremely sex-focused woman who gets some sort of

the girl in the painting

thrill from fucking anyone with a name or status.

She was attractive and horny. I wasn't blind. And we had some fun.

Before Naomi, there was an up-and-coming actress by the name of Ella.

And before Ella, there was Marissa, a backup guitarist for Bram's band. It's probably for the best he remains clueless about that last one...

"How long ago?"

"Over a year."

"Jesus," he mutters. "That's some dry spell you're living over there."

"Yeah, well, sex isn't the same when you can't physically see the woman you're fucking."

"Yeah, but you can hear her, you can *feel* her."

Instead of a response, I busy myself with another chug of whiskey.

I'd rather drink myself into oblivion than talk to my brother about my sex life.

"You do realize there's absolutely no need for that long of a dry spell, right?" he patronizes through a laugh. "I mean, we're in a bar that is practically swimming with women who keep looking over here...at *you*. You're the famous Ansel Bray. The sex god, broody artist," he adds, and his voice is etched with amusement.

Sex god, broody artist? An absurd laugh escapes my throat.

Sure, that might have been my life a year ago, but that's not my life now.

Now, I'm just the blind guy who doesn't want to be fucking blind.

"Seriously, Ans. There is no reason for you to have a dry spell."

"It doesn't matter. I'm not interested."

"Why the fuck not?"

"Because I don't want a pity fuck, Bram!" I yell, slamming a hand down on the table and knocking over my glass.

"*A pity fuck?* You really think these women are looking for a pity fuck?" Bram snorts as he scrambles to pick up the mess I've made. Fuck knows, I can't do it. "Just because you're blind doesn't mean you're not still the same good-looking fuck you were before the accident. Trust me, these women aren't looking to pity-fuck you. Fuck you and get their name added to your bank account? Sure. But you and I both know, there is no pity involved here."

"Still, not interested."

He sighs, and thankfully, drops the subject altogether.

And for a far too brief moment, we just sit back and listen to the music flowing in from the speakers of the bar. But just like most good things, it comes to an end.

"Why don't you want to do it?"

There it is. The big question of the day. The thing that's been on my brother's mind since we left Dr. Smith's office.

"Would you want to do it?"

"If I were you?" The incredulity in his voice annoys me. "Yeah, I would want to do it."

"Did you even hear the risks?" I question. "We're not talking some minor little surgery here. This is serious shit. This could literally mean life or death for me."

"Yeah, but you're a painter, Ans. A fucking artist," he says quietly. "And we both know losing your vision was like losing your soul. As far as you're concerned, you might as well be dead already."

I wish I could refute his words. I wish I could call bullshit.

But the truth is, I'm a shell of the man I once was.

Some might say a painter's most important asset is his hands, but I disagree.

The eyes are the windows to the soul, and once those windows are closed, darkness seeps in and spreads its roots like ivy. And without a soul to inspire and connect and create, hands are just hands.

Fucking hands I can't even fucking see.

chapter three

Ansel

"Well, look who finally decided to grace me with his presence." Unfortunately, my assistant's far too cheery voice is the first thing I hear as I step foot inside the entrance of my office and studio on the Upper East Side. "What's it been? Two? Three weeks?"

Her enjoyment makes me grimace, and my grimace pulls at my temples and, like a domino effect, the hangover headache that's been beating against my skull all morning is magnified.

"Apparently, not long enough," I retort and she laughs.

Last night, I let whiskey take the wheel. And while she proved to be quite the enchanting beauty then, this morning, she's serving up quite the sucker punch.

It took me a good two hours to get myself moving, shove enough coffee, ibuprofen, and toast into my body to quell the urge to vomit, and call Hank, my driver, to pick me up and bring me here.

Obviously, besides the whiskey last night, it's the worst idea I've had in the past twenty-four hours.

Lucy smacks her lips, and it sounds like a cat having a seizure. *Good God.*

"Are you chewing gum?" I ask with distaste.

"Yep," she answers and, as if the revolting sound isn't enough, my mind fills with an old memory of her sitting by the sleek desk in my front office, chomping on Bubble Yum like a heathen.

"Spit the gum out," I order.

"So," she says, ignoring my command completely, "do tell what brought you in on this rare occasion."

"Certainly not your office decorum."

She doesn't respond. Not with words, anyway. But I'm almost positive there were a few rude gestures.

"You've left me nearly fifty voice mails about assholes wanting to buy my paintings."

"Huh. Who would've thought fifty was the magic number that would *finally* drag your cranky ass into work?"

"I'd say it's lovely to see you again, but we both know I'd be lying," I retort with a shadow of a grin. "And that wasn't a blind joke either."

When it comes to Lucy, she is, hands down, the worst assistant who has ever assisted anyone. But what she lacks in proficiency and actual work ethic, she makes up for in the ability to handle my dickish tendencies.

Whatever I dish her way, she throws right back at me. The girl has the kind of backbone that would make even the biggest macho bastard look like a pussy.

And, the icing on the cake, she doesn't have a single sympathetic bone in her body.

Lucy cares about herself and no one else, and she's far too self-involved to help anyone else.

It's those qualities that have kept her on my payroll despite the nature of the last year.

I know I'll never sense pity or sadness in her voice. I'll never feel like she's going out of her way to accommodate me. Honestly, she's about the only person in my life who hasn't changed the way she treats me.

All of a sudden, the truth hits me, and I almost trip over my cane.

It's kind of a horrible discovery to find out I might actually like her.

"Don't be such an ass," she responds through a laugh. "And, for the love of God, make some decisions. *Sell your paintings. Don't sell your paintings.* It doesn't matter to me. But please figure it out, so I don't have to keep fielding all of these calls."

"It's tough, isn't it, Luce?" I retort. "Having to answer actual calls and do work."

If I were a betting man, I'd give some damn good odds that she's rolling her eyes right now.

"You know I *hate* answering the phones," she whines.

Yep. Definitely rolling her eyes.

"Yes," I agree. "Answering phones and doing pretty much anything on the computer."

"That too."

"And handling my calendar."

She groans. "God, that's terrible."

"And scheduling meetings and drawing up contracts," I add with a wry grin.

"You can shut up already."

Amused laughter escapes my lungs.

"Remind me, Luce, why did you agree to this job?"

"Because I like money," she singsongs without a single ounce of shame.

"Because of money?" My voice lightens around the edges with amusement. "And all this time, I thought it was because you loved my art."

"Stop being so annoying."

I laugh. Full out, this time. No doubt, Lucy loves money. She also loves makeup, plastic surgery, and Louis Vuitton.

But somehow, some way, the fake-titted twenty-four-year-old has become the closest thing I've got to a friend these days.

"Bring the most sought-after painting into my office."

"What?" she complains. "Right now?"

Still, she's a huge pain in the ass.

"You heard me," I call over my shoulder as I use the cane to guide myself through the doorway and around to the back of my desk.

Her groan of annoyance fades as she goes to do my bidding, and the sound of her heels on the tile amplifies as she makes her way back to me.

The wave of sound *almost* makes me feel like I can see her in motion.

"Here it is," she says and pops her gum between her teeth. "It's—"

"Don't tell me the name of it," I cut her off. "Describe it to me."

"What?"

"Tell me what's on the canvas."

"Are you screwing me with me right now? Why can't I just tell you the name of it?"

"*Luce,*" I demand. "Describe it."

"Fine." She huffs out a sigh. "Well…" She pauses, and her heels shuffle back and forth across the marble floor. "It's of an old woman. She's wearing pants and a shirt. She really needs to brush her hair, and she's, like, leaning up against a wall or something," she describes—poorly, mind you—in between obnoxious pops of her gum.

"That's it?" I question. "*That's* your description of it?"

"Yeah," she retorts without an ounce of uncertainty. "And I would guarantee you now know which painting it is, too."

"That's only because I painted it," I say through a raspy laugh. "Your description, *if you can even call it that,* provided absolutely zero visual. Hell, it was complete shit, Luce."

"I didn't realize I was supposed to write a poem about it," she sasses me. "Is that all you needed?"

"Yeah," I sigh. "You're free to go secretly watch Netflix behind your desk."

And as the sound of her laughter and heels drifts away, I assume she goes to do just that.

Meanwhile, I groan and run a hand through my hair as I visualize the painting Lucy just verbally assaulted.

Insomnia is the title. With a muted palette of black and white and the occasional soft touch of colors, the canvas appears dreamlike. The female figure feels as if she's fading away before your very eyes.

Her plump frame is hunched over, and her back rests against the stark wall behind her. The messy locks of her gray hair fall in front of her face and create a veil of mystery and secrets.

You can't see her eyes. Or her cheeks. Or her lips. But you can feel her looking toward you.

I think about the day I created it, and it's so…*vividly foreign.* My chest constricts around my heart at the loss.

Fuck, this is painful.

My fingers itch to paint, but my soul has no desire to create.

I miss my old life.

I miss losing myself inside my studio.

I miss the rush and comfort and adrenaline and solace that painting provided.

God, I *miss* being able to *see.*

Before I know it, I'm barking instructions at my assistant to call Dr. Smith and make an appointment for as soon as he can fit me in.

If I've been offered the chance to take my life back, I have to do it.

Dr. Smith is ever accommodating, and a few hours later, I find myself inside his personal office, waiting on him yet again.

The smell of mahogany wood assaults my senses, and when I run my finger across the top of the large wood desk in front of my chair, I understand why.

Leather. A gargantuan desk meant to portray power. And most likely containing a plethora of medical-related books, Dr. Smith's office is both a comfort and a cliché.

"Good afternoon," he says when he walks into the room. The door shuts with a quiet click after his words.

"Afternoon, Doc."

"I'm glad you decided to come back in for another visit." His soft footsteps move past me, and his chair squeaks as he settles into it behind his desk. "Alone today?"

Whether it was for moral support or the simple reality that navigating New York City with no eyes and a simple red-tipped cane isn't the easiest of tasks, prior to this visit, I've always attended these appointments with Bram at my side.

But I needed to do this one on my own.

"Observant, Doc," I tease, but I quickly drop the sarcasm and get to the reason why I'm here. "I'd like to apologize for my abrupt departure the other day."

I'm pretty sure I knocked over no fewer than three pieces of furniture and a nurse on my way out of his office, but there's no need to get lost in specifics.

"Not a problem," he responds, his voice the auditory equivalent of a neutral, friendly smile. "I can imagine it was overwhelming."

"Yeah," I answer around a choked, sardonic laugh. "Quite overwhelming, in fact."

Silence fills the room as I try to organize my scattered thoughts. Thankfully, the doc senses the need for quiet and stays patient through the lack of conversation.

God, where do I even begin…

"This surgery," I say, and I clear the cobwebs from my throat. "It's a bit of a risk, yeah?"

"Yes, Ansel. There are serious risks involved with it." He pauses, and I tense as I wait to hear the rest of what he has to say—what I *need* to hear him say. "But there's also a significant reward."

With a deep, calming breath, I force myself to move past the risks and focus on the reward.

"Do you really think it's possible?" I ask. "I mean, how confident are you? Do you really think you and your team can pull this off? Really restore my vision fully?"

"We've been successful in London, and we wouldn't have been fighting for approval from the FDA and the medical board for the past eight months if we weren't ready," he answers, and I don't miss the calm confidence in his voice. "We can do this surgery, Ansel."

"Why me?" The question falls from my lips before I can stop it. "Surely, you have other patients. Ones who are also blind *and* good candidates…"

Ones who aren't assholes.

"For one, your blindness wasn't caused by disease or a genetic disorder. It was caused by trauma from an accident," he explains. "We know going into it there's no risk for disease to come back and ruin the healthy eyes."

"Okay…" I pause and swallow hard against the anxiety creeping up my throat.

"And to be blunt about it—mostly, you're financially stable enough to handle the cost of this surgery and the therapy that's required after."

His words startle a laugh from my lungs. "You mean to tell me I'm a candidate because I'm rich?"

"That's not the only reason, but it's definitely an important factor."

"That's a little fucked, isn't it, Doc?" I retort.

The idea someone else deserving doesn't get this opportunity just because they're *less financially stable* coils anger around my nerves.

"I know it's not right, but that's just the way it is right now," he clarifies. "Insurance companies won't cover something like this because it hasn't been done before in this country. There are no statistics or prior cases for them to use as a guide. One day, though, they'll have the statistics they need. But we have to start somewhere."

"With me."

"Yes."

"And if I say yes, if I agree to the surgery, when would it happen?"

"Well, we'll have to do some extensive blood and genetic testing on you before we list you as an actual candidate for a donor, but I don't anticipate that taking more than a few weeks."

"And after that?"

"Then we wait for a donor."

His words hit me straight in the fucking gut. "You mean…we wait for someone else to die."

"Yes," he answers frankly.

I think about the risks and the possibilities. I think about the seriousness of what I'm about to do.

I think about opening my eyes and seeing the world around me.

I think about my art, my painting, and getting my life back.

And I think about the fact that if I go through with this, I could be paving a path for other people who are just as desperate as me to see again.

"Okay."

"Okay?" Dr. Smith questions.

"I look forward to *seeing* you, Doc."

chapter four

Ansel

The TV blares from the living room like a fire alarm, yanking me out of a dream and straight into consciousness. It's so loud, in fact, I can hear every word that comes out of the stupid newscaster's mouth.

"Good morning, New York! This is Louis Fallon coming to you live from Times Square with the eight o'clock morning news. Stay tuned for an interview with the mayor about the impacts of yesterday's storm, and the *Flash Five-Day Forecast* from our favorite meteorologist, Jenny Flash. It looks like the first official day of February is going to be a cold one, folks."

Fucking Bram.

You'd think as a lead singer of one the country's most popular up-and-coming rock bands, he'd be pulling late nights with groupies and shit and refusing to wake up before noon.

But, sadly for me, that's not the case.

Up with the sun even if he goes down with it too, the bastard has made it a habit of arriving at my house far too early, like some sort of stupid, macho, I-don't-need-sleep, show-off thing.

I can only assume it's for the satisfaction of torturing me.

"Bram!" I shout from beneath my covers. "Why the fuck are you here?"

He ignores my question completely, not that I really expected it to be anything but rhetorical.

"Morning, sweetheart!" he singsongs back toward me. "Want some coffee?"

"Go home!"

"Want some breakfast?" he calls over the television. "I've got bagels!"

I swear, this might be my brother's last day alive.

"Go away!"

Bram responds to my demand by turning up the volume on the TV to an ear-bursting decibel and tuning me out completely.

I pull the blankets over my face and try to remember why murdering him would be complicated with my physical limitations.

It's hard to check yourself for blood residue when you can't fucking see, and arson is probably a hobby better suited to someone who doesn't stand a risk of stumbling into their own damn fire.

Sure, I'd probably be a shoo-in for the eye donation, thanks to our matching blood type and genealogy and all, but would I really be able to enjoy my sight fully from prison?

When I'm convinced I won't shoot him, I pull myself out of bed.

"I hate you," I yell to my brother as I carefully cross the threshold of my bedroom and feel my way into the bathroom.

"Love you too, bro," he responds, his voice so fucking cheery, my brain starts campaigning for homicide again.

By the time I'm out of the bathroom and in the kitchen, Bram has finally turned the volume on the TV back down to a humane level. Still, I hold up my middle finger over my shoulder for good measure as I attempt to make some coffee.

He laughs, and the sound of it distracts me just enough.

"Ah, fuck!"

"I just made a fresh pot," he updates about thirty seconds too late. The sting of the red-hot pot delivered the message itself.

"Thanks for letting me know," I grumble sarcastically.

"In my defense, you didn't give me a chance."

Just before I find the exact right words to tell him precisely where he can stick his defense, a loud, undeniable ring echoes from the pocket of my pajama pants. From the phone I've been carrying on my person constantly since I left Dr. Smith's office two months ago. Sixty days of waiting for a donor to become available. Sixty days of wondering if it would ever happen.

I freeze and inhale a sharp breath into my lungs.

"Is that…is that *the* call?" Bram asks, the teasing tone of our sibling banter officially gone.

"Yeah," I manage to whisper through the tightness in my throat. "I think it is."

"Well, what in the fuck are you waiting for?" he exclaims. "Answer it!"

With shaky hands, I pull the phone out of my pocket by the fourth ring and answer the call.

"Hello?"

"Ansel." Dr. Smith's voice fills my ears. "It's time."

"Seriously, Doc?"

"Yes," he answers. "Our surgery window is now less than forty-eight hours."

"Okay…so what do I do now?"

"Head to the hospital."

"This is really happening?"

"This is really happening, Ansel," he says, and I don't miss the smile in his voice. "It's time to make you see again."

High heels click around my pre-op room in quick succession, and Bram's soft but annoyed chuckle grates on my already shredded nerves.

"Mom, everything is going to be fine," Bram reassures her.

Our stepdad Neil is quick to jump onto the comfort train. "It's all going to be okay, honey."

Mom sighs but offers up no response, continuing her pacing with renewed fervor.

For the past thirty minutes, Bram and my stepdad have tried to calm her down, but it's no use. She's a fucking mess.

Click-clack, click-clack. It's all I can hear.

If I could come up with a way to politely tell them all to fuck off without sending my mom into a spiral of hysteria, I would.

Instead, I try to be patient. I'm not exactly the king of cool sitting in this hospital bed with an IV in my arm and an itchy patient gown irritating my skin.

"Ansel," Dr. Smith's friendly voice bellows into the room.

Ah, fuck. Here goes everything...

"You ready to do this?" he asks and, instantly, I take a deep inhale of fresh oxygen into my tight lungs.

God, am I ready?

I'm ready to see again, I know that much.

Am I nervous as fuck? Of course. Scared shitless, even.

But it's time to get my life back.

"Yep," I eventually respond. "I think so."

"Hey, good to see you, Doc," Bram greets, and Neil and my mom follow suit.

Everyone exchanges their hellos and all three men offer more encouraging words for my worried mom, and then the sound of running water takes over. I presume it's the good doctor washing his hands.

"Mom, how about we go grab some coffee while Dr. Smith gets Ansel ready for surgery?"

"I think that's a good idea," Neil agrees, but my mother isn't convinced.

"I need to make sure I see Ansel before they take him back." Her voice quivers with emotion. "I just need to see him one last time before—"

"Mom," I interject. "I'm sure Dr. Smith will let you guys see me before they take me to the OR."

Though, it wouldn't be so horrible for me if he didn't.

"Don't worry, Della," the doc chimes in. "I'll make sure you see him before we take him back."

With a little more patient coaxing, my brother and stepdad manage to scoot my mom out of my room, and I'm left alone with Dr. Smith.

He fiddles in front of my face, pulling open the lids of each eye as he examines them.

"Making sure I really can't see before you give me the eyes?" I tease nervously. "The paperwork for that kind of fuckup is probably never-ending."

"It would be," he says, humoring me. "And I hate paperwork. Consequently, you can be sure I'll do my absolute best to make sure this goes off without a hitch, okay?"

He's coddling me, playing into my jokes to soothe my nerves, but for the first time since I lost my sight, I'm happy to have someone's pity.

I'm anxious and unsettled, and I'm not sure I'd be able to find my own ass at this point if someone asked me to.

"Appreciate it. I'd really hate to have to haunt you." An amused chuckle falls from his lips, and I take a deep, audible breath while he's providing the sound bite to cover it.

"I'll certainly miss your supply of sarcasm."

"Aw. Are you breaking up with me, Doc?"

"Yes," he says. "Obviously, we'll have several follow-up appointments after the surgery to monitor your progress, but I don't envision anything but a successful transplant. I'll be nothing but a bad ex-girlfriend to you soon enough."

A successful transplant.

God. There's really a chance. A chance I'll be free of the stigma of being the blind painter who can't paint.

I'll simply be Ansel again.

It's hard to feel deserving of something as monumental as this, but I'm going to do my best to make the most of it. Starting with acknowledging that in order for me to be where I am today—being given this gift—someone else had to lose all of their tomorrows.

"Dr. Smith?"

"Yes, Ansel?"

"Can I have a minute before you bring my family back in?"

"Ansel, I know I can't promise you a perfect outcome, but I assure you we wouldn't be attempting this today if I weren't confident—"

"It's not that," I interrupt and swallow thickly. "I'd just like to write a letter to the donor's family."

"You don't have to do that now. You're deserving of this, and you're not the reason for their misfortune. It's just a part of life."

"I know, Doc. Or, at least, I'm trying to. But if I don't write it now, I don't know that I'll ever properly put into words what this means to me. I might forget... I'm afraid I'll forget what this is like. What it's like to be a man..." I choke on the words, and emotion I didn't know I still had bubbles up.

Dr. Smith is nice enough to pretend he doesn't notice.

"Do you want me to write it for you?"

"No," I say, my voice softly dancing around the emotion in my throat. "I need to be the one who writes it."

Without question, he hands me a sheet of paper and a pen and promises to make sure it gets to the proper people at the donor organization when I'm done.

It doesn't matter that I can't see the paper or the pen.

I need to write this down even if it's a fucking mess of words.

I trace the edges of the page with my fingertip and guide my pen to the top left corner of the sheet of paper. Using my free hand as a guide for straight lines and to prevent myself from writing words on top of each other, I bleed words onto the page just like I used to bleed colors onto the canvas. There's no overthinking or questioning; it just is.

The day is a gift whether the surgery is a success or not, and I want the people who loved my donor to know that.

chapter five

Four Years Later

Ansel

Three knocks rap against the closed door of my studio, and I sigh.

Apparently, my assistant doesn't understand what *no distractions* means. I shouldn't be surprised, though. Lucy's priorities have nothing to do with her role as my assistant. Half the time, people who come to my studio don't even realize she works here. They probably just assume she's some sort of social media influencer wasting time in my lobby by taking cleavage shots.

Another two knocks ring out, and I ignore whoever is on the other side and focus my gaze back on the half-painted canvas in front of me.

As if my hand is on autopilot, I watch as it gently creates the soft lines of her hair. Stroke after stroke, dark brown and honey-beige and gold combine to make the flowing locks that cascade down her back.

Eventually, though, the knocks grow so persistent that I can hardly follow the rhythm of the soft background music serving as a medium for my artistic exploration.

Fucking Lucy.

"Go away!" I call over my shoulder, but the answering chuckle is not an annoyed feminine laugh. *No.* It's husky and deep and rough around the edges.

"Ans, it's Nigel," the disturbance answers back.

Nigel Marx. We grew up together on the outskirts of the Bronx and found our way into the art world during our college years. Where I've always had an innate ability to create, Nigel has a natural talent for seeking out beauty.

If anyone can find art worth seeing, it's Nigel. Or Nye, as I've grown to call him over the years.

Even though he's one of my oldest friends, I groan and contemplate at least ten different ways to tell him to fuck off. I may not be as grumpy as I was before the surgery, but being interrupted during the creative process brings me as close to that level of aggravation as I come these days.

But even the bad-tempered side of my personality knows a verbal middle finger is unwarranted.

Technically speaking, it's probably not even his fault. My assistant is undoubtedly too busy posting pictures of her new nose job on Instagram to follow my instructions and man the reception desk in the front.

So, eventually, I set my brush down beside my paints, move the canvas into the small, hidden nook near the windows, and tell him to come inside.

Dressed in a sharp black suit and tie, Nigel strides in as I head over to the sink to wash the dried paint off my hands.

"Did I interrupt?" he asks, and I glance at him over my shoulder.

"Yep."

A big, hearty laugh escapes his throat. "You don't even want to pretend I'm not being a huge inconvenience to you right now?"

"Pretty sure you know me better than that," I say with a grin and swipe the extra moisture off my hands onto my jeans. "I'm not a beat-around-the-bush kind of guy, Nigel."

He grins at that.

"What brought about this gloriously annoying visit of yours today?"

"Just want to make sure you're ready for the big opening," he says and slides his hands into the pockets of his dress pants. I don't miss the way he takes it upon himself to peruse my studio, his eyes taking in all of the empty canvases stacked in the corner and the finished works scattered along the floor and the walls.

"By all means, please feel free to browse. You know how much I love that."

He ignores my jab completely. "So, can I count on you to be there?"

"Be where?"

"You know where, you bastard." He glares. "Does January 31st ring a bell? The big exhibition some of us have been working so hard on."

"If I weren't such a big person, I wouldn't be able to ignore the fact that you're insinuating I, *the artist*, haven't done any work for the show."

He rolls his eyes. "You know that's not what I meant. Stop trying to distract me."

Now it's my turn to make a show of my new eyes' ability to move. "We've already been through this, man. There's no reason for me to be there."

Unconvinced, Nye presses on. "It's your opening, Ans. You need to be there."

"I don't need to be anywhere."

"Tell me this…why wouldn't you *want* to be there? This is your first exhibition in five years. Since *before* the accident. This is huge. If anything, you should be there to celebrate that you're painting again. That you're alive."

And just like that, he's answered his own question. He just doesn't know it.

Circuslike fanfare and a giant spotlight on my tragic past are the last things I want. I just want to paint without all of the fucking hoopla.

"How about this? I'll drink a glass of whiskey tonight to cele-brate. I'll even give myself a special toast."

"If you drink that glass of whiskey inside my gallery, on the night of your opening, then we have a deal."

It's my turn to laugh. "Not happening."

"The press will be there. Your fans will be there. People want to see you. They want to talk to you. Interview you. Why don't you want to be there?"

"For those exact fucking reasons, Nye," I answer honestly. "While I'm thankful people still want to see my art, I don't need the ego trip that comes with gallery openings and interviews. I don't need fans kissing my ass, and I sure as fuck don't need rich investors schmooz-ing me up because it makes them think they'll have a better shot at getting their greedy hands on one of my paintings."

Silence stretches between us, and I hope that means Nigel has *finally* come to terms with the reality of my absence at the opening.

Before the accident, I would've been there in a heartbeat. I would've been the guy with the big fucking ego and some random, superficially beautiful model attached to my arm. The douchebag looking at everyone inside that gallery and mentally giving myself a pat on the back.

But I'm not that guy anymore. I haven't been that guy since the day I went blind.

Do I claim to be the world's happiest, most-together guy? Fuck no. Like I said, on my best day, I'm still an asshole. But after living in the dark for what felt like an eternity, I've at least realized a few things.

For one, money, success—*material shit*—doesn't mean a fucking thing.

You can't buy happiness.

And, two? Friends are better to have than fans. Friends stick with you no matter what.

"Okay." Nigel's voice breaks our silence. "Fine. I won't ask you again."

I grin. "That sounds like a truly brilliant idea."

"Why haven't I seen this one?"

I follow his gaze to the far corner of my studio, and instantly, I know which painting he's talking about. My chest tightens with unease. *I can't believe I left that one out in the open like this...*

I run a hand through my hair and try to make myself sound at least somewhat disinterested. "Because it wasn't a painting I wanted to put in the exhibition."

My voice sounds slightly higher pitched, even to my own ears. *Dammit.*

About a year after my transplant, Dr. Smith cleared me to go back to my normal life—*back to painting.* I found myself inside this studio with a brush in my hand and a beautiful girl in my mind.

Crystal-blue eyes, dark, dimensional hair, and dimpled cheeks, every detail of her face and features vivid to the point of precision.

I couldn't stop picturing her. The way her full lips appear when they're curled into a smile. The way she looks mid-laugh. The way her eyes light up beneath the sun.

She was all I could see, this girl I've never met before, this girl I've never actually seen.

She was the first thing I painted after the transplant, and she's been locked inside my mind ever since—for nearly three years, to be exact.

But who's counting, right?

I nearly snort out loud. The truth is, my obsession is nearly pathetic and almost certainly unhealthy. But I can't seem to stop myself.

"This is...stunning," he says quietly as his eyes rake over the canvas. "*She's* stunning."

His words, while holding no harm or ill will, make me feel incredibly uncomfortable.

Like I need to shield her from his eyes. I feel too vulnerable. Too raw.

Nigel turns to meet my eyes. "Why didn't you want to put this one in the exhibition?"

"I don't know." *Because it's too special to me.*

He looks at the painting for a long moment before moving his eyes back to mine. "Should I know who she is?"

"No."

A figment of my imagination?

Some kind of angel muse?

I don't know, but I can't stop painting her.

"Is this the only one of her?"

"Yes," I flat out lie. Besides the one he's looking at, there are another four finished canvases hidden away and at least seven in progress. But I'm already pissed enough at myself for leaving this one out for him to see.

Strange and most likely fucking insane, I know, but it's the reality.

"You need to add this one to the exhibition."

I shake my head. "I don't think that's a good idea."

"Your other works are amazing, but this, it's something else, Ans," he says and glances back at the painting. "It *belongs* in the exhibition."

Silence stretches between us, and I'm torn about what to say.

Fuck no seems inappropriately callous, but I'm having a hell of a time coming up with any other words.

The artist inside of me agrees with his assessment. That painting—*and the other paintings of her*—is special.

She draws the viewer in just as she's done with me, like a mermaid luring sailors to their deaths.

But everything else inside me wants to keep her to myself.

"Ans, people need to see this painting," Nye urges.

I let out a deep exhale. "I don't know…"

"Ans, this one has to be in the show." His gaze is steady, unwavering. "You and I both know it would be a fucking travesty if it weren't in there."

My back tenses, but for some reason, the word "Okay" slips from my lips.

My stomach churns and my mind races and I don't know why I'm agreeing, but I am. I don't know why I feel sick over the prospect of other people seeing this painting, but I do.

The way I'm feeling, the way my emotions intertwine with her paintings, is a complete mystery to me.

Just like her.

chapter
six

Indy

The hardest part about being a music teacher at Great Elm in the Bronx is making lesson plans.

Okay, that's a lie, since the actual hardest part is keeping a room full of six-year-olds from burning down the classroom. Second-hardest is keeping eighth-graders from sticking their tongues down each other's throats, and *third*-hardest is making lesson plans.

I'm thirty years old, have been teaching for nearly two years, and I still have days when I can feel my eggs drying up in self-defense.

Seriously. I don't have kids of my own yet, but I send out nightly prayers to all of the moms and dads out there who have to spend the night under the same roof as some of these heathens.

The cursor on my Word doc flashes on the screen, and I put my head in my hands and watch the way a few loose pieces of my brown hair rise up into the air with the whoosh of breath that leaves my lungs.

Why did I think this was a good idea again?

I find *"Für Elise"* in my iTunes Library and hit play. If anyone can knock my ass into gear, it's Beethoven. And if he doesn't work, I'll make friends with Chopin or Erik Satie.

Usually, music is my saving grace in everything.

Horrible, awful day? Music.

Need to file my taxes? Music.

Started my period? Music. Music. Music.

It holds the key to my mind, my emotions, and my heart.

But, apparently, someone changed the locks because not even that is helping today.

I've been working on these lesson plans for my music classes for the past three hours, and I'm at a point where I might resort to banging my head against the wall. The vital clause in my lease contract that states my landlord, Betty, would lose her shit if I put a hole in the drywall is about the only thing that holds me back.

Literally. It says that. *Renter agrees to hold $1000 in escrow pending a damage inspection at move-out. Landlord does not agree not to lose her shit.*

Fine. I made the last sentence up, but if you'd met Betty, you'd understand.

"Mornin', babe. Coffee ready?"

I pause my music and squint my eyes at my boyfriend Matt as he walks into the kitchen. "Just brewed a fresh pot about twenty minutes ago."

"Fantastic," he says, rubs the sleep out of his eyes, and shuffles toward the kitchen counter. "Need a top off?"

I glance down at the nearly empty mug beside my laptop. "Yes, please."

It will be my third—*or is it fourth?*—cup of coffee of the day, but it's a necessary evil when you wake up before the sun.

Sadly, I'm not normally such an early riser. I prefer days where circadian rhythm is the only clock I have to answer to, but my job doesn't allow it.

Today, though… Today, I was already awake.

By the time the clock struck four, I threw in the towel, took a shower, and attempted to start my day.

Lessons plans that don't even really need revamping have been switched and reorganized five times, and I'm well on my way to a world record in coffee consumption.

But avoiding your insanity is much easier than facing the crazy train head on.

My boyfriend's hazel eyes sparkle as he grins at me from across the white marble-top island of my kitchen. Matt is what most would call classically handsome. With sandy blond hair and kissable lips, he reminds me of a *Fight Club* Brad Pitt, but replace the bad-boy vibes with softer lines and a kind face.

Without another word, he fills my white mug, and the steam from the hot brew rises and disappears into the air.

Before Matt can add sugar or cream to my mug, I hop out of my seat and finish the job.

He laughs and bumps my hip with his as he pours himself a cup. "You don't trust me?"

I shake my head on a smile. "Not with my coffee, I don't."

Too much sugar. Too much cream. Too much sugar *and* cream. No matter how hard he may try, my boyfriend of just over a year can never seem to get my coffee just right.

As I settle back into the seat in front of my laptop, he laughs off my teasing criticism and tops off his cream and sugar with a little dribble of coffee.

I'm not sure why he even bothers.

"What's your schedule like today?" he asks, leaning against the counter and taking a sip from his mug. "Any lessons after school?"

Not only am I music teacher for a little private school in the Bronx, but I also teach after-school music lessons. Piano, clarinet, guitar, you name it. My dad is a musician himself, and life with him readied me to play just about anything.

"I should be done around five or so."

"Dinner later, then?"

My ears perk up, and my tongue lolls out like a puppy. "The little Mexican restaurant across the street from your office?"

Matt's office is in Manhattan, my job is in the Bronx, and with my apartment all the way in Brooklyn, I spend a large part of my days in the Bermuda Triangle of hellish commutes. I'd damn near take a train to the moon for a chance to eat at the little Mexican restaurant by the name of El Torro, though.

Hands down, the best guac and tacos that have ever graced my taste buds.

"Consider it a date." He smiles and kisses my cheek just before grabbing the remote for the small TV in the kitchen and flipping on CNN.

Internally, I groan.

I loathe starting my day like this, with the harsh sounds of reality and all of the awful things going on in the world smacking me right in the face.

But Matt loves it. Something about being *informed* and shit. I'd much rather live in a bubble, thank you very much.

Fortunately, it's a rarity for him to stay at my place during the week, and when he's here on the weekends, I can avoid the onslaught of news trauma by getting out of bed an hour or so later than him.

Plus, he travels a lot for his job. It's not uncommon for him to be on the road for weeks at a time.

I'm not entirely sure what he does, but I know it has something to do with big companies and computer software. According to his boss, whom I met at the Christmas party last December, he's a thirty-three-year-old tech wiz. I like to think of him as the Chandler Bing of my alternate *Friends* universe.

"We have exclusive breaking news," the male news anchor announces on the television, and I cringe and roll my eyes.

Everything these days is breaking news.

Internet scams, church scandals, the bitter cold of New York in *January*. It's fucking winter. If you don't expect it to be cold when you go outside, you might be a moron.

Sometimes, I wonder if this twenty-four-hour, every day, constant access to news and social media is going to make us all lose our minds one day. Or, at the very least, develop a chronic case of anxiety.

The urge to bitch about the TV is damn near overwhelming, but instead of taking out my testy mood on Matt or my favorite *Zero Fox Given* mug, I bite my tongue and focus on finishing up this lesson plan for my first-graders. This week, we'll be working on keeping the beat with little drums and animal sounds.

It doesn't take long, though, before Alisyn Camerota, the annoyingly perky news anchor is back on the screen rambling about some famous artist.

You guessed it—more *breaking news.*

"The art world is buzzing today, Phil. It's been nearly five years since we've heard from world-renowned painter Ansel Bray, but his long period of silence has been broken, and the world is mesmerized again."

Blah, blah, blah.

"And now," the male news anchor continues the story, "everyone is wondering about the inspiration behind his paintings. While his signature style used to be that of a muted, melancholy palette, Alistair Frank, the curator at the Met, is calling Ansel Bray's newest works highly romantic and tender."

I know absolutely nothing about art, nor have I ever heard of this artist, but yet, here I am, listening to this boring report.

Probably because you're avoiding lesson plans…

"His works will be showcased in an exhibition at Aquavella Gallery in New York," the male anchor updates. "And tonight will be the first official showing. Although, we've been told tickets are nearly impossible to get."

"Shit," Matt mutters and glances over his shoulder to meet my eyes. "I forgot."

Oh God. I hate that tone. I can almost guarantee he's about to say something I don't want to hear.

"What?" I ask timidly.

"We need to change the plans tonight, babe."

I scrunch up my nose at him. "Why?"

He nods toward the screen. "Because I forgot one of my clients gave us tickets to this art exhibition."

I knew it wasn't going to be good news. My stomach was already preparing for tacos!

"Can't you just act like you're sick or something?"

He grimaces. "I'd feel like an asshole if we didn't use them."

"An art exhibition? Really?" I whine. I want to stuff my face with guac.

"I know." He shrugs one meaty shoulder. "But he gave us four tickets, Indy. We have to, *at the very least,* use two of them."

"You do realize you've already promised me tacos, right?"

A laugh escapes his throat. "I promise we'll still get the tacos. We just need to go to the gallery first."

Even with the taco addendum, I almost refute that option, but an idea pops into my head and reverts my mind-set.

"How many tickets did you say you have?"

"Four."

"If you keep the taco plans and let me bring my sister, we have a deal."

"That works." Matt smirks. "You and Lily can meet me at the gallery. I have a late meeting, and it'll be easier to come straight from work. Is that okay?"

"I think we can manage," I say and grab my phone to shoot my sister a text.

Me: You're going to an art exhibition with me and Matt tonight.

A minute later, she responds.

Lily: What art exhibition?

"What's the artist's name?" I call toward Matt, who is now heading toward my bathroom to take a shower.

"Ansel Bray."

Me: For an artist named Ansel Bray. Meet me at my apartment around 7.

43

Lily: HOW DID YOU GET TICKETS TO ANSEL BRAY'S SHOW?? ON OPENING NIGHT, NO LESS!

I blink at her overexcited text. Maybe I'm not the only one who's had too much coffee this morning?

Me: One of Matt's clients.

Lily: Well, that was FUCKING GENEROUS. I write an arts and entertainment column for the New York Press, and I couldn't get tickets.

Me: I'm not really seeing what all the excitement is about.

Lily: Seriously, Indy? He's a HUGE deal. And now, thanks to Matt, I get to write my next column about Ansel Bray's FIRST SHOW BACK!!!

Me: So, it's a yes?

Lily: SAVE A TICKET FOR ME OR DIE.

Ah, sibling love.

Me: Fine. Also, we're getting tacos afterward at El Torro.

Lily: WHO THE FUCK CARES ABOUT TACOS RIGHT NOW? WE'RE GOING TO ANSEL BRAY'S SHOW!

Me. I care about tacos.

Not even a minute later, my phone starts vibrating across the kitchen counter with *Incoming Call Lily* flashing across the screen.

"Hey, Lil," I greet, but she's already off to the races.

"Oh. My. God!" she shouts so loudly, I have to pull the device away from my ear. "Indy! You have no idea how excited I am now! I can't believe we're going to this show tonight!"

I swear, sometimes Lily is like a little Chihuahua all hopped up on speed.

She's only eighteen months older than me, but it's almost as if we have completely different DNA. She's boisterous, super outgoing, insanely chatty, and I'm mellow, a little bit introverted, and prefer to keep my emotions close to the vest.

Obviously, our parents didn't mix at all. They split chromosomal donation cleanly by alternating children. Lily is Holly Davis to a T, and I'm one hundred percent Mac Davis's daughter.

"Well, I'm glad you're excited."

"Excited?" she shouts. "I'm over the fucking moon!"

I grimace. Her current mood is a bit too much for me this morning.

"Okay, well, I'll see you tonight…" I attempt to end the call, but she doesn't let me off the hook that easy.

"Wait a minute…are you okay?" she asks. "You sound off…"

"It's nothing." I shrug and pick at a piece of invisible lint on my pants. "I'm fine." There's no way I'm going to drudge up old demons right now. I've done pretty well this morning, and after this many years, you'd think I'd at least be moving in the direction of getting over it.

"Well, then liven up, buttercup," she commands. "We've got tickets to the hottest show in town, and there's no way I'm going to let you ruin it by moping before eight a.m."

I swallow against the pull of melancholy and take her advice. The day hasn't even started yet, and at least I'll get to spend the evening with my sister. "You're right."

She groans. "Of course, I am."

"And so humble."

"Who needs to be humble when they've got tickets to see Ansel Bray's long-anticipated collection?"

"Not you."

"Fucking right."

I roll my eyes and, despite myself, even manage a little laugh. "I'll see you tonight."

"That's right," she says, and her voice jumps in octaves. "You'll see me tonight at Ansel Bray's show!"

At seven on the dot, my always on-time sister shows up at my apartment, dressed in a sleek white pantsuit and tapping her watch impatiently at my lack of readiness.

It takes me another fifteen or so minutes to fix my long dark locks into somewhat manageable waves down my back and decide on my outfit of choice—a simple blush shift dress, heels, and a vintage cape with gold buttons.

My sister bitches at my lack of timeliness for most of the Uber ride to the gallery, but once we pull up in front of the building, she drops the attitude and goes straight into journalist mode.

I, on the other hand, take a weird nose dive into anxiety.

I have no idea what has me so on edge. Maybe it's the crowd? The day? Because I'm already hungry for tacos?

Who knows, but I breathe through it and show the tickets Matt had couriered from his office to my classroom this afternoon to the security guard at the entrance.

We're barely five feet inside the front doors when Lily is stopped by a gray-haired gentleman holding a complimentary glass of wine. He animatedly asks her about a recent column she published about the Guggenheim, and my sister goes into her full smiley, outgoing, extrovert mode.

As their conversation barrels into journalist mumbo jumbo, my phone buzzes inside my purse with a text.

Matt: Sorry I'm running late, babe. I'm still stuck in the meeting, but trying to leave as soon as I can.

Internally, I groan. The only reason I'm here is because Matt said we *had* to make an appearance. And yet, here I am, without him.

But when I glance back at my sister and find her totally in her element, chatting it up and smiling at her number one fan, I realize the evening isn't entirely lost. *At least someone is gaining something from this boring art exhibition.*

Me: It's okay. Just let me know when you're headed here.

I hit send on my text to Matt, and when I see my sister is still balls deep in a conversation I know nothing about, I quietly shuffle away and walk around the gallery by myself.

Ironically, it's so crowded and stuffy that it takes an insane amount of jockeying and work just to stand in front of one of Ansel Bray's infamous paintings.

Good thing, as Matt once pointed out to me, I have extra pointy elbows.

Starting at the front, I work my way toward the back of the gallery, standing in front of each painting and trying to figure out what all the hype is about.

The first is of a window that frames the outside of the canvas, and the almost heavenly beyond that lies within it. I notice the attention to detail is intense, but none of the objects look like anything I've ever seen before. There are no roses or lilies in the garden; there are only vibrant flowers I'm almost positive couldn't exist in nature.

The second is much less abstract. An image of a tattered woman lying at the base of a fountain. The water spills over her body and soaks the rags she has for clothes.

The third is a complex swirl of color only, dying in the center and fading into what seems to be a pit of darkness.

There's an ease in the strokes of each painting, but the colors are complex. It's like he's layered a mix to make the end result, instead of just using the color in the first place.

I've never really understood this kind of art, though. It's pretty, I admit. Pretty enough to validate the fact that my sister nearly comes in her pants every time she hears the artist's name? I'm not convinced.

With each step I take deeper into the space, the whispered conversations get louder. The artist's tragic absence from the art scene when a car accident turned him blind. His miraculous recovery.

And, every once in a while, a poetic rave about the art. *Brilliant. Fragile. A beautiful mélange of softness and story.*

The crowd in the back space is different, though—more intense—and I have to wait in line for a few minutes to see the painting.

At last, the crowd in front of me clears and reveals the canvas framed in gold. And this time, the illustration before me reaches out and grabs me by the throat. Three abrupt coughs come out unbidden, and I have to cover my mouth with my hand to prevent my saliva from spraying the expensive art.

Long brown hair with ribbons of gold, blue eyes, and two dimples pressed into the center of her cheeks, she's nearly the spitting image of me.

Dear God, I feel like I'm looking in the mirror.

Jesus.

I blink my eyes several times to refocus.

Surely, the lack of sleep and the six cups of coffee I drank today have affected my eyes...

But the more I stare at the painting—a delicate visual of what looks like me from behind while I glance over my shoulder, bare skin all the way to the curve of my left hip—the harder it gets to breathe, and my heart all but hurtles out of my chest and onto the gallery floor. It's so fragile and tender, and so goddamn distantly familiar that my hands begin to shake against my legs.

I can almost remember when I last looked this carefree.

I've never met Ansel Bray.

Never even heard of him until today.

So why does the girl in his painting look so much like me?

Seeing this woman...seeing so much of my old self in her to-day...it's nearly too much to bear.

A young guy wearing a fedora bumps my hip as he tries to shuffle through the crowd behind me, and I'm stunned out of my silence.

"I'm so sorry," he apologizes as I meet his eyes.

My voice—my very being—feels trapped in the tight hold of my chest, but somehow, someway, I manage to push out the words, "It's okay."

"It's too crowded," he says, but then pauses. His gaze shifts between me and the painting hanging in front of us. "Wait..." Excitement lights his eyes. "Is that you?"

My heart all but collapses in on itself at his words.

"No!" I snap with something that was meant to be a laugh. It sounds more like a small animal in distress. It may not be what I'm going for, but it perfectly embodies what I'm feeling.

"Are you sure?" he asks and keeps alternating between examining the painting and my face. "Because it sure looks like you."

"I'm sure. I don't even know the artist. Hell, I don't even really like art."

A wrinkle forms between his brows, and I realize my hysteria may have loosened my lips just a little too much.

"I mean...the paintings are great, but this is my first time at a show. It's not me."

The scrutiny of his gaze makes my chest grow tight with anxiety. I feel vulnerable. Exposed. Like I'm having that awful dream where I'm standing completely naked in the middle of my high school, ex-cept replace the school with this gallery. I rub my now sweaty palms across the material of my dress.

He grins, and I take it as my cue that I need to get the *fuck* out of there. "If you'll excuse me, I need to find my sister." I don't give him time to respond and push through the crowd, paying absolutely no at-tention to the rest of the paintings, until I reach the rear of the gallery.

I rest my hip against an empty wall which is connected to a long back hall with a small sign that says restrooms resting above its archway and try to get myself together.

My chest is tight and my head feels fuzzy, and I don't know how much longer I can stay here while my mind races with confusing thoughts and questions and memories I'd much prefer not to think about right now.

I stare at the tops of my nude pumps and force myself to take slow, deep breaths.

There has to be an explanation for this, I tell myself. *It's probably just some sort of weird coincidence.*

And then I start to question the likeness of it all. *Does that painting really look like me? Isn't that kind of a narcissistic thing to think, Indy? That a beautiful painting looks like you?*

Surely, I'm mistaken...*right?*

That guy in the fedora didn't seem mistaken...

"Where did you go?" Lily asks, bumping me with a playful hip. I look up from my shoes to meet her eyes, and I find Matt standing beside her.

Looks like he finally arrived.

"We were looking everywhere for you."

"Sorry, I was late, baby." Matt grins and steps forward to plant a soft kiss to my lips. I feel oddly annoyed by it, but I swallow down the feeling with the rest of the intense emotions running through my veins.

"I thought you were going to text me when you were on your way?" I ask, and he wraps his arm around my shoulder, tucking me into his side.

"I did, but I guess you didn't see it."

Oh. Whoops.

"I guess so," I mutter, but my mind is mostly just thinking that his body is too warm and I am too warm and, goddammit, is this gallery on the surface of the sun?

"You feeling okay?" Lily asks, and she scrutinizes my face.

"Yeah, it's just a little crowded in here," I say with a little shrug and a tug on the material of my dress. "I might need to step out and get some fresh air soon. I'm feeling overheated."

"Well, if you can hang in there for a little longer, I just need to see a few more paintings. Maybe then I can walk outside with you while Matt finishes making his rounds?"

I want to tell them I'm ready to go right the fuck now, but I bite my tongue.

Matt wants to be here and Lily is here for work, and I want to respect that. I don't want to be the emotional asshole who wrecks everyone's evening.

So, I suck it up.

"Okay."

Lily smiles and leads the way, with Matt and me in tow behind her.

All is well, until she leads us right back to that *fucking painting.*

Instantly, my heart flutters and flips beneath my rib cage, stealing the breath from my lungs.

Maybe they won't notice.

"Holy shit," Lily mutters, and she glances back and forth between me and the painting. "Indy, she looks like you!"

"Yeah." Matt grins and squeezes my shoulder. "She really does look like you, baby."

I try to shrug it off, but on the inside, I'm dying.

"You don't see it?" Lily asks and I shrug again.

"Maybe a little," I force out a lie.

"A little?" my sister questions on a laugh. "If I didn't know you better, I might ask if you were Ansel Bray's secret mystery muse or something."

My heart drops to my stomach, and I think the words *I am no one's muse* in my head. *No one's.*

Matt grimaces but laughs at the same time. "Well, fuck. I don't think I'd be too happy with that scenario."

"I'm kidding!" Lily says and gives him a teasing pat to the shoulder. He takes it all in good humor. All in all, really, he's happy.

And Lily's happy.

Everyone's just having the fucking time of their lives.

Everyone but me.

I try to laugh along with them, but I'm almost certain all I've managed is a silent grimace that has all the feminine appeal of Voldemort.

While my sister takes notes and pulls her camera out of her purse to take a photo, I stare at that damn painting, picking it apart for all the details I surely don't share.

"Look, babe," Matt says and points toward the painting, "she even has dimples and that little beauty mark on your cheek."

"That's crazy," Lily chimes in just before she lifts her camera in front of her face to snap a photo.

I couldn't respond if I wanted to. My lungs are too tight with shock, and my heart has migrated its way into my throat. So, all I do is nod, but on the inside, I'm rocks and dirt and dust crumbling to the ground.

Vivid memories assail me, and I grab at my chest to find what surely must be a knife. And closer and closer the walls of the gallery come, suffocating me until I can't breathe.

My fingers tremble, and my flight response kicks in.

"I think I'm g-gonna walk outside," I say through the tightness in my throat.

"What?" Matt asks, but when his eyes lock on to my face, his gaze goes wide. "Indy? You okay, babe?"

I shake my head. "I don't feel so well."

I turn on my heels and push through the crowd until I reach the long white hall that leads to the bathrooms.

I'm in the stall and barely getting the door shut when a rush of nausea overwhelms me, and I almost don't make it to the toilet in time.

Fucking hell. What just happened out there?

What did I just see?

By the time I get myself together enough to step out of the stall, my sister is standing beside the sink with concerned eyes.

"Are you okay?" she asks and hands me a wet paper towel to wipe my mouth.

I nod and take in my pale and clammy reflection in the mirror as I move the towel across my forehead and lips.

"What happened?"

That fucking painting happened.

"I don't know." I shrug and throw the towel into the wastebasket beneath the sink. "All of a sudden, I just felt nauseous."

It's at least partially the truth.

The rest, I can't even understand myself, much less try to explain it to someone else.

"Wait…" Her eyes go wide. "You're not pregnant, are you?"

"Don't be ridiculous." I roll my eyes and turn on the faucet. "You have to have sex to get pregnant."

"You have a boyfriend, Indigo Davis," she retorts with a furrowed brow. And I know when she uses my full name, she means business. "A boyfriend whom you've been with for over a year, by the way. I sure as fuck hope you're having sex. One of us should be."

"Well, he travels a lot," I retort, trying to cover over my embarrassing truth. "And, plus, I'm on the pill."

To be honest, I can't even remember the last time Matt and I had sex.

Has it really been that long since we've had sex?

I try to count the days in my head, but when I reach three weeks, I stop altogether and choose to explore that shocking realization another time. Preferably one that doesn't involve me puking in a public restroom.

"Well, if you're not pregnant, then what's wrong with you?"

"I don't know." I shrug and wash my hands. "I think it was just a bad combination of it being too hot and crowded inside this gallery and the fact that I ate tuna salad for lunch."

"Ew." She grimaces. "I can't even think about tuna fish after hearing you hurl into the toilet."

"How do you think I feel?" I question on a laugh. "I was the one hanging over said toilet, doing all of the hurling."

Lily's bright-red lips crest up into a smile. "What do you say we head out of here and get you home? Pretty sure your stomach isn't going to be able to tolerate tacos right now."

For once in my life, I can agree that tacos are a bad idea.

"Definitely not." I dry my hands with a paper towel and turn off the faucet. "Let's head home."

When we leave the bathroom, I find Matt standing at the end of the hall, worry written all over his face.

"Everything okay?"

"Yeah," I say and force a reassuring smile to my lips. "I think I just got overheated, and the tuna fish I ate for lunch didn't respond too well to that."

"You sure that's all it is?"

"Positive." I nod. "But I *am sure* I want to go home now."

Thankfully, Matt doesn't give any pushback, and it doesn't take long before we're heading toward the front doors of the gallery. But this time, I'm smart enough to keep my eyes toward the ground as we pass through the exhibition. Avoiding everything and everyone inside the building.

My heart has had enough for the day.

Tomorrow, I'll try to wrap my head around the girl in Ansel Bray's painting.

chapter seven

Ansel

"First, I want to thank you for taking the time to chat with me this morning," *Just Debra,* as she's introduced herself, with the *Los Angeles Times* says, and I rein in my inner asshole and focus on remaining cordial.

She's just doing her job, I remind myself.

"Sure," I respond in the friendliest voice I can manage. It sounds a little too much like I'm imitating Clark Griswold, but at least it's devoid of irritation and annoyance.

I run my free hand across the leather of my favorite chair and stare lazily at the floor-to-ceiling windows of my living room. The bright morning sun magnifies the specks of dust floating in the air, and I think briefly about hiring a housekeeper.

It's barely ten, this is already my fourth phone interview of the day, and my mind has started to wander.

I make a mental note to threaten Nigel's life if he ever does this to me again. There's already a sticky note filed in the back of my brain with that exact message on it, crinkled from overuse. I add an asterisk and date it for today, bringing it back to current.

No doubt, this is his version of payback for my refusing to attend the exhibition opening the other night.

I used to have a publicist who handled this kind of shit, but he quit. There was "nothing a publicist can do for an angry blind man who doesn't want to speak with anyone," and he wasn't thrilled with conditions."

ently, my good friend Nigel thinks he can stick his big fuck-
e into the empty publicity role, and I either won't notice or
t say anything.

The bastard.

His gallery may be running my show, but that doesn't mean I'm going to roll over and let him feed me to the media wolves.

"Last night was the first official opening of your exhibition at Aquavella," the reporter informs me—as though she's telling me something I don't know.

Thank you, Mrs. Obvious.

"It was."

"Early reviews from the opening are absolutely phenomenal, with the one complaint seemingly about the space. Why is that you've chosen to hold the exhibition in such a small space and for such a short amount of time? You could have sold out MoMA, yet you chose Aquavella."

"Because the paintings in this exhibition aren't meant to be show-cased in a large empty room with fluorescent lights glaring down on them. They're too vulnerable, and their scale is too small. They needed a space that was intimate."

"An intimate space. It's interesting that you use that word."

I roll my eyes and lean back in my leather chair. "And why is that, Debra?"

There's one question I've been asked in every single interview, and Debra's version of it is circling, readying itself to make a landing.

"One painting seemed to fit that bill in particular."

I hum.

"The girl in the painting, Ansel. Who is she?"

"She's simply a girl in a painting."

She laughs, as if she can't believe I'm being this obtuse. As if I'm fucking feeding her lines.

"Her phenomenal presence in your show has raised a lot of

questions and curiosities. That painting seems to be the one that is drawing the most attention out of all of your works."

"Interesting observation," I muse.

Her incredulous laugh fills my ears. She's done with our dance around the bush. "Is she real?"

"She's as real as any of my other works. I take little parts of my life and put them into everything I paint."

What I don't say is how big of a part this particular mirage has had. After being locked inside the black abyss, she is what guided me back to the light. Back to painting again.

"Somehow, you've given me an answer that only raises more questions," she responds, and it's my turn to laugh. I haven't made a point to be cryptic, but apparently, I've played right into the curious mass's hands.

"My brother would have a field day with this right now."

"Is that so?"

I swipe off a piece of lint from my jeans. "It's a certainty."

"Speaking of your brother, what does he think of your exhibition?"

"I don't know," I say with a cheeky smile. "You'd have to ask him yourself."

"I'd love to do just that, but I'll have to pull a few strings before I can get an interview with Bram Bray on the books."

Instantly, I get an idea.

"How about I pull those strings for you?"

"Excuse me?"

"Sit tight for a minute, Debra," I instruct, and already, I'm pulling the phone away from my face to prepare to dial the number I know by heart with a smile on my face. "I'll be right back."

I don't give her time to respond, and a minute or two later, I have my brother on one line, while Debra is on hold on the other.

"What's up?" Bram asks by way of greeting.

I make the conscious decision not to explain. It'll really be better if this is a surprise. Well…better for *me*, anyway.

"Hold on, Bram," I say and tap the screen to merge the calls together.

"Debra? You still there?"

"Uh…yes," she responds immediately.

"Bram?"

"What's going on, Ans?" he asks, but I ignore him.

"Debra, this is my brother. Bram, this is Debra, an interviewer from the *LA Times*. She has a few questions for you."

"Wait…what—?"

"Looks like we're all set here." I cut my brother off, my grin so big now it's a second away from being a full-blown smile. "It was great talking to you, Deb. Have a lovely day."

I remove myself from the call before my brother can protest, and I shout victory into the crisp emptiness of my brownstone.

And that, ladies and gentlemen, is exactly how you end an interview early.

By the time I'm almost ready to head into my personal studio on the second level of my house, my phone vibrates with a text message.

Bram: You're such a dick.

I chuckle and type out a quick response.

Me: Consider it payback for that time you sent a car full of your groupies to my house at three in the morning.

Bram: But they wanted to meet the illustrious Ansel Bray. Who was I to say no?

That fucking night. It took me nearly an hour to get the drunk, extremely loud, and scantily clad ladies inside my driver Hank's Escalade and on their way home.

Me: Well, Mr. Accommodating, I'll keep that in my mind the next time someone stops me on the street to tell me how much they love New Rules...

Next time that happens, I'll personally escort them to his fucking house.

Bram: And I'll be sure to get you on the line every time someone asks me about the girl in your painting...

I cringe. The one painting I didn't want to put in the show, the one painting I hoped would fly under the radar, is the one painting everyone appears to be fixated on.

Me: People are asking you about her too?

Bram: Apparently my publicist is up to her ears today with calls about the girl in your painting.

I click my phone to sleep and walk into the bathroom to take a shower and get ready to head to my studio.

I've got more visions of *her* to paint.

But before I hop in the shower, my phone pings with another text.

Fully prepared to see Bram's name, I tilt my head to the side when I read the name Lennon Quill on the screen.

Fucking hell. I groan, already annoyed.

Lennon Quill is a guy I've known since I was in my early twenties and is a complete fucking mess.

A cocaine-dabbling, fedora-wearing, self-proclaimed hipster who tries to chase other people's fame because he can't find an artistic voice of his own.

The only reason his number is programmed into my phone is to ensure I avoid his toxicity. Because that's exactly what he is—*toxic*.

Unfortunately, given the amount of time that's passed since I last heard from him, I'm too damn curious *not* to open his message.

Lennon Quill: Great show, dude. Truly impressed with the new works. And it was clever to have her at the opening, but not admitting she's the inspiration.

What is he talking about?

I shake my head as I read the message again. When it still doesn't make sense, I have to assume it's being brought to me courtesy of a bender.

It's an easy decision.

Ignore. Delete. And go on about my day.

chapter eight

T wo hours ago, I gave Matt a kiss goodbye and watched him hop into a black town car and head for the airport. He's on his way to another business trip that includes big European companies and the installation of some sort of high-tech computer program.

Considering my knowledge of computers revolves around how to find Microsoft Word and my iTunes library, it's all a bit over my head.

He will be gone for twenty-one days, and his itinerary will take him through several stops in Europe—France, Italy, Germany, and a few other countries I don't even remember.

No doubt, it's a long time to be away from my boyfriend, but I'm used to it.

My phone vibrates across the coffee table, and I pause my mindless search for something to watch on television and check the screen.

Sally. *Again.* This is the second call in the last three weeks. It's way more than her usual twice a year, but not enough to make me hit accept. I'm not ready, and something emergent would surely warrant more calls than this.

I slide my phone back onto the table, and it vibrates again immediately. I'm almost scared to look, but something about being in my thirties means I'm not allowed to be a total baby anymore.

This time, it's a text from Matt.

Matt: Getting ready to board now. Here's to hoping these next three weeks fly by. Miss you already, baby.

Baby. My lips turn down at the corners.

Terms of endearment have never really been my thing, but they're sort of Matt's thing, so I try to oblige.

But I can't deny it grates on my nerves a bit. Or *a lot*, if I'm really being honest with myself.

Me: Have a safe trip and let me know when you land. XOXO.

Matt: I will. Promise if you start feeling bad again, you'll go to the doctor?

After my abrupt departure from the gallery the other night, he's been urging me to get checked out.

It's been a long forty-eight hours of reassuring him I'm fine and him obsessing over stomach viruses and weird diseases.

In his defense, when it comes to illness, he's biologically prone to worrying too much, courtesy of his hypochondriac mother. And, well, he doesn't know the real reason I ended up puking in the bathroom at Aquavella.

I mean, how do you tell your boyfriend you got sick because of the painting you saw? In hindsight, even I feel like I overreacted. Seeing myself in one random painting that some guy painted shouldn't produce such a physical reaction.

It's just a coincidence. Nothing more.

Me: I'm fine, Matt. It was just a weird blip of nausea. Nothing to be concerned about.

Matt: Okay, sweetheart. Getting ready for takeoff now. Talk soon.

I toss my phone back onto the coffee table and scroll through the channels for another few minutes before I set down the remote and get off the couch.

It's Saturday. I should be doing something fun. Something that gets me out of my house. Something, *anything,* besides sitting on my couch.

I think about calling Lily or my mom or even a few of my girl-friends from work, but being with people seems like too much work.

Instead, I decide to go it alone, take a little walk, and see where the day takes me.

Maybe I'll grab some lunch at my favorite diner up the street. Or maybe I'll be adventurous and take the subway toward the city for a stroll through Washington Square Park. The day is an untraveled road, and I get to choose the destination.

Before I talk myself out of it, I get dressed, put on a little makeup, fix my long locks into a ponytail, and bundle up in my favorite pea coat, scarf, and boots.

I tap on one of my favorite playlists, put my earbuds in my ears and my phone in my back pocket, and head out the door. With Camila Cabello serenading me, I step outside, and the frigid February air punches me right in the face. If the bitter wind had a fist, I'd officially have a black eye. I adjust my cream scarf to cover my mouth and nose and force my feet to move across the sidewalk.

Shit. Maybe I should've just stuck with Netflix?

It doesn't take long for me to realize the subway station is closer than the diner, and I let the harsh winter weather lead my way down the stairs to the waiting platform and onto the next train.

Looks like a trip into the city it is…

Packed to the brim with other Saturday-goers, I stand in the center of the metal-enclosed cart, my fingers clutching a silver pole for balance, and let my eyes rake discreetly over my ride companions.

A family with two small children and a stroller takes up the entire back wall. A group of giggling teenage girls stare down at their phones and take up nearly an entire row of seats on the left side. And a couple holding hands and smiling into each other's eyes stand to the right of me.

But it's the couple that I can't seem to stop watching.

He reaches out, brushes her auburn hair out of her eyes, and her pink-coated smile grows.

They're so beautiful, so in-the-moment, so lost in each other, it kind of hurts to witness.

Not because I don't like seeing people so lost in love that the world around them dissolves, but because I *do*. I love to see it. I just don't like to think about how much I want it for myself.

Which leads my thoughts down a dangerous path toward that fucking painting and the carefree version of me inside it and back into the emotional tailspin I've been trying desperately to ignore.

The subway screeches to another stop and people start filing off, but the couple stays rooted to their spot and fixated on each other's eyes. Their decision to stay solidifies my decision to go, and I walk off the subway in the name of self-preservation.

I don't even know what stop I've chosen, but I don't care. I'll make it work.

Once I make my way up the stairs and onto the sidewalk, the surroundings give me déjà vu, and it isn't the good kind. I feel sick almost instantly, and the taste of tuna flashes in my mouth even though I haven't eaten it since.

Of course, I took this fucking stop.

The gallery is a scant two blocks away, and I hate myself for not paying enough attention to end up anywhere but here.

Hell, even the claustrophobic crowds of Times Square would've been a better option than this. At least I could have popped into M&M'S World and left with five pounds of chocolate I don't need.

After that night at the gallery, I've resisted the urge to find out anything about Ansel Bray. I told myself the girl in his painting wasn't really like me, and it was all just a freakishly weird and mind-blowing coincidence. It was for the best that I retreat back to my art ignorant bubble and go on about my life.

Yet, here I am.

One foot after the other, two blocks are gone far faster than they should be.

With cold hands and a nearly frozen nose, I pull my earbuds out of my ears and stand in front of the building, peering through the windows to the right of the entrance.

It looks empty, completely vacant of movement and people, so I nearly jump out of my skin when one of the big wooden doors opens unexpectedly.

A man dressed in a smart suit steps out of the front doors and glances over his shoulder as he pulls a key out of his pocket. "We're closed."

"All day?" I ask, and he shakes his head.

"The next exhibit is this evening, but it's completely sold out," he answers matter-of-factly. When I don't acknowledge his statement or take any steps to move away, he glances at me over his shoulder again. "Did you need something else?"

"I've already seen his exhibit."

"Okay…?" He pauses, and confusion creases his brow. "And you wanted to try to see it again?"

What is it I'm trying to do here? See the painting again?

Jesus. I don't even know.

You want to see him.

That last thought stirs something inside my belly, and the words are out of my mouth before I can stop them. "I…uh…I need to speak with him. With Ansel Bray."

The guy chuckles. "You and everybody else, sweetheart."

Sweetheart. Jesus. There's only one thing I dislike about terms of endearment more than hearing them from my boyfriend, and that's hearing them from complete fucking strangers.

"It's really important," I continue.

I have no idea what I'm doing. I have no idea what I'll say.

But I can no longer ignore the fact that something is pulling me here.

The guy turns on his heels and scans my face. His brow furrows deeper as he takes in my eyes and my hair and my lips. And just before I attempt to toss out some ridiculous lie to try to persuade him, his gray eyes turn big and wide.

"Well, looks like someone is a liar," he mutters to himself, slides his key back into the lock, and opens the door. "Come inside and give me a minute to get in touch with him."

chapter
nine

Ansel

"Ansel!" Lucy yells from the front office, and I groan.

She's blatantly ignoring my request for no distractions, and I have a feeling it's in direct protest of having to come into work on a Saturday to finalize a contract with a museum in San Diego.

Never mind it's her own ineptitude that's forced her here. The contract should've been finalized Thursday.

It's my turn to play the ignore card, and I tap my brush against the side of my large easel three times, my eyes focused while my brain visualizes hues of pink and nude and cream.

"Ansel! You have a phone call!"

I set down my brush and run a hand through my hair. "Goddammit, Luce, I'm a little busy!"

"But it's Nigel!" she shouts back. "I think it's important!"

Nigel. I've been ignoring his text messages since he scheduled a bunch of phone interviews that I didn't agree to. Boy oh boy, the mental Post-it note about ways to kill him sure is looking worn.

He better hope he's calling me for a specific, vitally important reason.

I wipe my palms against my jeans and head toward the main office located at the front of my studio.

Lucy sits behind the desk, her lips pursed into an "I told you so" expression, and I roll my eyes as I grab the phone.

"What?" she chimes in before I answer the call. "No apology?"

I can't not grin at that. "You've got some balls, you know that?"

She flutters her eyelashes dramatically. "So, I'm free to go home now?"

"Did you send the contracts?"

"God, you're like a tyrant," she groans, and my grin turns into a full-on smile.

While most days—*like today*—my assistant is a sarcastic, stubborn pain in my ass, I know for a fact that she is the only person in the world who would tolerate working for me for all these years.

I was a real bastard during those tragic months when I didn't have my eyes and the vines of despair and bitterness had taken root within my heart, and I'm not all that much better now.

I'll have to acknowledge her commitment at some point. Maybe some extra time off and maybe some bonus money to finance one of her many cosmetic procedures.

I grab the phone and put it to my ear.

"Hey, Nigel."

"I know you're in the studio this afternoon, but...uh..." He pauses, and I don't miss the way amusement curls around his voice. "The model from your painting—the one that you specifically said doesn't exist—well, she's here..."

"Model?" I furrow my brow. "What model?"

"The girl in your painting," he says, and I can actually hear the smile in his voice. "She's here. In my gallery. Right now."

I let out an annoyed sigh. "Stop fucking around, and tell me why you really called."

"I'm not fucking around," he retorts. "I'm literally standing here, in my office, looking at her through the glass."

Now, he's starting to piss me off. "I'm going to give you about ten more seconds, then I'm hanging up."

"Honestly, Ans, I feel a little betrayed that you lied to me about your muse," he says through a soft chuckle. "Here I thought she was just some fictitious angel inside your mind, but come to find out, she's actually real."

It's on the tip of my tongue to call him a half-dozen less-than-flattering names, but then I think about the strange text Lennon Quill sent me. *It was clever to have her at the opening, but not admitting she's the inspiration.*

My heart makes itself known inside my chest, pounding against my ribs like it's trying to make an escape from my body.

"The girl from my painting is at your gallery?" I ask, my voice a mere whisper.

"Yep," Nigel answers like it's not the most insane, unbelievable thing that's ever left his lips. Because, in fact, it is.

The girl in my paintings, the angel inside my mind, she doesn't exist.

At least, I didn't think she did.

Does she?

"She said she wants to speak with you," he adds.

Good God, what if she's real?

"Tell her I'm on my way." The words fall from my lips without a second thought. If she's real, if Nigel isn't fucking around with me, if Lennon Quill's message actually held some truth to it, I need to see her with my own eyes.

"But…"

"Just tell her I'm leaving my studio now, and I'll be there shortly, okay?"

"Okay." Finally, all traces of amusement have left his tone. Probably because I foolishly haven't done enough to hide how shaken I am.

I don't waste any time after that, hanging up the phone, grabbing the essentials, and rushing out the door.

"If you're leaving, I'm leaving!" Luce yells as I push it open. I'm too fucking consumed by what Nigel's just told me to give a shit.

"Do whatever you want!" I yell back without a second thought.

Two stairs at a time, my feet move like they have a mind of their own, but I don't protest.

They're headed to the right place. To Aquavella.

Thirty minutes later, and my hands are close to shaking by the time I reach the front doors of the gallery.

Get it together, you fool, I tell myself.

Rationally, I know the odds of this woman being the woman from my paintings, the constant presence inside my mind, are impossible. I know this, yet my gut churns with this irrational elation. This undeniable surge of relief and excitement and palpable joy.

Usually, I'm the least excitable man I know. But today, right fucking now, I'm damn near high off the possibility of finding her. Of meeting her. Of seeing her in the flesh.

My mind has traced the lines of her face, her lips, her eyes, her hair, her soft skin a million times. I've seen her smile and her sadness and her melancholy. I've seen what her eyes look like when passion flashes within them.

I've never met her, but I already feel like I know her.

It's insane, I know, but somehow, she's become a part of me.

I inhale a deep, steadying breath and grab the large, distressed-wood handle of the gallery door. The wind whips through my leather jacket as I step inside, and when the door closes behind me with a quiet click, two sets of eyes turn to look at me.

One set of eyes are of a man who's been a friend for most of my life.

The other are the sparkling blue of a woman I didn't know could really exist. Even the gold flakes laced artfully within the blue are familiar, and it makes my heart ache and race at the same time.

Every nerve inside my body wakes up until I'm a walking live wire.

I rake my eyes down her cheeks and her lips and her hair and the slender lines of her neck. I think I've lost my mind because it's *her.*

The girl in my paintings.

Her wide-open gaze turns guarded when her eyes lock with mine, and the urge to stride toward her and wrap her up in my arms overwhelms me.

I want to protect her from whatever it is that's making her uncomfortable.

But I quell the nearly overpowering impulse because, in all likelihood, *I* am the thing that's making her feel that way.

"Here he is," Nye says as he stands up from one of the lobby chairs. "You made good time, buddy."

"Hello," I say to her. Nye has ceased to exist to me. There is only her and me, and…and I probably need to tone down the intensity a little, for fuck's sake.

She looks like I'm scaring her.

Forcing the stiffness out of my jaw and the crazy out of my eyes, I put my hands in my pockets to seem less threatening and try again. "Hello."

"Hi." Her voice is so soft, so smooth, so melodic to my ears, it could be its own fucking instrument.

God, my heart is racing so fast. So fucking fast.

I have *got* to calm down before I make her run.

Hell, if I were her, and some strange man told me I was his muse even though we'd never met before, I'd probably run too.

"I'll be in the back if you need anything," Nye says, but I hardly notice when he quietly extracts himself from the room.

I step toward her and hold out my hand. "I'm Ansel Bray."

Tentatively, she accepts it with her own.

It feels tiny and delicate and like the easiest comfort I've ever experienced in my life.

This is crazy. Fuck, I feel crazy.

"I'm Indigo Davis," she responds.

"Indigo," I mouth, and just a hint of a grin curls the corner of her mouth.

"My dad is a fan of the blues. He thought my name was a cheeky take on an ironic tribute." She shrugs. "But everyone calls me Indy."

"Nice to meet you, Indy." Her name rolls off my tongue like it was always meant to be there.

She releases my hand, and I don't miss the way her shaky fingers scratch at the fabric of her pants in quick, awkward strokes.

Silence stretches between us, and it takes everything inside of me not to let it grow while I feast my eyes on her face. On her eyes. On her lips. On her porcelain skin.

How can this be?

How is she here?

How is she real?

I blink my eyes and clear my throat. "So, you wanted to see me?"

She nods, but when her lips start to move, no words come out.

She has to know. She has to know she looks like the girl in my painting.

I take it upon myself to break the ice. "So, I'm not sure if you've noticed, but I've been painting someone who looks exactly like you."

She nods again.

"I have no fucking clue why." It's a soft statement, despite the vulgarity, and it's apparently just what she needs to hear.

Her eyes light up with relief, and a nervous giggle escapes her lips. "God, I'm so glad you said that. I have no clue why either."

I grin at the small victory.

"I'm sorry if you were busy," she continues and pauses for a brief moment as she glances around the gallery before meeting my eyes again. "But...I saw the painting, and I just wanted to meet you."

"I wasn't busy, and I'm glad you came."

"Really?"

I nod. "Of course."

The fact that she's even questioning my desire for her presence is mind-blowing, but I keep those details to myself. I can tell she's nervous and scared and guarded. Like a beautiful little hummingbird locked inside a cage.

And that's the exact opposite of how I want her to feel.

"I was here the other night," she admits. "For the exhibition. With my sister."

That explains the coke addict's text.

"Did you enjoy it?"

"I did," she says and then giggles awkwardly as she fidgets her fingers together. "And I also didn't."

My lips crest up into a grin when she puts a hand over her mouth in surprise.

"Oh God, that sounded bad," she grumbles, dropping her head fully into her hand before looking up to meet my eyes again. "I mean, I don't know much about art…at all, really…but your paintings seem pretty great. It was just a little weird for me, you know?"

"I knew what you meant," I say, and my smile grows. For some reason, I love that she doesn't seem to know much about me. "I can imagine it's a little weird having a man you've never met before paint a portrait of you."

"Yeah…uh…it's definitely not the norm, you know?"

"I know. I didn't think the imaginary muse inside my mind was real, yet here you are, looking so much like her. Pretty much identical, if I'm being truthful about it. It's a bit crazy."

"Yeah," she whispers. "Crazy is probably a good word for it."

I chuckle, and I watch the way her eyes open wider, her guard slowly crumbling.

"Maybe we've passed each other in the street or seen each other on the subway." She shrugs. "Or who knows, maybe I have a doppelgänger out there somewhere."

I furrow my brow. "A doppelgänger?"

"Yeah," she says with an uncertain little nod. "Someone who looks just like me. People post about their celebrity doppelgänger all the time on social media."

"I don't have any social media profiles."

"Really?" She seems shocked, and the wide-eyed look that goes with it makes me want to laugh.

"Nope," I respond. "I'm not much for social interaction."

"Me either," she agrees, which surprises me given how shocked she was about my lack of an Instagram account.

"An imaginary muse," she repeats my earlier words, like she's testing them out on her tongue.

To my soul, I know this isn't some random coincidence. This beautiful woman standing in front of me, Indy Davis, is *her.* The girl I've been picturing inside my mind over the past year.

She is the girl in my paintings.

I know it in the way she moves her mouth and the way she smiles and the way her eyes reflect the light of day.

I *know* it's her. It's the whole, not-knowing-why part that has me reeling.

Though, my mind and my heart are fanatical in their pursuit to figure it out.

I've never been the type of man who believes in fate. But I know to my core that there is a reason for Indy.

A meaning. A purpose.

Her gaze is locked with mine, so tight, so strong and powerful, and I sense the way she's searching my eyes for something. For answers to unknown questions. For reasons and truth. For something she's hoping I know.

Her blue eyes turn hazy, and all at once, she blinks and averts her gaze.

"Well, I'm sorry for bothering you today," she whispers, "but I just had to meet you."

"You didn't bother me, Indy," I reassure her.

And then I do the only thing I can think of to reassure myself that this isn't the last I'll see of her. "I was thinking about grabbing a late lunch. Would you like to join me?"

She opens her mouth and closes it, trying to make words come out, but instead, another quiet moment spreads between us, and I let it.

The caged little bird can't sing right now. She's too uncertain. Too overwhelmed.

All of the things neither of us has said are written all over her face in shaky script.

"Um…I really appreciate the offer, but I have somewhere I need to be. It was nice meeting you," she mutters, shrugging on her coat and heading for the door without delay.

I follow her as calmly as I can manage until she turns back to look at me over her shoulder.

"Goodbye, Ansel," she says softly, and I have the insane urge to chase after her even after the door has closed.

Instead, I let her go.

But I know this won't be the last time I see her.

Indy Davis.

It can't be.

chapter
ten

Indy

"*amily Feud?*" Lily questions in outrage between bites of lasagna. "We'd be horrible. We're more *Wheel of Fortune* people than anything else."

I nearly choke on my garlic bread. *Wheel of Fortune?* The whole lot of us would get slaughtered. We'd be lucky to walk away without *owing* Pat Sajak money.

This, right here, is family dinner at the Davis's. A night with too much wine, the soft sounds of my dad's favorite jazz bands playing in the background, my mom's delicious food, and arguments over ridiculous shit like which game show my family could win.

The real answer? None of them. But I keep my thoughts to myself.

While I normally enjoy the company of my family, tonight feels like more of a task than anything else, and the last thing I want to do is incite a riot because I don't think we're smart enough to spin the big wheel with Vanna White.

"Don't be dramatic, Lil," my father says, and a piece of cheese from his last bite of lasagna dangles from his beard. It's normally good manners to let someone know they have food on their face, but when it comes to Mac Davis, we've all learned just to let the man be until he finishes his meal. Otherwise, we'd be busy all fucking night.

"We'd kick ass at the Feud," he adds after a sip of wine. "And your mother would be our ace in the hole."

"Aw, thanks, Mac." My mother smiles, and the slight waves of the laugh lines around her lips appear. "But I'll be honest, if I'm going on any game show, it has to be *Jeopardy*."

Instantly, my sister bursts into laughter.

It's completely warranted. Our mother's knowledge of history goes as far as 1990, and her literature expertise ends with Rachael Ray cookbooks and *The Notebook*.

"*Jeopardy*?" Aunt Bethany, my mom's sister, questions with hilarity in her eyes. "Have you lost your mind? You'd have better luck coming up with an invention for *Shark Tank*."

"I'll have you know, I'm *really* good at *Jeopardy*, Bethie." Mom is unconvinced *and* offended. "Tell her, Mac."

"She's good." Another bite of lasagna. Another piece of cheese added to the beard. "Really good."

It's safe to say everyone at this table has had too much wine.

Besides me.

The conversation switches to who Alex Trebek would like the best, and I can hardly focus on the chatter.

I push a bite of my mom's lasagna into my mouth and force myself to chew.

My appetite is nonexistent, which is rare considering lasagna night usually concludes with me feeling like an overinflated balloon.

But I can't stop thinking about yesterday.

About the gallery.

About *him*.

I met the man behind the painting. Yesterday morning, I barely knew who Ansel Bray was, and now I can hardly think about anything else.

I hate it.

One glance in his direction and you know he's incredibly handsome.

Like a modern-day James Dean. He filled the role perfectly when he walked into the gallery yesterday, an exquisitely worn black leather jacket covering his strong torso, with jeans and boots finishing off the look. His brown hair was perfectly messy, and he had the fullest lips I've ever seen on a man.

But it's his eyes that are the most prominent in my mind.

Honey-brown with sparkles of gold, they suit him incredibly well. And I instantly felt comfortable looking into them.

Seeing him, talking to him, it was equal parts thrilling and terrifying.

I wanted to crawl inside his brain and try to understand why. Why does the girl in his painting look so much like me?

But I could barely find the words to introduce myself, much less ask him all of the questions racing through my mind, and I don't think he would have had the answers if I'd managed.

He seemed just as shocked to see me in the flesh as I was to see myself inside his painting.

By the time I left the gallery, I was overwhelmed.

It was too much.

He was too much.

But now that I've had some distance, I regret declining his offer to go to lunch with a stupid fucking excuse.

Too much or not, I want more time with him.

"Earth to Indy." My sister's voice pulls me from my daydream, and I look up from my plate to meet her eyes. "You okay over there?"

"Yeah," I say, clearing figurative cobwebs from my throat. "Of course."

"You sure, sweetie?" my mom asks, and I sigh.

Great. Now they're all going to get involved.

"I'm just a little tired tonight, that's all," I excuse and then toss in a little white lie to sweeten the deal. "I was up late last night working on lesson plans."

I've heard that the best lies are founded in truth, and this one fits the bill. Because I *was* up late last night. I just wasn't thinking about anything even remotely related to work.

I was trying not to Google.

The impulse last night to search anything and everything about Ansel Bray was so intense I could hardly stand it, but I just couldn't let myself fall down that rabbit hole.

What if I found something that terrified me? Drew me to him?

Hell, I'm not entirely sure those questions aren't the same thing.

I silently groan at the mental battle and pop a piece of garlic bread into my mouth. It's savory and warm and just the right size to keep word vomit from spilling out.

"Where's Miller?" Aunt Bethany asks, and my mom tilts her head to the side in confusion.

"Miller?"

"Indigo's boyfriend," my aunt clarifies, and my mom rolls her eyes.

"Pretty sure you mean Matt," Lily corrects with a wry grin.

The mere mention of Matt's name makes my stomach drop with guilt. I haven't thought about him at all today. Truthfully, I've barely thought about him since he left yesterday morning.

At least you remembered to check-in this morning and make sure he had a safe flight, I try to reassure myself, but it only magnifies my guilt. *Oh, yeah, world's best girlfriend, right here…*

"His name is Matt?" Aunt Bethany looks at me, and I nod. "Well, shit, maybe if you brought him around more, I'd remember his name."

"I do bring him around," I counter, but my sister flashes me a look that says I'm full of shit. "Well, I *try* to bring him around, but he travels a lot for work."

Aunt Bethany purses her lips. "It'd be nice if at least one of you girls managed to find a husband. I'd love a great-niece or nephew, you know, while I'm still alive."

Lily snorts. "You're sixty, Aunt Bethie. Pretty sure you've got a few more good years in you."

Our aunt shrugs and takes a hearty drink of her wine. Her *third* glass of wine, mind you. "I guess we should at least be thankful this one—" she nods toward me "—has a boyfriend. You, on the other hand, I'm starting to wonder if you're a lost cause."

Uh oh. The storm is a-brewin'.

Wine, Aunt Bethie, and Lily mix like oil and water.

"A lost cause?" Lily questions, her voice rising in irritation. "That's a little harsh, don't you think? I'm only thirty-one, for fuck's sake."

"Lil!" my mother screeches. "Language!"

But they ignore her completely.

My aunt clucks her tongue. "Thirty-one is only four years away from thirty-five, and you know what they say about thirty-five…" My aunt tsks, and Hurricane Lily is now headed for landfall.

"If it's something about my eggs going bad, then I don't want to hear it."

"Well, it's true," Aunt Bethany continues. "Fertility plummets by the time you reach your mid-thirties. Hell, by that time, menopause might even be kicking in, and you're more likely to be killed by a terrorist than to get married. I saw it in *Sleepless in Seattle*."

Lily slams her fork onto the table. "Well, God forbid I don't get married or have kids, you know, like *you*, Aunt Bethie. And *Sleepless in Seattle* is a damn movie, not a representation of fact."

I cringe.

Oh boy…

If there is one thing Aunt Bethany is good for, it's pissing off my sister with her old-fashioned mind-set on things like marriage and kids. Which is insanely hypocritical considering she's a sixty-year-old spinster who has never been married and has exactly zero children.

Instantly, my mom tries to put out the flames. "How about we… uh…change the subject?" I'm impressed by her diplomatic nature's ability to overpower her love for Tom Hanks.

My sister and aunt engage in some sort of stare-off.

And my dad, well, he just keeps eating. Dinner is Mac's favorite meal of the day. It'd take something like a meteor crashing into Earth to distract him from his food.

"Lily." Mom continues to fight for peace. "What kind of article should your dad and I look forward to next?"

The stare-off continues for another moment or two, but eventually, my sister pulls her eyes away from our aunt.

"I'm working on a piece about Ansel Bray."

"Ansel Bray?" my mom asks. "His name sounds familiar. Why do I know him?"

My stomach dives into my shoes at the sound of his name.

Shit...maybe we should go back to bad eggs and menopause.

"Ansel Bray, you say?" my dad finally decides to join the conversation, cheese beard and all. "Isn't that the artist who's blind?"

"Oh yeah!" my mom chimes in, equal parts cheery and relieved that she's managed to remember how she knows him and change the subject all at once. "He's not blind anymore. He had transplant surgery a few years back."

"That's him." Lily nods. "The other night, I went to his art exhibition with Indy and Matt."

"Matt?" Aunt Bethany scrunches up her nose. "Who's Matt?"

"Indy's boyfriend, Bethie," my mother repeats on a sigh. In addition to being a shit-stirrer, Aunt Bethie has a memory that's only slightly better than Dory from *Finding Nemo*.

"Oh, right. The one we never see."

Dear God, it's me, Indy. Please send help.

"You know," Lily continues, and I'm not so sure I like the smile that's sliding its way across her lips. "One of Ansel Bray's paintings looks like Indy."

My dad's eyes perk up. "Is that right?"

"Yep." Lily turns her stupid smile to me, and I kind of want to stab her with my fork. "The girl in his painting looks almost identical to her."

"N-no." I nearly choke on my own tongue and lie through my teeth at the same time. "Don't be ridiculous, Lil."

"Oh, come on," she retorts. "You know it looks like you. Hell, even Matt thought it looked like you."

"Maybe a little," I continue the lie, because what else am I going to do?

Tell the outrageous truth?

The girl in the painting looks so much like me that the sheer shock of it made me vomit. And, oh, by the way, I went ahead and tracked down Ansel Bray. We talked. He's beautiful and nice, and he's been on my mind ever since…

No thank you. I'll keep that crazy shit to myself.

"I'm hoping to get an interview with him," Lily adds, and my jaw goes slack.

"What?" I question. "Why?"

"Why wouldn't I?" she answers like I'm crazy. "He's the hottest topic in the arts right now. Although, I have to admit, he's not the easiest man to get in touch with. His assistant is pretty much the worst."

Dear God, it's me again. Can you do me a teensy tiny favor and make sure this interview never happens?

If there's anything I've learned in the past two minutes of this dinner, it's that I never should've invited my sister to that opening.

Also, my family is crazy, and my dad's beard can hold a surprising amount of mozzarella cheese.

When my mom starts asking Lily more questions about Ansel Bray, I excuse myself from the table and take my barely eaten plate of food into the kitchen.

It's all too weird, and I already feel guilty about not telling my sister, *my best friend in the whole wide world*, about my little day-trip to see Ansel yesterday.

But how can I explain something to her that I don't even understand myself?

Once my plate is scraped clean and in the dishwasher, I quietly sneak into my dad's "office." He calls it that, but it's really just a television room with a lot of books and a desktop computer he hardly uses.

I run my finger along the edges of his books and savor the one room in the house that's devoid of conversations that stress me out.

But it doesn't take long before I'm not alone.

"So, tell me, Indigo, how is teaching going?" my dad asks and sits down in his favorite leather chair. "Still happy at that private school?"

"I can't complain." I shrug. "I love the kids."

"You still giving private music lessons, too?"

"Uh huh."

"You have a lot of students taking them?"

I nod. "More than I have time for, if I'm being honest."

"That's good," he says and taps his fingers along the armrests. "It's nice to hear not all the kids in this country are killing their brains with video games and YouTube videos."

I grin at that.

"The world always needs more music, Indy. It's what keeps us going. It's what inspires us. It's what connects us all."

Mac Davis, while retired now, was a music professor at NYU. He also played saxophone in a jazz band for most of my life and is an expert on the piano.

The only time music isn't playing in this house is when he's sleeping. Miles Davis, Billie Holiday, Bach, Frank Sinatra, and Led Zeppelin, I heard them all for the first time because of him.

His tastes are about as eclectic as they can get, and there is no doubt his love for all things music was passed on to me. Ever since I was a little girl, music has had a pivotal presence in my life. My first true love.

"You know, I sure do miss seeing you play," my dad says softly, and my heart clenches tight in my chest.

I don't respond, but he's too lost in whatever memories flit about inside his mind to see my visible discomfort.

"I don't think I'll ever forget the night you graduated from Julliard and the New York Orchestra found out you were something special." His words are wistful and sad at the same time.

Tears threaten to prick my eyes, but I discreetly pinch the skin of my thigh with my thumb and forefinger to distract myself from the emotional pain even the idea of playing publicly brings me.

"I hope one day I'll get to see you play again, Indigo," my dad adds before he eventually drops the subject altogether and turns on the nightly news on the television.

I wish I could tell him he will.

But I can't.

The tragic truth? I don't know if I'll ever be that girl again.

chapter eleven

Ansel

've only managed to get half of my body into the front office of my studio when Lucy holds out her hand and wiggles her fingers, demanding, "Give me your phone."

She's obviously been waiting on my arrival for a while, but she's going to be waiting even longer for me to follow orders she barks at me.

Like, however long it takes for hell to freeze over.

"No."

"Seriously." She purses her silicone-filled lips. "Give me your phone."

"*Seriously*, no," I emphasize.

Luce is unaffected, and apparently, willing to take her life into her own hands because, without care or caution, she reaches into the pocket of my jacket and grabs my phone herself.

What. The. Fuck.

"Jesus Christ. You're fired!"

My anger is an inconvenience to her, and she shows it through a scowl. "Someone named Lily Davis has been demon-dialing the studio, and I'm literally done trying to avoid her and her obnoxious calls. You need to speak with her because I'm positive she is going to drive me insane until you do."

"Who is this woman?"

"A columnist with the *New York Press*."

"*Luce,*" I growl, but she ignores me completely and uses one dramatic, red-painted fingernail to tap send on the call.

"Talk to her," she orders, placing the phone to my ear.

"You really are fired," I mouth as it rings.

She rolls her eyes in the face of my glare and steps away—out of reach.

Probably a smart idea.

I'm about to end the call when a woman answers. "This is Lily Davis."

I'm still half tempted to hang up, but if Lily is even half as dogged as Luce claims she is, she'll just call back. This time, thanks to my soon-to-be *ex*-assistant, on my *personal* phone.

"Hello," I say as I glower at Luce. "This is Ansel Bray."

"Wow. What a pleasant surprise," she replies. "I've been trying to schedule an interview with you, but your assistant is the opposite of accommodating."

"Tell me about it." Luce sure as hell didn't accommodate me when she saddled me with this phone call.

"What?"

"Never mind. What is it you want me to do for you?"

"An interview."

Jesus Christ.

"I went to your exhibition on opening night, and I'd really love the opportunity to sit down with you."

An in-person interview? Fuck, I can barely tolerate them on the phone.

"I'm not much for interviews." I sigh heavily into the receiver. "And, no offense, but I doubt you're going to ask me anything that hasn't already been asked."

"Well..." She pauses and clears her throat. "I mostly want to know why you're painting portraits of my sister."

I furrow my brow. "I'm sorry, *what?*"

"The girl in your painting could be my sister's doppelgänger."

86

Her words reach out and slap me across the face with déjà vu.

"Your sister's doppelgänger?"

"Yes," she answers without the slightest bit of nervousness or hesitation. "It's nearly identical to her."

"What did you say your name was?"

"Lily Davis," she tells me, and a soft laugh leaves her lips. "I have a feeling your assistant will probably never forget my name with how many times I've called your studio over the past few days."

"My assistant is incompetent at best," I comment, and I'm rewarded with a middle finger right in front of my face.

My heart rate kicks up ten notches, and I've never been more interested in getting an interview on the books than I am right now.

"And what is your sister's name?"

"Indy Davis." She verifies what, deep down, I already know.

I wonder if she knows that just two days ago, her sister tracked me down at the gallery. And if Indy told her, what did she say?

Was she as affected as I was?

Is she still thinking about it like I am?

Hope bubbles inside of my chest, and I decide there is only one way to find out.

"Tomorrow night," I say without hesitation. "I can fit in an interview over dinner. But do me a favor and make sure your questions are worth my time, yeah?"

"Holy shit," she mutters more to herself than me. "I can do tomorrow."

"There's just one condition," I add with a smile. If I'm doing another fucking interview, I'm going to make sure Lily Davis isn't the only one who's going to get something out of it.

I tell her where to be and what time to be there, and then I tell her what I want. And I end the call before she can say an opposing word.

A dick move? Yes. But the reward could be well worth the consequences.

Lucy stares up at me from her desk, her eyes squinted into tiny little lines.

I smile at her for the first time today.

"Good news, Luce. You're un-fired."

She laughs. "That's good. Because I wasn't leaving anyway."

And then I go to work.

My muse is alive and well, and my color palette might as well be preordained.

"Hmm," I mutter to myself as I survey my selection of paints. "I'm thinking indigo."

chapter twelve

Indy

The lunch bell rings, and just as the last eighth-grader leaves my classroom, my phone buzzes inside my desk.

Matt: How ya doing, baby? Hope your day is going good.

My day? Well, it leaves a lot to be desired.

Firstly, every single one of my morning classes was filled with boisterous, antsy kids, hopped up on Pixy-Stix speed and stir-crazy from the cold weather. I swear, if it's been one day without recess, it may as well have been a million.

And secondly, the name Ansel Bray has been following me around all day.

It started this morning while I drank coffee in my kitchen, and it hasn't let up since.

With Matt gone, I forwent CNN and put on E! News. All was normal as they talked about the Kardashians, but then, while I was distracted with getting my Eggos out of the toaster, they segued and ended up showing a picture of Ansel from five years ago, out with some model at a restaurant in Manhattan.

Two blocks into my walk to the subway station, I stopped at Pauly's Newsstand to buy a pack of gum and came face-to-face with *him* again. On the front page of the freaking *New York Post*.

I kept my head down for the rest of the commute, but when I

got to school, I let my guard down. *Big mistake.* Two steps into the faculty lounge and Sherry from the math department, propped unavoidably against the counter in front of the donuts, was reading said newspaper.

He is everywhere, all around me, and that doesn't even include my own ridiculous thoughts.

Needless to say, I now know I never should've sought him out.

Coming face-to-face with Ansel Bray didn't do anything but raise more questions, more intrigue, *more of these fucking thoughts*, and feelings I don't understand.

Guilt churns in my gut when I realize that it was *my boyfriend's* text that launched my current Ansel-driven crazy plane.

God, I'm the worst, and I don't even understand why.

With a mental slap, I pour my focus back into the man on the other end of my phone.

Me: It's going okay. How's your trip?

Matt: So great that I just got word a large bank in Spain wants us to add a software consultation with them to our itinerary. It would extend my trip for another week or so, which sucks, but it's almost too good to pass up.

I know Matt well enough to understand there's no maybe about it. His three-week trip has just been extended.

Me: Sounds like everything is coming up roses, then.

Matt: It is, but I miss you. You wouldn't by any chance want to take a week off from work to come visit me, would you? ;) I've heard Paris is lovely this time of year...

Me: LOL. Pretty sure Paris in February is just like New York in

February. COLD. And you know I can't take time off last minute in the middle of the school year.

Matt: I know, but I figured it wouldn't hurt to ask. Well, I'm going to head out and grab some dinner with Tom and Conrad. Another FaceTime call before you're headed to work tomorrow morning?

Me: Sounds like a plan.

I set my phone back in my desk drawer and glance at the clock. *Thank God. Lunchtime.*

I head for the faculty lounge as covertly as I can without employing an army crawl, and I snag my lunch from the fridge. I'm just about to make my getaway when Mary calls toward me, "You're not going to eat with us today, sweetie?"

I shake my head. "Sorry, but I have way too much work to catch up on."

A flat-out lie, but I'm pretty sure when it's for self-preservation, it's excused. With the way today has gone, I just need to hole up in my classroom, away from everyone and everything.

The instant I shut the door to my classroom, the breath I didn't realize I was holding escapes my lungs, and my shoulders sag as I plop down into the chair behind my desk.

Remnants of kindergarteners are scattered across the center of my classroom, on the rainbow rug where we compose musical renditions of "Old MacDonald Had a Farm" and "The Wheels on the Bus," but I don't even consider cleaning up.

It can wait. My next class isn't for another hour.

My phone vibrates inside the top drawer of my desk, and truthfully, a large part of me sees the merits of ignoring it. It's just that the smaller part of me is yappy, like a little dog, and I can't stand the sound of it.

Incoming Call Lily

I sigh, but I still manage to hit accept and force myself to answer.

"You're coming to dinner with me tomorrow night."

No hello or how are you. Just demands. So far, this phone call with my audacious sister is going just as I expected it would.

"What if I have plans?"

"Pffft," Lily snorts. "Eating Chinese food and grading papers while watching Netflix doesn't count as plans. Plus, Matt is out of town. Surely, you want some company."

"That's not all I do," I retort, and she laughs. A little too hysterically for my taste. I mean, it wasn't *that* funny.

"You're going with me."

"Lil," I whine.

"Consider it a girls' night. Just the two of us. We haven't done one of those in so long, Indy. C'mon, don't be such a grouch!"

I don't respond. I know from experience that anything I say will just give her a foundation on which to build her argument. I'm pretty sure she missed her calling as an attorney.

"Pretty please go with me?" she begs.

I sigh. She knows I won't say no to her begging. Probably because she won't stop until I agree, and it's a lot better time management if I just give in at the start.

"Fine," I mutter, "but I'm not getting dressed up."

"At least brush your hair and put on a little makeup."

"What's it matter to you?" I question. "It's not like I'm trying to impress anyone."

She groans. "Just don't dress like a complete slouch, okay? Pretty it up a bit. That's what girls' nights are for. To drink wine and tell ourselves how pretty and awesome we are."

I squint my eyes. "You're acting so weird right now."

"Just be ready around six tomorrow night, okay?"

"Fine."

"Love you! Bye!" She hangs up before I can get another word in.

I contemplate texting her and backing out of girls' night the cowardly way, but I know it would be a huge waste of time and have the same ending—*me going to dinner tomorrow night.*

Ugh.

She's lucky she's my sister.

Nestled beneath the Brooklyn Bridge, we are cocooned by a sweeping view of the New York skyline and what feels like a million twinkle lights creating a path toward the front entrance of Bistro, the hip little restaurant my sister picked out for girls' night.

Fucking girls' night. It's so cold, it might end in frostbite.

The temperature drops as we get closer to the water, and I tighten my pea coat around my body. I know I said anyone who doesn't expect New York to be cold in the winter is a moron, but this is on a whole other level. The wind whips past my body and pricks at my bones.

"God, I'm freezing," Lily mutters as we step up to the entrance. She opens the door with a heavy hand and gets us inside as quickly as possible.

Chatter and clanking cutlery and lively conversation fill the air. I shiver when the chilly outside breeze meets the warm cocoon of the restaurant in an electric swirl, and I rub my hands up and down my arms. "Maybe eating by the river wasn't the best choice on a ten-degree day…"

"I know," she says through chattering teeth. "But, in my defense, it wasn't my choice."

"What are you talking about?" I scrunch up my nose at her and laugh. "This whole damn evening was your choice. If it weren't for you, I'd be at home, incredibly warm and in my pajamas."

Lily ignores me entirely and steps toward the hostess desk. "I have a reservation for six thirty. It's under Davis."

The teenage hostess is fresh-faced, and her name tag reads Marley. She smiles her understanding and looks down at her clipboard. "For three, right?"

"Yep." Lily nods.

"Three?" I look between Lily and myself, counting like one of my kindergarteners. *One. Two.* "I thought it was just the two of us?" I ask while the hostess grabs two menus.

"Well…that was kind of a lie…"

If she invited our Aunt Bethany, I'm leaving. It's one thing to watch them verbally spar with each other inside the safety of my parents' house, but it's a whole other thing to take the freak show out in public.

I open my mouth to question her further, but I'm interrupted.

"Looks like the other person in your party is already here," Marley says, and I glare at Brutus, the backstabbing sister formerly known as Lily.

"Who's here, Lil?" I whisper, and she grimaces.

"Don't be mad, okay?"

Marley gestures toward us with a polite hand. "If you'll follow me, I'll take you to your table."

Lily averts her gaze entirely and follows Marley's lead, giving me no other option but to do the same.

Past the bar area, through the main dining room, and toward a back room that has an incredible view of the river, we follow the hostess until she stops at a booth in the corner.

"Here you are," she announces and sets our menus down on the table.

When Marley finally shuffles aside to head back toward the front of the restaurant, I damn near fall on my face. His honey-brown eyes twinkle like the reflections on the river behind him.

My heart starts training for a fucking marathon inside my chest.

Ansel Bray is here. Sitting at our table.

One. Two. *Three.*

chapter thirteen

Ansel

nside the sapphire-blue depths of Indy's eyes, I watch as recognition turns to shock and confusion. The woman standing beside her—the one I shamelessly bribed to get Indy here—smiles a million-dollar smile.

I stand up to greet them, and since Lily seems more amenable, I extend my hand toward her with a friendly curl of my lips. "I take it you're Lily Davis."

"I am. It's a pleasure to finally meet you," she says and shakes my hand with a firm grip before turning toward her sister. "Indy, I'd like you to meet Ansel Bray. This is the artist whose exhibition we saw at Aquavella."

Indy worries her bottom lip with a nip of her teeth for a moment, and then two, and when the silence between us pushes past normal and veers right into awkward, Lily offers a discreet nudge into her sister's arm.

Instantly, Indy blinks and clears her throat. "It's…uh…nice to meet you," she responds, acting like I'm a complete stranger, and shakes my outstretched hand.

So that's how it's going to be.

Obviously, she didn't tell her sister about meeting me, and her sister didn't clue her in on the details of this dinner. I, Ansel Bray, am the center of their Venn diagram of deceit.

And I'm not going to be the one to expose any of it.

"It's nice to meet you, too," I say instead. "Please, sit down."

The girls settle into the seats across from mine, and after quickly studying the menu, Lily doesn't hesitate to dive right into the meat of her interview. "So, tell me, are you painting my sister on purpose, or is it a coincidence?"

"Lily!" Indy snaps, her back stiffening and the muscles of her shoulders locking tight with tension. "What are you doing?"

Lily rolls her eyes. "Interviewing him. That's why he's here."

I nearly laugh at Lily's boldness, but Indy's discomfort is far too palpable. So, instead, I offer a kind smile and rub my fingers across the five-day-old scruff on my chin.

"Well, while I can definitely see the resemblance, I don't know the reason for it."

It's not a complete lie. I may have an overwhelming certainty that it's Indy—and not just someone who looks like her—but I *don't* know the reason.

"See, Indigo?" Lily nudges her sister. "Even the artist thinks you look like her."

Indy tries to glare and fake a smile at the same time. It's quite possibly one of the cutest things I've ever seen.

Lily, finally noticing just how uncomfortable Indy is, sighs heavily and puts her elbows on the table to lean toward me. "Okay. I have a *bit* of a confession to make…" She pauses and pouts slightly. "I *may* have told my sister a little white lie to get her here."

Yeah, that's pretty apparent.

I turn my gaze to Indy. "And where did you think you were going tonight?"

"To dinner," she says, and one corner of her mouth turns down. "But I was told this was a *girls'* night."

The way her annoyance reddens her cheeks makes me laugh. "Didn't expect a cock in the henhouse?"

The flush in her cheeks deepens. "*No.*"

And what she really didn't expect was *me.* An unspoken statement but true all the same.

"You wouldn't have come along," Lily argues. "And you being here was a condition of getting the interview!"

Ah, shit. Looks like the cat's out of the bag.

"Is that how it went?" Instantly, Indy locks her gaze with mine. "Did you *blackmail* my sister?"

"Off the record?" I ask, and Lily nods, a smile curling the corners of her lips. "I'd really call this more extortion than blackmail."

Lily laughs, and Indy's blue eyes brighten as if she's amused by my candid admission.

She keeps looking at me like that, and I might just adopt a life of crime.

Our server stops by the table with the wine I ordered before their arrival, pours everyone a glass, and writes down our dinner orders, and I use that time to steal glances in my real-life muse's direction while Lily dives back into her list of questions.

Who are my inspirations?

What influences my color palette?

Have I always been artistic?

They're a lot of the same questions I've been asked a thousand times, but I'm surprised to find myself enjoying it.

Lily is likable and endearingly pushy, and Indy's lack of understanding of everything her sister is talking about is fun.

No doubt, it'd be different if she were the slightest bit self-conscious, but thanks to our smiles and the wine, Indy has embraced it completely.

In fact, since the initial awkwardness, there's been an impressive amount of eye contact.

And fuck, if those beautiful blue eyes of hers don't give me a rush. They speed up my heart and put a fire inside my belly. I could paint those eyes of hers over and over, *stare into them for the rest of my life*, and I don't think it'd be enough.

I've never had a woman affect me like this. But fuck, I'm *affected*.

"Not gonna lie." Lily pulls me from my overpowering thoughts. "I'm a little surprised you're this amenable. You have a reputation for being…"

"A dick?" I offer, and a burst of hilarity leaves her lips. Indy actually snorts.

"You said it, not me."

"You're not much for social interaction," Indy says, repeating my words from the first time we met at Aquavella. A thrill runs down my spine.

"Exactly."

A mischievous smile kisses her lips, and she nudges her sister. "Lily *loves* attention. I bet she would love being a celebrity."

"No doubt about that." Her sister damn near cackles. "If I could change my name to Kily and join the Kardashian clan, I'd do it in a heartbeat."

"Pretty sure Kily would be a PR nightmare." Indy snorts again, and good God, why is this woman the most adorable creature I've ever encountered?

The Davis sisters are both classically beautiful, but there's a reason Indy is my muse.

The way she moves. The way she fidgets her fingers when she's nervous or uncertain. The way she worries her teeth against her bottom lip when she's trying to find the right words. And when she smiles, *really fucking smiles*, it steals my goddamn breath.

I feel as if I've known her all my life, yet I've been in her presence all of two times.

"Do you mind if I ask a question?" Indy requests, and I've never been more excited for a fucking question in my life.

"Of course."

"Occasionally, you use models for your paintings, right?"

I nod. "Yeah. Sometimes."

"Have you ever been on the other side of things?"

I furrow my brow as I try to understand her question. "Are you asking if I've ever been the subject?"

She nods and, for a brief moment, I admire the way her long lashes sweep across her pretty face.

"Well…" I pause and search my mind. "Actually, no. I don't think I have."

"That seems a little unfair, don't you think?" she questions, her voice teasing. "I mean, in order to really understand your subjects, don't you think you should try being on the other side of the canvas?"

"You know," I say and run my fingers over my chin, "I've never really thought about it like that before. But I guess, yeah, I probably should, huh?"

Indy grins. "You should."

Before I can add to it, our server steps up to our table and begins to set our meals in front of us. Steak for me, grilled chicken for Lily, and chicken fingers and fries for Indy.

The mere idea of chicken fingers and fries makes me laugh, and Indy looks up from her plate to meet my eyes. "What?" she asks. "What are you looking at?"

"I didn't realize Bistro had a kids menu," I say, and I'm rewarded with another ridiculous snort.

"Mind your own business, pal," she orders with a smile. "Chicken fingers and fries are delicious."

It takes Lily interrupting our banter with another question to make me remember we're not on a date.

"Have you sold any of your paintings from the exhibition?"

I finish chewing my bite of steak and take a sip of wine. "Not a single one."

"That sounds like a lie," she guffaws. "I happen to know there are a *ton* of people out there vying to get an Ansel Bray."

"Yeah, but you asked me if I'd *sold* one of my paintings, not if there was *interest* in them."

Lily raises a pointed eyebrow. "Those two things are normally directly linked. Are you not planning on selling any of them?"

"I don't know." I shrug and meet Indy's curious eyes. "I'm not sure if I can part with any of them. Most of the people trying to buy them want them for the status, not for the art."

And in some form or another, the paintings are all inspired by Indy. They deserve to be cherished by someone who sees their real value.

"When you're in your studio, do you have a specific routine when it comes to painting?" Lily asks, and lamentably, I take my eyes off her sister to look her in the eye.

"A certain routine?" *Like fucking jumping jacks? What in the hell is she talking about?*

She nods. "Like a certain time of day you always paint, or do you just paint when inspiration strikes? What's a normal day look like for Ansel Bray?"

"Let's see." I hum. "When I'm inspired, I'm generally in my studio for hours, surviving off water and granola bars and the musical genius of Chopin or Vivaldi, while I paint until my fingers threaten to fall off."

"So music is a must for you in the studio."

"Definitely."

"You know," Lily continues and glances at her sister. "Indy is a classically trained musician. She's even played with the New York Orchestra."

My heart trips over its own rhythm, and it takes everything inside of me not to choke on my wine.

A specific painting pops into my head, and I force myself to push it away and act like I haven't just been punched in the gut with the undeniable realization that I know Indy Davis far more than I even realized.

Holy shit.

Indy's shoulders are rigid with tension and discomfort again.

"I don't play professionally anymore," she comments faux-casually. There's a pain rooted there, deep in the bowels of her response, but I don't pry. Clearly, the last thing she wants is to go into it.

"What do you do now, Indy?"

"I'm a music teacher."

"Really? Where?"

"Great Elm School. It's a private school in the Bronx."

I grin at the thought of her with children. "Do you like it?"

"I hate my commute, but, yes, most days I do like it." She shrugs and smiles at the same time. "Although, there are some days I wonder why I didn't try harder to become a YouTube Influencer instead."

What the hell is a YouTube Influencer?

I raise my eyebrows, and she laughs. "It's a thing, trust me. You'd think it's the kindergarteners that give me the most trouble, but honestly, it's the smartass eighth-graders. Especially, the boys."

I laugh. "Hormones and puberty, a deadly combination."

Indy opens her mouth to respond, but the sounds of a phone ringing pull her attention toward her purse. When she takes it out of the front pocket, her mouth forms a tiny little O of surprise. "Shit," she mutters, and her sister glances at the screen.

"You should get that," Lily says. "I'm sure Ansel will understand that you need to answer Matt's call."

Matt?

Who the fuck is Matt?

Indy glances at the screen and then at me, and eventually, she gets up from the booth. Her eyes are apologetic, but I offer an understanding smile as she excuses herself from our table.

Once Indy is out of sight, Lily gives me all the details I wish I could unhear. "Her boyfriend is on a work trip in Europe for the next few weeks, and the time change isn't the easiest to manage."

I nod, but on the inside, I'm dying.

I'm officially jealous of a man I've never met.

chapter
fourteen

Indy

glance up at the clock above the door to my classroom and see it's already 2:15. Only ten more minutes to go until I send my last class back to Mrs. Thomas's homeroom and finish up my day.

For a Friday, this day is dragging on like a migraine.

The morning started off a bit rough when I had to discipline Austin, one of my second-graders, for singing "Mary Had a Little *Fart*" instead of "Mary Had a Little Lamb."

When I sat him down for a nice little chat and asked him what prompted him to come up with his own creative arrangement instead of following the one provided, he told me that "snitches get stitches."

Is it just me, or are second-graders seeming older these days?

It took pretty much everything inside of me not to laugh.

Unfortunately, Austin set the tone for the day, and I've had to spend the last six or so hours trying to wrangle what might as well have been a hardened, gang-sign-repping herd of feral cats.

Needless to say, these kids are ready for the weekend, and I am too.

While the first-graders from Mrs. Thomas's class put their instruments back in the bins, I grab my mug from my desk and take a sip.

"What are you drinking, Ms. Davis?" Olivia asks, and I look up to find her back in her assigned seat.

"Coffee."

"Ew, gross!" she exclaims, and her face pinches in disgust. "Coffee gives my mom bad breath!"

"You should drink beer instead, Ms. Davis," Kyle chimes in as he settles into his seat. "My dad does all the time. He says it takes the edge off."

Kyle's dad is the father of three rowdy boys who are all under the age of ten. Surely, the man deserves to have something in his life that takes the edge off.

I swallow my urge to laugh and smile. "Thanks for the tip, Kyle."

"No problem!"

Conversations like these are probably my favorite thing about the little kids.

They're so innocent and sweet, and yet they never hesitate to tell you exactly what's on their young minds. They also never miss an opportunity to throw their parents or siblings under the proverbial bus.

The warning bell chimes through the intercom, and my students stand up excitedly from their seats. With a lot of deep breaths and grit, I wrangle them into a line and lead them to their homeroom.

Once they're safely inside Mrs. Thomas's room, I head back to my classroom and decide to make an early escape for the day. No music lessons on the books for the afternoon means I'm a free woman until Monday.

Five minutes before the end-of-day bell rings, I'm turning off the lights in my classroom, waving goodbye to the ladies in the front office, and walking out the front doors of the school before anyone can stop me for small talk.

The subway station is a short walk, five blocks or so, and once I make my way down the stairs, I wait on the platform for the next train and check my phone for emails, missed calls, and text messages.

The monthly school newsletter from our principal.

A text from Lily.

A missed call from my mom.

A text from Sally.

The last one makes me decide to avoid all of them for now.

I open my purse, dump my phone inside, and then look up and directly into the familiar golden-brown eyes of Ansel Bray.

My heart kicks up in speed and I blink a few times to comprehend if what I'm seeing is real or a hallucination. I know I've been thinking about him a lot—*okay, nonstop*—but what are the odds that he'd be here, in the Bronx, at the same subway station as me?

Probably about as good as you ending up in one of his paintings…

The ridiculous, unbidden thought almost makes me laugh.

God, he looks handsome. The same leather jacket. The same boots. The same perfectly messy hair. And those eyes.

Hi, he mouths toward me, and a smile kisses my lips without my permission.

God, who is this man? I silently wonder to myself. *Who is he and where did he come from?*

After I got home from Bistro two nights ago, I finally gave in and internet-stalked him. Per my Google research, Ansel Bray is a thirty-four-year-old, world-renowned artist whose paintings sell for insane amounts of money. But it was only after he was in a tragic car accident and lost his sight that his success *really* skyrocketed.

Some people even call him the Leonardo da Vinci of his time.

He's also the brother of Bram Bray, a member of the rock group New Rules. Which is…*big* news for a fan of New Rules like me.

And now, a modern-day da Vinci with his brand-new eyes and his handsome smile is walking toward me.

His long strides are unhurried but unbelievably efficient, and before I know it, he's standing right beside me.

He slides his hands into his pockets and stares toward the tracks. It's only then that I notice the earbud cord that peeks out from beneath his black hoodie.

He doesn't say anything, just stares expectantly into the dark void of the tunnel, and I don't say anything either.

Normally, I'd feel compelled to say something, do something, but rather than give in, I decide to trust that his silence has some sort of purpose.

I don't know why he's here, inside this subway station, waiting beside me, but I can only assume it's because he needs to be somewhere.

Maybe he's headed to his studio?

Does he even have an art studio?

Of course, he has an art studio, Indy. He's a famous painter. It's not like he's creating masterpieces in his fucking kitchen.

A small sliver of relief fills my chest when the lights in the station flicker. I'm committed to the silence, but that doesn't mean it's easy to go against my habit to fill it with words.

With an audible screech, my train arrives, and I step inside.

Ansel steps inside too.

The doors close behind us.

I sit down in an empty seat.

He sits down beside me.

I look at him expectantly, search his steady gaze to try to will him to end my torture, but he doesn't cave. Instead, he smiles this soft, warm, cozy, fucking perfect smile, and I break out in goose bumps.

What is it about this guy?

Ansel slides his earbuds out of his ears, and before I know it, he's slipping them inside mine.

"Brindo" by Devendra Banhart, a song I know to my bones, starts up, and my heart threatens to crawl up into my throat as the music both haunts and soothes my nerves.

I'm surprised he knows this song, much less has it on his phone.

His brown eyes lock with mine, and my breath stutters inside my lungs.

My hand shakes in my lap, and for some unknown reason, he reaches out and interlocks our fingers. His sturdy hold quells the earthquake of nerves beneath my fingertips.

I should pull away, but I don't. *I can't.*

Instead, I savor the feel and relief of it.

With two long fingers, he brushes against my cheek and slips one earbud out of my ear. "I want to show you something," he whispers, and I watch the way his long, dark lashes swipe gently over his eyes.

Show me something?

I blink. "Right now?"

He nods but doesn't say anything else.

God, this is insane.

I hardly know this man, yet I feel like I do. And I should probably be concerned about him being some kind of secret serial killer or something, but before I know it, I'm whispering "Okay" back to him.

Okay. Simple as that. No questions. No concerns. Just *okay*.

What is wrong with me?

I nod toward the phone in his hands. "Can I see?"

He tilts his head to the side as he follows my line of sight. "My phone?"

"Your music."

You can find out so much about someone just by hearing their favorite songs.

Their fears. Their ambitions. What moves them.

And there is something inside of me that wants to know everything about him.

Something that is pulling me toward him.

He obliges, but before I let my curious mind have at it, I pull my phone and my earbuds out of my purse. I slip my earbuds into his ears and scroll through my favorite playlist until I find the perfect song.

"You're playing me a song?" he asks and I nod.

"Yes, but this one needs to be played as loud as your ears can tolerate." I turn up the volume, and with one tap to the screen, I watch his eyes as he reacts to the opening piano notes of *"Comptine d'un autre été."*

To my surprise, he takes the phone from my hands and turns up the volume even more. He closes his eyes and drifts away, straight into the music.

No questions asked.

chapter fifteen

Ansel

I've never stalked anyone in my life.

A statement, ladies and gentlemen, I could only candidly make until today.

Truthfully, I've never even had the urge to track someone down. I'm more of a people-avoider than a people-tracker, but everything I've ever known seems upside down when Indy's around.

I feel a bit like a creep. Like an evil bastard. But here I am, sitting beside her on the subway, and I have no one to blame but myself.

I ignored the fact that she has a boyfriend, completely put the bastard named Matt out of my head, and took a day-trip to her school—*after finding said school on Google Maps.* And I might have also timed said trip to have me arriving near the end of the school day *and* hung out inside the closest subway station that would take some-one—*Indy*—in the direction of Brooklyn.

I was seconds away from scrapping the whole thing, finally hav-ing found a little morsel of morals at the bare bottom of my con-science jar, but when I saw her step into the station, I was powerless to stop myself from doing something about it. Seeing her, talking to her again, *being fucking near her*—all things I now feel like I *need*.

She's a red string tied to my finger, and I can't forget her. Can't shake her. It doesn't matter what I'm doing, what I'm focused on, she's always in the back of my mind, her name is always on the tip of my tongue.

It's crazy.

I'm probably fucking crazy.

But here I am, and I can't stop looking at her.

Her petite hand grips my phone, and I watch with rapt attention as she scrolls through my library. Her teeth sneak out to scrape across her bottom lip as she pauses mid-scroll to tap on a song called "I See You."

I nearly laugh at the irony of it.

These days, she's all I fucking see. Hell, I haven't stopped seeing her since the day I opened my new eyes.

Her tongue sneaks out and licks across her pretty little lips, and I watch the tiniest hints of a smile crest her mouth up at the corners.

I wonder if she even knows just how beautiful she is.

The way she moves, the way she breathes, and her perfect blue eyes. I could swim in them.

Her long lashes brush across her cheeks as she blinks once, twice, and three more times before averting her gaze from my phone across the aisle of the subway.

I wonder if she even remembers she's given me her phone. Or that it's my phone gripped between her fingers.

With one tap of my index finger, I open up her message inbox and proceed to pull up a blank text and type in my phone number as the recipient. It doesn't take long before I'm hitting send, and the phone in her hands vibrates with a new message.

Me: What song should I play next?

Indy furrows her brow as she looks down at my phone, and then her tiny smile grows. Her fingers tap across the screen until the phone in my hand buzzes.

I glance down to see a message from her.

What are you in the mood for?

What am I in the mood for? The real answer? Pretty much anything she wants to throw my way, but I don't say that. If Indy knows how deep I already am with her, about the crazy thoughts I'm feeling, I'm confident she won't stick around to find out anything else.

So I dial it back a few emotional notches and stick with something a little more fun and lighthearted.

Me: The Beach Boys.

A laugh escapes her throat when she reads my message, and her big blue eyes meet mine.

"What?" I ask through a smile, but instead of answering, she just shakes her head and types out another response.

You don't really seem like a "Beach Boys" kind of guy.

Me: That's blasphemy. I'm all kinds of laid-back and beachy.

Indy giggles and snorts, and my smile stretches until it consumes my face.

And instead of waiting for her response, I send her another text.

Me: What kind of guy do I seem like?

She reads the message, and without even looking at me, she responds.

An emotional, deep, broody artist.

Indy isn't wrong. The last time I listened to something like the Beach Boys, I was probably eleven and cruising down the highway with my stepdad. That doesn't mean I'm not open to turning over a new leaf. Open to having fun every once in a while.

Indy makes me want to have fun.

Me: You're right. The Beach Boys are really more of an occasional thing. What would you recommend for someone who is an emotional, deep, broody artist, and a little bit of a dick?

She looks up, laughs, and takes the phone from my hands for a brief moment. Just as she slides it back into my fingers, the opening beats of her song choice fill my ears. It's haunting and sweet and melancholic. It is a daydream and a nightmare.

And it is perfect for someone tortured. Someone who's been through the wringer like me.

In fact, this isn't a new-to-me song.

Gently, I grab my phone out of her hands, find the exact song in my library, and hit play.

Now, we're both listening to a song named "Dust it Off."

Indy looks up at me through her big, dewy blue eyes, and my breath gets tangled up in my lungs. She's both shocked and awed, and this crazy connection between us burrows a little bit deeper.

I want to bask in this moment and stay there for a while, but the wheels of the train screech to a stop over the music flowing in my ears, and I know this is the stop. My stop.

Our stop.

I stand up from my seat and hold my hand out for her, maintaining the rhythmic trance between us the music has created.

She hesitates for a beat, her gaze jumping between my face and my hand, but eventually, she slides her petite fingers between mine and lets me lead the way.

We climb the stairs to the sidewalk and stroll until the very end of the song. Once the music bubble is broken, Indy lets go of my hand to take the earbuds out of her ears and hand my phone back to me.

I do the same with hers.

"So, uh, where are we going?" she asks at precisely the right time, and I smile.

"Right here, actually." We've stopped in front of my favorite little coffee shop, and this is step one in my two-step plan.

The sign reads Not-So-Average Joe, and Indy squints her eyes up toward the sky as she takes in the building.

"You're showing me coffee?" she questions, and her little nose scrunches up in the cutest fucking way.

I grin. "Do you not like coffee?"

"What? No." She bends her chin into her neck and puts a concerned hand to her chest. "Are there people who don't like coffee?"

"Maybe. But they're not people I want to know."

She laughs and glances back at the building again, her face a mask of confusion, and if I'm not mistaken, a little bit of disappointment. "Is this coffee shop really what you wanted to show me?"

"No." I chuckle and shake my head. "First, coffee," I add. "Then, I'm taking you to my studio."

chapter
sixteen

Indy

"Here we are," Ansel says as he stops us in front of a brownstone in Greenwich Village.

The stairs are ornate concrete with a heavy black iron railing, and a mature tree shades us from the direct sun. It doesn't look like an area where anyone would want to have a place of business because, for New York City, this is off the beaten path.

"Your studio is here?" I ask as he unlocks the door.

"Well, one of them. My most important studio is here."

I raise my eyebrow and follow him inside. "What's that supposed to mean?"

"It means this is my private studio."

"Where's the other one?"

He nods. "On the Upper East Side. It's where all the pretentious people come in and view my paintings and, subsequently, try to buy them," Ansel says with a grin. His opinion of his buyers might make him sound pretentious himself if he hadn't already explained his reasoning at the dinner with Lily. As it is, it just makes me laugh as he leads us into the house.

It only takes me a moment of being inside to realize he's sold this place short in its description. Not only is this his private studio, it's also quite obviously his home.

And it's gorgeous.

Modern fixtures and furniture with clean lines and a neutral color palette fill the space, but the exposed brick and paintings hung along the walls create just the right amount of vintage charm.

Busy taking it all in, I almost trip as Ansel guides me to the bottom of a set of steps. Two flights of stairs lead into a massive room that takes up two whole floors. The winter sun flows in through the windows that stretch from the floor to the ceiling, and one lone, worn-out leather couch sits dead center.

The rest of the room is littered with blank canvases, painted canvases, and enough art supplies to last a lifetime.

It's chaos. It's order. And for some crazy reason, it's exactly how I would have imagined it to be.

"This is…" I pause and let my gaze take in every corner, every canvas, every brush, and jar of paint. "Well, it's kind of messy. Beautiful, but messy."

His answering smile turns my insides to melted caramel.

"That might be the best compliment I've ever received."

I snort at that. "Liar."

"No, really," he says as he walks across the large space and turns on the rest of the lights throughout the room. "It's honest. And real. That kind of response is rare these days."

"You don't think people are honest with you?"

"Sometimes, they are. But a lot of times, they're not." He shrugs and leans down to pick up a blank canvas that rests against the wall. "Let's put it this way—you're the first person in a long time to admit to me that they don't know anything about art." His boots tap across the hardwood floor as he carries the canvas back toward the center of the room.

"Really?"

He sets the blank canvas on an easel and pulls up a small stool to sit in front of it, a smile lighting up his entire face. "Once you reach a certain level within the art world, people start catering to what they think you want or expect rather than being real. It's hard to tell if people even really like what you create, or if they're just going along with it because everyone else is."

"That's a bit self-deprecating."

His grin doesn't fade. "Most of us artists are self-deprecating fools, Indy."

The ease of our conversation isn't lost on me.

I feel like I've known him all my life, yet I've merely just met him.

It's strange and would be overwhelming if Ansel gave me any time to explore the anxiety building beneath my skin. As it is, I barely have time to take a breath before he's pulling me another step further outside my comfort zone.

"It's your turn," he says and points toward the empty canvas.

I scrunch up my nose. "My turn?"

"I've been thinking about what you asked me the other night at dinner, and I feel it's only fair if I put myself on the other side of things. You know, fully grasp what it feels like to be the subject."

I look at the blank canvas and then at the leather couch and then back at him.

"That's great and all, but who's going to paint you? I can't paint. Like, *at all.*"

A handsome smirk lifts up the corners of his mouth, and he waves off my words with a nonchalant hand. "Anyone can paint. You just pick up the brush and put it to the canvas."

"You and I both know it's not that easy."

Ansel points toward the couch in front of the canvas. "Do you mind if I sit, or would you prefer me to stand?"

I silently wonder if I asked him to get naked, would he do it?

That might actually make doing this worth the embarrassment of the garbage I'll no doubt create…

Oh. My. God. Don't be such a pervert. I quickly squash that ridiculous thought and focus on my lack of skill.

"There is no way I'm painting you," I declare. "I mean, I can hardly draw a stick person, much less create a portrait that would do you justice."

"Who says it has to be a portrait?" he asks and sits down. He stretches his arms out along the back of the couch and makes himself comfortable. "Just because I'm the subject doesn't mean my face has to be on that painting."

I laugh at the absurdity of a famous, incredibly talented artist acting like anyone can paint. "Ah, see," I say with a snap of my fingers, "that's where you're going wrong. You're forgetting that I know nothing about art."

"Just think of all the paintings inside the Met—" he begins to say, but I cut him off.

"I've never been to the Met."

Ansel's brown eyes widen in shock. "You're kidding me, right?"

I shake my head and suck my bottom lip between my teeth. "I told you I don't know anything about art!"

He rubs an agitated hand across the top of his head and barks a laugh. "You did. I just assumed that meant you didn't know anything current. *Everyone* should go to the Met."

I blush and shrug again.

"Okay, so don't try to picture the Met," he says through a soft laugh. "Do you know who Jackson Pollock is?"

I'm pretty sure I do. "The guy who did those drip paintings?"

"That's him." Ansel grins and nods at the same time. He's proud again, like maybe I'm not a total lost cause. I decide not to tell him I only know about Jackson Pollock from that movie with Ben Affleck, *The Accountant*. "Think about his paintings and compare them to a painting like the *Mona Lisa*."

"Okay…"

"Well, just because da Vinci painted a portrait of an actual female and Pollock didn't, doesn't mean Pollock didn't have a muse that inspired him. It *doesn't* mean he wasn't actually painting a subject."

I glance back and forth between the canvas and the handsome man on the couch.

I have no idea what I'm doing here. Hell, I don't even know if I should be here.

But here I am, standing inside Ansel Bray's private studio, and I'm so fucking intrigued by him, so damn curious about this man, that I don't think about anything else.

Eventually, my brain absorbs all of his advice and guidance, and an idea takes over.

I take off my coat and set it and my purse at the top of the stairs, sit down in front of the canvas, and while I choose my paints, Ansel picks up a remote from a wooden table beside the couch. With one small click, the exact piece of music I played for him on the subway starts to echo inside the room—*"Comptine d'un autre été."*

It's already halfway through the composition, and I look up to meet his gaze. "Did you play this on purpose or...?"

"Do you want the truth or a sugar-coated lie?"

What is that supposed to mean?

"The truth, obviously."

"This was the last song I was listening to when I was in here painting the other day."

My heart kicks up a rhythm inside my chest, and I have to inhale a deep breath just to make the damn thing relax.

What is it between us? Why do the two of us, people I wouldn't have thought would cross paths in a million years, have so much in common?

"That's..." Crazy. Weird. *Makes me feel nearly drunk I'm so consumed.*

"Yeah." A secret smile kisses his mouth. "I agree with that." He doesn't need me to finish the statement to know what I'm saying. He feels it too. "Tell me, Indy, why do you like this piece of music?"

"For a few reasons, I think," I answer honestly as I try to wrap my brain around what it is about Yann Tiersen's composition that touches me the most. "For one, it's on the soundtrack of one of my favorite movies..."

"*Amélie,*" he provides, and I nod. Once again, we're so in sync it scares me.

"And, mostly," I continue, "I like it because when a piano composition is done right, it is nearly painful how beautiful it is."

"Music is a passion of yours."

"It has been since I was a little girl." A wistful smile kisses my lips. "My dad is a talented jazz musician and always had music playing in the house. I'm pretty sure he's on a lifelong mission to hear everything that's ever been created."

Ansel chuckles. "That reminds me of my friend Nigel. But only, his mission involves every piece of beautiful art."

"Whatever I'm about to create right now—" I point the tip of my brush at him to emphasize my threat "—your friend Nigel doesn't need to see."

He grins at me and crosses an X over his heart. I focus my gaze back on the canvas. Maybe if I just take an abstract approach, I might come up with something that's not entirely embarrassing?

Fingers crossed.

The music switches over to something with a soothing beat, while a woman with a pretty voice sings softly in Spanish. My head sways back and forth to the relaxing lull, and my fingers guide the bristles of the brush across the stark-white canvas.

Blue turns to gray turns to yellow turns to splashes of gold and brown.

Occasionally, I glance at Ansel, but mostly I just focus on the canvas.

One song bleeds into another and into another until I don't know how much time has passed. But the sun has set, and the only light coming in through the windows is from the streetlamps and nearby buildings.

By the time I set my brush down, the canvas is a kaleidoscope of colors.

Without question or exchange, Ansel senses the finality and stands up from the couch.

Once he's standing behind me, he rests his hands on my shoulders, and I can feel the warmth of his fingers through my sweater.

"Is that me?" he asks, and I glance up to meet his eyes.

"If you were a rainbow, I think these would be your colors."

His smile lights up the whole fucking room. "It's brilliant."

I laugh at that. "Now, that's a lie if I've ever heard one."

He shakes his head and reaches down to grab my hand and help me to my feet. Standing directly behind me, he pulls my back against his chest and places his lips near my ear.

"I'm not lying," he whispers, and the heat of his breath triggers goose bumps that start at the back of my head and slowly move down my neck and arms. "It's heartfelt yet cool and both soft and rough. It's pensive and maybe even a little irritable around the edges, but there's also a lightness to it. If I were a rainbow, this would most certainly be me. There's just one thing missing."

"What? Something missing? I've gotta tell you, buddy, I think the ol' Indigo creative well has run dry."

He laughs and runs an intimate hand through my hair. My stomach lifts itself into my chest, and I have to swallow just to keep myself from moaning. Ansel either doesn't notice or pretends not to.

"You need to sign it."

I glance at him. "Sign it?"

"Yeah," he says and points to a nearby canvas resting against the wall. "Every artist needs to leave their signature."

I look at the canvas and see the inscription in the right-hand corner.

AB.

It's simply his initials. A messy script with an A and a B.

I pick up the brush near my hip and put it to the canvas. Only instead of my initials, I sign **Indy** in the bottom right-hand corner of my creation.

"*Perfect,*" he whispers near my ear, and every nerve ending beneath my skin comes to life.

My eyes flutter shut, electrified by the way I feel when his body is pressed up against mine. The insane urge to turn on my tiptoes and press my mouth to his full lips damn near consumes me.

God, he makes me feel so good...

Across the room, the sound of "My Boyfriend's Back" by the Angels starts to play inside my purse, and everything—and I do mean everything—comes crashing down around me at once.

It's Matt's ringtone—the one he set for himself on my phone—and the lyrics are entirely too ironic for my liking.

I blink out of my stupor and step forward to put a little distance between us.

"I'm glad you like it," I whisper hoarsely, the realization that I've completely forgotten my boyfriend for almost an entire day making me feel sick.

When Ansel caresses the skin of my cheek with a rough, sexy hand, I realize just how badly I need to get out of here.

chapter seventeen

Ansel

I f Indy's desire to run were a volleyball game, the ringing phone was the set, and the feel of my hand on her cheek was the spike. And just like that, it overcomes her.

"So, it's getting late," slips from her pretty little lips as she heads toward the top of the stairs to collect her jacket and purse. I follow in her wake but do it slowly enough so as not to make her even more uncomfortable. She's putting her arm into the sleeve of her coat when I come to a stop in front of her, and she verbalizes what her actions have already made pretty clear. "I think I should probably be heading home."

Even though I don't want her to go, I understand why she needs to, so I don't even entertain the idea of pushing her to stay.

Instead, I concentrate on making sure she gets home safely.

"I'll call my driver," I say without hesitation.

She slides the last button on her coat through its hole and settles it into place while shaking her head. "No, I can—"

"Indy, I'm not taking no for an answer on this," I say softly but firmly. "I'm making sure you get home safely."

It's a Friday. The city is bustling, the sidewalks and subway are crowded, and the roads are slick with black ice. As a survivor of a traumatic car accident and a realist with a grasp of just how much evil there is in the world, I'm completely unwilling to yield on this particular issue.

Before she can protest again, I pull my phone out of my pocket and call my driver, Hank. He's been with me for years, and while I don't need him twenty-four seven now that I've got my sight back, it's a rare occasion when he can't accommodate my request.

"Ansel," he greets on the second ring. "What can I help you with this evening?"

I tell him the situation, and he doesn't hesitate to oblige.

"Give me fifteen minutes, and I'll be there."

"Perfect," I respond into the receiver and hit end on the call.

Indy's mouth turns down at the corners. "You really didn't need to do that."

"Yes, I did."

With my hand at the small of her back, over the material of her jacket, I lead her out of the studio, down the stairs, and toward the entryway of my home. The entire way, I can sense something is on her mind, on the tip of her tongue. Several times, she glances back at me and opens her mouth, but then snaps it shut before words come out.

"Everything okay?" I ask as we stop in the small foyer near the front door.

Indy glances down at her boots and then at me and then back at her boots, and it only takes about three more circuits before she finds the strength to meet my eyes and stay there. "I enjoyed spending time with you today."

"I can assure you the feeling is mutual."

"W-why do you think I look like the girl in your painting?" she blurts out the question, and her own surprise slides its way onto her face in the form of parted lips and widened eyes.

Why do you look like the girl in my painting?

That, my sweet Indy, is a question that's been on my mind ever since I came face-to-face with you.

"I don't know." It's the only answer I have right now.

Her big blue eyes stare up into mine, and her voice drops to an almost whisper. "I don't know what your intentions are—and I'm definitely not assuming you have any sort of intentions—but I should probably let you know I'm in a relationship, and the only thing I can offer you is friendship."

Her words are weak at best, feeble and flimsy. It's like she doesn't even believe them herself, but the ins and outs of her relationship are none of my business.

"Matt, right?" I ask with a forced smile, and she tilts her head in confusion. "Your sister mentioned he was your boyfriend at dinner, remember?"

"Oh." She purses her lips, and her mouth forms a tiny, exquisite heart. "Right, yeah."

"And, Indy?"

"Yes?"

"I'd be honored to be your friend."

If friendship is all she can give me, then friendship it is. Even if I fucking hate it.

"Maybe that's why it feels like the universe is pulling us together," she adds. "So we can be friends."

Friends. *Fuck.*

Do I like that she has a boyfriend? Hell no.

But when it comes to Indy, I'll take what I can get.

Even if that means I have to put my own emotions aside.

It isn't long before I'm saying goodbye and helping her into Hank's Escalade. I don't make a big thing of it, and I don't press for the next time I can see her.

I'll see her again. It might be the one of the only things of which I have no doubt.

Once Hank's Escalade is out of sight, I head back inside my house and lock the door behind me. I make my way back up the stairs and into my studio, and I don't stop my progress until I'm standing in front of her painting.

Maybe I'm biased, but Indy Davis is better at art than she thinks.

With the light of the moon filtering in through the windows, I stare at the wet paint of her work.

She may be gone, but I can still feel her in the room.

My private studio.

The one place that is my safe haven.

Indy and Bram are the only two people other than me who have ever been inside.

I can't decide if it's all a bit John Cusack holding a boombox over his head or completely batshit crazy.

With careful fingers, I take Indy's painting and carry it downstairs with me. Once I reach the first floor, I set it on an empty bench by the window and head into the kitchen to make some fresh coffee.

I've got several missed calls and texts and even more emails to answer, and I'm going to need the bitter bean's assistance if I have any hope of getting through them all.

Nigel asking if I want to sell a painting I most likely will not sell.

Lucy bitching at me for cutting out early today and not signing the paperwork she left out for me.

My mother asking me God only knows what.

Bram letting me know his band is playing at Rookwood Music Hall tomorrow night.

It's an endless list of people who undoubtedly deserve at least a cursory response. But I don't bother with any of them. Instead, I open up my texts and find the one and only person I feel like talking to right now.

Me: Did you make it home okay?

Her quick response surprises me.

Indy: I did. Hank was very accommodating.

I grin and type out a pithy response.

Me: Exactly how accommodating?

My phone vibrates with her response a moment later.

Indy: He stopped at Taco Bell on the way home and bought me dinner.

A laugh escapes me when I read her message. Apparently, I'm not the only one under Indy's spell. My fingers fly over the electronic keyboard, and before I know it, I'm doing the exact thing I claimed to be above during her exit—pushing her to see me again.

Me: Are you busy tomorrow night?

I watch the text bubbles appear and then disappear several times, and I know she's mulling over my question. She probably doesn't know what to say, and I'm coming to find, with Indy, it's a lot of push and pull. Even when she wants to do something, she has to consider it carefully before allowing herself to concede.

I don't know why I know these things about her, but I just do.

All I can do is let it guide me.

Indy: I guess that depends…

I grin at her cryptic text.

Me: On what exactly?

Indy: On what you're about to ask me to do.

Me: Let me guess, if it's something you don't feel like doing, then you're going to be conveniently busy…

Indy: Good guess. If it's something I'm into, then I'm free.

Another laugh escapes my throat at her cheeky response.

Me: My brother is playing a show tomorrow night. Rookwood Music Hall. 8 p.m.

Indy: Is that so? How neat.

Neat? My eyebrows pinch together with suspicion.

Me: Yeah. He's the lead singer for New Rules.

Indy: Oh wow. That is brand-new information!

I chuckle and type out a teasing message.

Me: Crazy thought here. Did you, by any chance, already know who my brother is?

Indy: It's possible that I've seen it before on the Google.

The Google. Hah. I wonder if that means she's been Googling me. *God, I hope so.* Seeking out information via an internet search may not be the way a man usually wants a woman to learn his secrets, but I can only see the positive. It would confirm that she wants to know more about me.

Me: So, does that mean you'll go?

Indy: Yes. It turns out I'm free, after all.

Tomorrow night, I'll see Indy again, thanks to my brother's concert. Maybe his help isn't so bad, after all.

chapter eighteen

Indy

've been a ball of emotions all day. A pressure cooker of excitement and guilt and anxiety, all of which turns to complete overload where I feel one thousand moods all at once and everything falls apart. Kind of like a rump roast.

And Ansel is at the forefront of it all.

My new bestie.

Good grief.

Friendship really is all I can offer. I know that, and I *mean* it. But post-declaration of that, my heart feels sluggish and my skin is clammy, and I'm so confused about what I want out of life that my willpower seems to have completely left the building.

So, despite the doubts, not once do I ever consider canceling my evening. *Nope.* Instead, I rationalize.

Friends go to concerts together all the time. If anyone else had tickets and backstage passes to see New Rules, I'd be there in a heartbeat. We'd sing and dance, and nothing else would matter.

If I'm going to commit to being friends with Ansel, we have to really act like friends, and that means doing things like going to the concert and supporting his brother.

It's completely innocent, and assigning it any more consideration is way more offensive to my relationship with Matt than going to the concert.

Right?

Right.

I dress for the weather, slipping on my favorite pair of jeans, brown ankle boots, a cozy cream sweater and the soft pink pleather jacket that I've had for at least three years but love dearly. I keep my hair and makeup simple—a natural color palette and my brown locks long and wavy.

The living room is quiet as I sit down on my sectional, dressed fully and ready to go—almost an hour early.

My knees bounce and my fingers fiddle, and when I finally can't take the silence anymore—a whopping fifteen seconds later—I turn on the TV and mindlessly flip through the channels. The episode of *Mike and Molly* where she's trying to write a book is on, so I settle on that, knowing it'll make me laugh.

About thirty minutes before Ansel is supposed to pick me up, I get a text message from Matt.

Matt: Sorry I missed our FaceTime call today, baby. I was stuck in meetings all day. It's close to one in the morning and I'm dead on my feet, but I'm also missing you. Do you want to chat real quick before I go to bed?

I glance to the clock and back to the show. I *really* like this episode. Who knows when I'll get the chance to see it again, and Ansel could be here anytime. It would be rude to keep him waiting.

Me: How about you get some sleep, and we'll chat tomorrow? I know you have to be exhausted.

Matt: Okay. Talk to you tomorrow, my beautiful girl.

Me: Sleep well, Matt. XOXO.

I feel a little guilty about forgoing the call, but Matt's exhausted and I'm going through something. The last thing I want is to make him start worrying I'm sick again while he's so far away. I just got him to stop asking me to go to the doctor.

There'll be plenty of time to talk to him tomorrow after I've spent the evening with Ansel as friends. I know I'm in a relationship. He knows I'm in a relationship.

Everything will definitely be different tonight.

Fifteen minutes later, when I finally have my needlessly guilty conscience persuaded, my sister calls me. I stare at her name flashing on the screen, but I don't answer. Instead, I tap decline on the call, put my phone on silent, and slide it into my purse.

I'm avoiding her. But what if she would have asked me what I was doing tonight?

I haven't even told her I've been spending time with Ansel Bray, so dropping the news of his brother's concert would be a little too reminiscent of a bomb.

The reporter in her would have all sorts of questions, and I don't have the kind of time to devote to the call that it would take to answer all of them.

Plus, she's shameless when it comes to celebrities, and she'd end up wanting to come along. Ansel and I really need the time alone to find our friendship groove.

I will eventually tell her. I silently resolve my guilt. *Just not right now. Just not today.*

And, lucky for my subconscious, I don't have the opportunity to think any more about why I'm avoiding everyone because two knocks against my door grab my full attention. Molly's in the middle of her dramatic flip through the pages of her book, trying to tear the pages apart because of how much she feels like it sucks, but I grab the remote and flick it off without hesitation.

When I open the door, Ansel stands across the threshold, a soft smile on his lips and a lightness to his brown eyes. The way the moonlight hits them tonight makes me wonder what color his eyes used to be.

He greets me with a gentle hello and a friendly hug, and it takes all of my willpower not to shove my nose into the leather of his jacket and inhale the familiar, delicious scent I'm coming to find is his signature. A heady combination of mint and leather and soft vanilla, and my nose is a fucking fan.

"Excited to see New Rules?" he asks, and I smile like a loon, equal parts thankful for the distraction from my annoying thoughts and eager to see his brother's band play.

"You have no idea."

Instantly, all of my doubts and concerns and second-guessing pretty much go poof and disappear into thin air.

We don't waste any time at my apartment, and once I grab my purse and lock the front door, we're walking out into the frigid February air and into Hank's Escalade.

It's all very friendly, very laid-back, and I mentally give myself a little pat on the back.

As the car rocks us with the gentle lullaby of the road, I let go of all the tension I've been holding. We're going to see New Rules at Rookwood Music Hall, and I can't think of any other place I'd rather be.

Our commute isn't too bad, a brief twenty minutes or so, and once we reach the venue, it isn't long before we're inside and Ansel is playing his "I'm related to the band" card. I cling to his arm in an effort to play a card of my own—*I'm with him.*

"Are you ready?" he asks as we step past security and head toward the backstage area of Rookwood Music Hall.

"Uh huh." He doesn't miss the ridiculous smile all but tattooed across my face, but honestly, I'm pretty sure the astronauts on the International Space Station don't miss it either. It's been forever since I've done something this fun, this young. I'm prepared to go full fangirl.

The building is a relic, a bit old and rickety around the edges, but that only seems to add to its charm. Rookwood Music Hall is a shrine to famous musicians who started their careers in this very building, their memorabilia cluttering the walls around us, and I have to fight the urge to squeal as Ansel leads us toward a room in the far back.

The instant we step inside, I nearly have a stroke.

New freaking Rules is standing right in front of me.

Bram and Lee and Nix and Tom. The entire fucking band is in this room, and I'm not sure whether to laugh or cry. This is a band I've been following for the past six or so years. I fell in love with their indie rock vibe and haven't stopped listening to them since.

It was literally love at first listen.

Holy shit, I'm backstage with New Rules.

"Well, look who decided to make an appearance at one of our shows!" Lee, the drummer, bellows when he spots Ansel in the doorway.

The rest of the band turns around, and similar jabs and teasing ensue.

From what I gather, it's been a while since Ansel has been to a New Rules concert, and I bite my tongue when the words *what the hell?* threaten to slip past my lips.

I mean, his brother is the lead singer, for fuck's sake.

If that were my brother, I wouldn't miss a single show.

Bram steps up and gives his brother a friendly hug and a playful fist to the bicep. I'd probably bruise like a peach if he hit me that hard, but Ansel doesn't even blink.

My eyes flit back and forth between the brothers, taking in their similarities. They have the same nose and strong jaw, and they're both tall. Deep and raspy, their voices even sound alike.

No doubt, they're both incredibly good-looking, and I have to imagine Mr. and Mrs. Bray are no slouches either. I mean, you don't create human beings that look like this without some damn good genes.

"When you said you were coming, I honestly didn't believe you,"

Bram says, and Ansel rolls his eyes. "I mean, I told security you might show up but not to hold their breath."

Ansel scoots me out and more into his side when one of the backstage runners bumps into me, and the subtle movement makes Bram take real notice of me for the first time.

"It appears you've brought a friend."

"Yes."

The obvious interest Bram then takes in me makes me feel slightly self-conscious.

His eyes narrow as they run the circuit of my features one more time. "You look familiar, friend. Have we met before?"

Shit. I really don't want to think about the painting tonight. I came to see New Rules play, not discuss the ins and outs of the already confusing, completely mysterious situation.

Thankfully, Ansel bypasses the whole "you look like the girl in the painting" conversation, answers for me, and then introduces us. "No. You haven't met before. Indy, this is my asshole brother."

"The pleasure is all mine," Bram says with a sly grin and reaches out to shake my hand. "Indy, this is Lee and Ni—"

"I know who you are," I cut him off before he can finish, and my eyes go wide when I realize how rude that probably sounded. "All of you…I mean, I'm a…I'm a fan. Of New Rules. Your band," I ramble and trip over my own words. "It's, uh, yeah, it's nice to meet you guys."

The rest of the band offers hellos and smiles before going back to doing whatever it is famous musicians do in backstage rooms.

Talk to pretty girls.

Throw back a few beers.

Smoke something that smells a lot like weed.

Yeah, those sorts of things. Being in a room with a famous rock group is a little like being in a room with the sun. Everyone is better off if you don't look directly at it.

"A New Rules fan, huh?" Bram grins and winks at his brother. "I like your new friend already, bro."

Ansel laughs, joking, "She didn't really know anything about you. I fed her that information in the car." The energy between the two of them is fun and welcoming, and I settle into the ease of it all so much that I'm caught off guard when Ansel looks down at me with amusement filling up his striking brown eyes.

A choking cough escapes my lips, and immediately, I feel like the biggest, most awkward idiot in this room. In the country. On the entire planet.

"You okay?" Ansel asks, and his brow furrows in concern.

Oh yeah. Just a bout of unexpected déjà vu.

"I'm fine. I'm fine," I mutter, clearing my throat and making an excuse instead of going into something literally no one will understand. "Apparently, I haven't mastered the art of breathing yet."

And I'm officially an idiot.

Both Ansel and Bram chuckle at my words.

"How about you not encourage my brother's ego?" Ansel suggests, and I stick my tongue out at him. Casually, his arm comes up and around my shoulders, and he tucks me into his side. I don't pull away. "We'll let you guys do your thing. See you after the show, yeah?"

"Sounds good," Bram agrees and moves his gaze to mine. "It was nice meeting you, Indy. Enjoy the show, all right?"

Enjoy the show? *Pffft.* He does know he's in New Rules, right? They could be singing my grocery list in my kitchen, and I'd be having the time of my life.

"Break a leg?" I say, but it's more of a question than anything else. "Does that apply?"

Bram chuckles and shrugs. "A little? I guess?"

"What about *break all the fucking rules?*"

Ansel's brother raises a brow, and it's my turn to shrug.

"That's what Led Zeppelin always used to say before they walked onstage."

"No shit?" Bram asks and I nod.

Bram looks at his brother. "Keep her around, yeah?"

"Shut up." Ansel laughs, and his fingers tighten ever-so-slightly around my shoulder. "We'll see you after the show."

We offer our goodbyes to the rest of the band and head back down the hallway toward the inside of the venue.

"Led Zeppelin really said that?" Ansel asks just as we walk past security.

I lift my shoulders under his arm. "Hell if I know. It just sounded good."

His chuckle is so big and hearty, it echoes off the walls. "What am I going to do with you?"

His question is meant to be teasing, but I can't stop myself from wondering, *what is he going to do with me?*

My unbidden thought puts me at the edge of the slippery slope of reality, so I back away slowly. Rock crumbles and tumbles down the cliff into the deep-seated complications of the question, but I find firmer ground just a few inches away by focusing on the here and now.

On the literal answer to his abstract question.

"Take me to the bar," I say with a smile. "I could use a drink before the show."

By the time New Rules takes the stage, I am one shot of whiskey—*Ansel's choice*—and three beers deep. For most people, that probably doesn't sound like a lot of alcohol, but it's about four times as much as I've had to drink at any given time in the last two years.

But goddamn, I feel good.

The music feels good.

And Ansel, well, he feels good too.

We're facing the stage, and his arms are wrapped around my waist and his chin rests on my shoulder as we watch Bram and his band finish a song from their latest album.

The venue is packed to the brim, but since Ansel is related to the band, we're standing in our own little VIP area located on the right side of the stage.

Bram sings the final lyrics of "Temple," and the crowd pretty much loses their shit—including me.

He grins toward the audience and reaches down to take a swig of water from the bottle sitting on the ground near Lee's drums.

"Thank you," Bram says into the mic. "Did you know that, ten years ago today, this is the exact spot where we got our big break?"

Everyone hoots and hollers and claps their hands, and a woman in the back screams, "I love you!"

"Love you too, honey," he responds as he adjusts a few chords on his guitar. "All right, so we're going to play another tune, but we're doing things a little different tonight. I'm feeling nostalgic, so we're going to play a cover of one of my favorite Dire Straits songs. A song we played before we knew how to play much of anything else. Here goes something awesome…"

The band starts into a rhythm, and the soft and sweet sounds of "Romeo and Juliet" fill my ears.

I sway my hips, and Ansel moves to the music with me. His warm breath is right beside my ear as he sings along to the lyrics.

I don't know if it's me or Ansel or the alcohol making the decisions around here, but I turn on my heels and wrap my arms around his neck. Our faces are inches from each other, and our eyes feel chained together.

He moves his hands to my lower back, and a shiver runs the distance from them to the back of my neck.

He mouths the words to the song. *How about it?*

My gaze moves from his eyes to his lips to his eyes again, and the urge to stand up on my tippy-toes and press my mouth to his is potent and overwhelming.

Just one little taste. That's all I want.

Closer and closer, I shut off my mind and lean. Toward Ansel. Toward the kiss. Toward satisfaction.

"Can I get you anything else to drink?" a bar waitress yells over the music, stepping up and into our area and breaking me out of my stupor.

I shoot away from him like I've been tased, and the truth is, I have.

Her interruption is the only thing that stopped me from making a criminal mistake.

"Another beer please!" I pretty much shout toward her.

Surely, another beer will serve as a good distraction, right?

I may be a little tipsy, but in my slightly inebriated opinion, that's a brilliant fucking idea. Drink beer and dance and don't do anything stupid.

I can handle that.

Right?

chapter nineteen

Ansel

The cab driver starts the meter and heads toward the Brooklyn Bridge.

Being inside of a cab makes my stomach churn and my skin crawl with unease, but Indy was swaying on her feet and it's nearly two in the morning. Visions of her stumbling around the subway platform—maybe off of it—made me suck up my discomfort. Plus, I didn't want to call Hank and make him get out of bed at this hour.

Now that I'm sitting inside of this godforsaken cab, I'm kind of regretting that.

A little over five years ago, I innocently hailed a cab to head to a showing for one of my friends at a gallery in SoHo—and ended up in an ambulance with broken bones and eyes filled with glass.

My mind barely remembers any of the middle of the story, but somehow my body does. Every time I'm inside a cab now, I would need a jackhammer if I wanted a chance to break apart the tension in my muscles.

Indy rests her head on my shoulder, and I give the cab driver the address of her apartment.

"And, please, take your time," I urge and reach across Indy to buckle her seat belt before moving to mine. "Getting us there safely is better than not getting us there at all."

The cabbie nods and smiles at me in the rearview mirror. "You got it."

Thankfully, traffic is nonexistent at this hour of the night, and the driver doesn't appear to have a lead foot as he pulls out onto the road.

I stare out the window, and without even realizing it, I start to smile.

This fucking night. It was perfect. *She was perfect.*

New Rules brought the fucking house down, and I actually enjoyed seeing my brother in his element. He was happy and at ease, and for as much shit as I gave him while he was doing it, he deserves one hell of a life after the way he helped me through my loss of sight.

After the show, Indy and I met the band backstage for a few more drinks and some laughs. In hindsight, now that I've gotten Indy into the cab and we're heading toward her apartment, I'm realizing a few more drinks *really* weren't needed.

I glance down to see her eyelids drooping and her long lashes fluttering down across her cheeks.

"You okay?"

"Mmhmmm…jus sleepy," Indy whispers toward me and wraps her hands around my bicep, snuggling her head into my skin.

She's drunk, nearly sloppy she's slurring and swaying so much, but I don't hold it against her like I would someone else. To be honest, she's an adorable drunk. All cutesy smiles and rosy cheeks, apparently this woman does no wrong in my eyes.

I gaze down at the angel crowding my personal space and smile.

God, what it is it about this woman?

It's like she has me under some spell, and I crave more. More time. More words. More stolen glances. More smiles. *More Indy.*

I wrap my arm around her shoulders and pull her closer to my side.

"Are you going to be able to wake up when we get to your apartment?" I ask softly into her ear.

No response.

"Indy," I say a little louder this time. "Can you wake up for me?"

Still, no response. Only the soft, lulling breaths of a woman who's ly

succumbed to the alcohol and exhaustion and passed out.

"Looks like you've got a goner back there," the cab driver says over his shoulder, and I catch his smile in the rearview mirror.

"Yeah, well, I don't think this was the plan, but pretty sure those are famous last words, huh?"

"Exactly." The cab driver chuckles. "Tomorrow, your girlfriend will be saying she's never drinking again. They always do."

My girlfriend. I don't correct him.

I look down at her again, and my amusement turns to unease. The more I think about leaving Indy in her apartment by herself in this condition, the more uncomfortable I become.

After two more attempts to wake her up, I make an executive decision.

"Mind if we switch up the destination?" I ask the cabbie. "Can you head toward the Village instead of Brooklyn?"

"It's going to end up costing you more," he says, but I wave him off. I don't give a fuck about the money as long as Indy is taken care of.

"Understandable."

Thirty minutes later, we're pulling up in front of my place, and Indy is pretty much down for the count.

I pay the cabbie, tip him generously, and with gentle arms, pick up Indy and carry her toward my front door.

She doesn't budge as I fumble for my keys or when I get us inside or when I carry her up the stairs and into my bedroom. Hell, she doesn't even budge when I remove her shoes.

Thankfully, though, her eyes peek open as I adjust her head on a pillow and pull the sheets and comforter over her body.

"Ansel?" she whispers.

"I'm here." I brush her long locks away from her face. "Just get some rest, okay?"

"Is the show over?"

I grin. "Yeah, it's over."

"It was a good show," she whispers.

"It was."

Her blue, slightly out of focus eyes gaze up at me. "Why do I have so much fun with you?" she asks and blows out a slightly frustrated breath. "Most fun I ever had." Her eyelids start to droop again as she adds, "I'm a stupid moth."

I smile at her words, half of which I don't understand. But I figure that's on par for drunk rambling. It's best if I encourage her to sleep.

"Good night, Indy," I whisper, and because I can't fucking help myself, I gently brush my lips across the soft skin of her forehead. "I'll see you in the morning."

I know I'm crossing a line, but this girl, *this beautiful fucking girl*, affects me in ways no one ever has.

I start to stand up and leave the bedroom, but she wraps her arms around my neck and doesn't let me go. "You know what?" she asks, and I tilt my head to the side.

"What?"

Without warning, she presses her full, pink, perfect lips against mine.

Shock electrifies every inch of my skin, and my eyes widen, but she doesn't stop or pull away.

Soft and slow at first, her mouth just barely explores mine, and I let her. I'm a bastard for not being the sober, responsible adult, but it feels so fucking good.

Her inhibitions left unchecked thanks to her lack of a clear head and reason, her lips turn needy and hurried, and she slips her tongue past my lips to take a taste.

A groan starts in my chest and rattles seductively up to the top of my throat.

Indy moans against my mouth and slides her hands into my hair, her arms digging into my shoulders and neck.

It takes everything inside me not to coax this kiss into something more.

Because, fuck, I want to.

But she's drunk…

Fuck, you need to stop this. Right now.

I let her keep the lead for another moment or two until I finally find the strength to take control and slow down her momentum. Once, twice, three times, I gently press my lips to hers and end the kiss before anything more can happen while she's this intoxicated.

Silence stretches between us as I hold her in my arms and let her search my eyes.

Eventually, she releases her arms from my neck and snuggles into the covers, dropping straight into the deep sleep of a woman who's had too much to drink.

At least, I think she does. Just before I reach the doorway, her voice stops me in my tracks.

"Ansel?"

"Yeah, Indy?"

"I've been wanting to do that all night."

"Do what?"

"Kiss you."

I know she's drunk and I know she doesn't know what she's saying and I know she probably won't remember any of this, but like a bullet, those two words hit me straight in the chest, and I don't bother to guard my words.

"I've been wanting to do it a hell of a lot longer than that."

chapter twenty

Indy

Sleep pulls and pushes, clawing me closer to the sweet sounds of my dreams and then releasing me to drift back into reality. The cycle is long and my eyes are heavy, but after several attempts, I finally overturn the magnets on my eyelids.

Music soothes and rolls, much like it did in the depths of my dream, but the cold of the room around me feels much different from my fantasy's warm womb.

Who's playing music in my apartment?

I blink a few times to moisten my eyes and focus on the squares of the coffered ceiling.

Wait. When did I get a coffered ceiling?

Abruptly, I sit up, and as soon as I do, the truth is obvious.

I'm not in my apartment. Not in my bedroom. Not even in my own bed.

Holy shit.

Although this is the first time I've seen his bedroom, it doesn't take me long to attribute ownership to Ansel. Two leather club chairs face a fireplace in the corner, a glass-and-gold side table filling the space between them. Exposed brick runs the length of the back wall, and the sleek king bed I'm in is low to the floor and beautiful in its simplicity. A white comforter covers my body, and a cream throw rests on top of that for good measure.

Oh my god, did I sleep with him?

My hand creeps up to my mouth, an involuntary reaction to the shock of my poor decisions, and I try like hell to recall all the details of the last twelve or so hours.

Ansel picking me up at my apartment.

Meeting New Rules. The concert. Dancing. Drinking.

I grimace and move my hand to my forehead as the pounding in my temples puts another tally mark next to the drinking.

Fuck, why did I drink so much last night?

I scrap and jockey, trying valiantly to cut through enough of the fog from my hangover to remember what happened next—what happened that made me end up here in his *bed*—but the effort is fruitless.

The last thing I remember is being backstage after the concert.

Surely, I didn't sleep with him, right?

I slide the covers off my body, and I'm relieved to find I'm still fully dressed in last night's clothes.

Okay, that's a good sign. In order to have sex with someone, clothes have to be removed. There's no way I had more than one wrestle with my clothes last night, so the fact that they're on must mean I never took them off in the first place.

"Good morning."

Hysteria makes me pull the covers back up over my fully clothed body as Ansel leans into the doorway of his bedroom. He rubs a towel through his wet hair, and the soft smile of a man who *isn't* hungover and *doesn't* have a splitting headache crests his lips. I kind of hate how good he looks fresh out of the shower and wearing a simple T-shirt and pair of sweat pants…and the fact that he probably remembers what happened last night with a touch more clarity.

Seriously? Why can't I remember what happened?

"Good morning," I croak out through the cobwebs in my throat.

"How are you feeling?"

All sorts of manic comments about hysteria and leaving the country come to mind, but I don't let any of them overflow the surface as I shrug. "I mean, I've been better."

His smile grows in response. "Well, do you think some coffee might help take the edge off?"

"God, yes."

"All right, then." He chuckles. "Meet me downstairs?"

I nod and watch as he turns on his heels and heads for the first floor of his house.

As soon as he's out of sight, I shoot out of the bed with a speed I immediately regret. After a quick sway with my hands on my knees, I head into the bathroom, pee, and do a half-assed job of fixing my hair. I mean, what's the point now? I pretty much ruined the allure of a woman who has her shit together last night when I decided to test my ability to hold my alcohol like a frat boy.

Fucking hell, I failed.

I make the best of my situation and brush my teeth with toothpaste and my index finger. Then, I take one last glance in the mirror, groan at my borderline-horrid appearance, pull up my proverbial big-girl panties, and head for the stairs. Luckily, I have the delicious aroma of bacon to guide my way to the kitchen like a lighthouse beacon shining in the night.

When I get there, Ansel is by the stove, flipping said bacon and scrambling up some eggs.

Jesus, he cooks too?

"You made breakfast?"

"I did." He grins at me over his shoulder. "Take a seat and have some coffee." He nods at the already poured steaming mug sitting on the kitchen island. "This will be ready in a minute or two."

I do as he says and sit down on the stool directly behind my mug. I'm almost scared to taste it, but when I do, it's *exactly* the way I like it.

"Coffee good?" he asks with a wry grin, and I nod.

"Perfect," I whisper. I'm clutching the cup in my hands like it's the key to the queen's castle, and the tips of my fingers start to feel weirdly numb.

It's just a cup of coffee, Indy, I tell myself. *Then why doesn't it feel like it?*

I blame my weird thoughts on all of the alcohol I shoved into my body last night and focus on the plate full of bacon and eggs that Ansel slides in front of me. Not to mention, the three ibuprofen he discreetly sets down beside my coffee.

Ah, yes. Pain killers.

He has literally thought of everything.

I quickly down the pills, and my stomach growls hungrily at the sight of the delicious food. The eggs are fluffy and light and just what I need to cut through the consequences of the alcohol.

"Breakfast is served." He winks, and I giggle.

"Thank you," I say and pick up my fork. "This looks delicious."

He sits down beside me and digs into his food. He's almost finished, and I've only managed four bites of eggs when I finally decide to address the big, fat elephant playing soccer with my mind.

"So, uh, what exactly happened last night?"

He glances at me out of his periphery as he takes a sip of coffee. "What do you mean?"

"I mean…how did I end up *here?*"

"Oh." He nods and sets down his mug. "You were a little too drunk last night to be on your own."

"God." I drop my head to the counter and groan before looking back up to meet his eyes. "I'm so sorry about that. If it's not obvious, I almost never drink alcohol. Pretty sure my tolerance is equivalent to a toddler's."

"No apology necessary." Ansel chuckles, and a whole new set of butterflies takes flight in my stomach. I thought it'd be easy—that we would naturally segue into the conversation about whether anything physical happened. But we didn't. And now I have to put myself out there all over again.

Christ, Indy. You are banned from alcohol for the rest of your life.

"So…uh…did anything…*happen?*"

He searches my eyes for a long moment, and my breath freezes in my lungs.

Oh God, I start to panic. *Something happened.*

I swallow thickly and chew at the inside of my lip. Ansel finally sighs. "Besides you sleeping in my bed and me sleeping on the couch? No, Indy," he says. "Nothing happened."

Okay, good news. I didn't sleep with him.

I expect myself to settle, to fall into the embrace of relief and breathe again. I mean, I should be happy nothing happened between us. Thrilled, even.

But for some reason, I just feel even sicker.

"You don't need to feel bad or guilty, okay?" Ansel insists.

His brown eyes are worried, and I get sucked so deep into them that I forget to answer.

"Okay?" he asks again.

"Okay." I nod to ease his discomfort. "You didn't have to give me your bed."

He shrugs. "It's the only one in the house. I never got around to putting anything in the other bedrooms."

I manage a half smile.

"Now, let's just enjoy our breakfast, and when you're ready to go home, I'll give Hank a ring."

"Okay," I repeat and lift a piece of bacon to my mouth for a bite.

"But I should make it clear," he continues with a secret smirk, "if you start going on and on about how awesome you think my brother is again, I might as well just give Hank a call now."

An abrupt laugh escapes my throat, and a bite of bacon shoots out of my mouth and onto the table. "Oh my god, I didn't mean to do that." I cover my mouth with my hand about two seconds too late, and it only makes me laugh harder.

"Well, shit," Ansel mutters through an amused chuckle. "You don't have to spit your food out over it. I mean, I guess I can at least listen to what you thought of the concert..."

I giggle-snort. "Just eat your breakfast and forget that ever happened."

"Okay, but before I do that, there's something I need to do…" He grins and grabs a fresh paper towel from the kitchen counter.

Two seconds later, that damn paper towel is tucked into my sweater like a bib.

"There." The handsome jerk grins. "Perfect."

And in an instant, I go from anxious and confused to smiling and laughing my ass off.

All because of him.

God, what is this man doing to me?

chapter twenty-one

Ansel

"Look who finally decided to show up! And only twenty minutes late!" Bram bellows from inside my mom's house the second I open the front door. He can't even see me, but already, he's laying into me. "Come inside, sweetheart, and grace us with your presence!"

I laugh even though I'm the butt of the joke.

In my defense, I didn't mean to be late, but my mom and Neil's house is an hour outside of the city, and I had a meeting with my accountant that lasted longer than I expected.

I take my boots off just inside the door—a rule of my mother's—and pad across the hardwood floor of the entryway in my socks as I make my way inside the house.

"Ansel." My mother's gentle voice is music to my ears, and I smile when I find her standing in the kitchen, setting a pot roast on a serving platter.

"Hey, Mom."

"It's so good to see you." A smile lights up her face, and faint laugh lines make their appearance around her mouth. She steps toward me and wraps me up in a tight hug. "We're just about ready to eat."

"Pretty sure you mean, we *are* ready to eat, but we've been waiting on Ansel to get here," Bram chimes in, and our mom scowls toward him. "Guy gets his sight back, starts to paint again, has one successful show, and forgets all about the little people."

"Stop being so ornery, Abraham."

"Yeah, *Abraham*," I tease. "Stop being such a prick around your mother."

"*Ansel.* Behave."

Thirty-four-years old and Della never hesitates to knock me or Bram into line.

The thought of it makes me smile. Even when you're an adult, *a grown-ass fucking man*, you can still count on your mom to put you in your place.

She may have a kind, sweet face and the voice of an angel, but if someone pisses her off, she'll go from zero to rage in five seconds flat.

She also runs a tight ship, and I have no doubt raising two rowdy, asshole boys only contributed to that.

My stepdad Neil walks into the kitchen and gives me a hearty pat on the shoulder. "Good to see you, son."

"You too, Neil."

Neil Wallace has been my stepdad since I was ten years old.

My mom and dad went through a messy fucking divorce when Bram was seven and I was nine, and thankfully, she met Neil about a year later.

He is the complete opposite of my dad.

Where Cal Bray is a self-involved, work-focused, money-hungry CEO and mostly absent from our lives, Neil is loving and family-oriented and supportive and would do anything for me, Bram, and my mom.

The last time I spoke to my dad was about three years ago, and our conversation was short and distant and reaffirmed the status of our relationship—*we don't have one.* And before that, it had been over two years since we'd spoken, and his urge to contact me stemmed from the accident.

Bram, on the other hand, stays in frequent contact with him and occasionally updates me on his status. Last I heard, he'd followed his latest business venture—a profitable cellular company—to London and appeared to be making waves in the European market.

As far as I'm concerned, Neil is and always will be the father in my life.

"How've you been?" he asks and grabs a stack of dishes from the cabinet. "I've been following the buzz on your exhibition, and it sounds like everyone is loving your latest works."

"I can't complain," I say and take the dishes from his hands. "What about you? Everything going well with you and mom?"

"Retirement is treating us well, and your mom's found a new hobby."

"Oh yeah?"

He nods. "Yep. Making lists of things for me to do around the house."

I chuckle. "Sounds like she's keeping you busy."

"Yeah." Neil smiles. Hell, he always smiles when he talks about my mom.

"All right!" Bram hollers from the dining room. "It's time to eat!"

"Jesus, Bram," my mom chides. "Do you have to be so loud?"

"I'm a rock star, Mom," he teases. "We're supposed to be loud."

"Yeah, well, in this house, you're my son. And right now, you're too loud. We're not trying to call the whole fucking neighborhood to dinner."

Neil and I walk into the dining room just in time to hear my mom dropping f-bombs. The three of us men grin and steal glances at one another.

"Don't even say it," Della threatens. "Just keep your opinions to yourselves, sit your asses down, and enjoy this delicious meal I've cooked for you."

I set the plates on the table and do as I'm told, *sitting my ass down* in one of the dining chairs. Smartly, Bram and Neil do the same.

Eager for the pot roast, carrots, and mashed potatoes with fresh biscuits, we all dig into the hot meal, and it doesn't take long for me to remember why I love my mom's cooking so much.

Eventually, once we've showered Della with enough "this is delicious" compliments, she softens around the edges and is back to her sweet-as-honey self.

"So, Mr. Rock Star," Neil pauses and looks at my brother with a cheeky grin. "How was your concert the other night?"

"Good. It's a shame you and Mom couldn't make it."

"We wanted to be there, sweetie," Mom chimes in. "We tried to get back from Barbados in time, but our flight kept getting delayed."

Mom and Neil have spent the last two years of retirement being world travelers, scheduling a trip to a new destination every three months or so.

"It's okay," he reassures, and a mischievous smile stretches across his face. "Ansel made it, *and* he brought someone with him…"

I toss a glare in my brother's direction.

"Oh, really? Like a date?" my mom asks and Bram nods.

"Yep."

"But Ansel doesn't date…" Immediately, she turns her curiosity to me. "Who did you bring with you?"

"Don't get all excited. She's just a friend."

Bram's smile turns challenging. "Her name is Indy and she's beautiful, and Ansel is completely smitten."

"I'm sorry, but did we somehow end up back in time? Because I swear to God that's exactly what ten-year-old Bram would've said…"

He just smirks. *Such a fucking shit-stirrer.*

"You know," my mom says with a wistfulness to her voice. "I knew there was something different about you, Ans. But I just couldn't put my finger on it."

I roll my eyes. "Don't be ridiculous, Mom. There is nothing different about me."

This is exactly why I didn't want to bring up Indy at dinner.

For one, I'm not in a relationship with her. And two, my mom gets far too excitable over any relationship prospects for her sons. If she could marry us off and get grandkids out of the deal, she would've done it five years ago.

Sometimes, I wonder if my track record of never dating and being *seemingly* incapable of falling in love with a woman has fed into this. Sometimes, I also wonder if my DNA—*specifically, those genes that came from my father*—have fucked up my ability to commit to anyone.

I've never been interested in progressing things past a short fling or one-night stand.

Until now. *With a woman who's unavailable.*

"Yeah, there is…" My mom pauses, and her knowing gaze searches my face. "There's a lightness to your eyes, and that signature scowl of yours is practically nonexistent."

"Do you want to know what she looks like?" Bram asks, but he doesn't give anyone time to respond. "She looks exactly like the girl in the painting that people are going so crazy over."

My eyes skitter to Bram, and he smirks, mouthing the taunting words, *I figured it out.*

Fucking nosy prick, I mouth back.

"Ansel's painting? The painting with the pretty, blue-eyed girl?" our mom asks, and my bastard brother keeps this insane conversation going.

"That's the one."

Della's gaze shoots to mine. "Is she the girl in your painting?"

I shake my head. "I met her after I painted it, Mom."

I know they say the truth will set you free, but in this case, the truth would only lock me inside an interrogation room with Della.

"Talk about some coincidence," Neil contributes, and my mother nods her agreement.

And, like a fucking miracle, my phone starts vibrating in my pocket. I pull it out as if it is the one and only key to my eternal salvation.

Incoming Call Nigel

"Shit, sorry," I mutter and hold my phone up in the air. "I need to take this."

"*Ansel,*" my mother sighs. "But we haven't finished eating."

"I'm sorry, Mom—" I stand up from my seat "—but it's important."

I'm not sorry. I'm fucking thankful.

"Bullshit," Bram mutters through a cough, but I flip him the bird and answer Nigel's call by the third ring.

"Hey, Nye, just give me a second," I greet, immediately making a beeline for the entryway. But before I'm able to shrug on my jacket and step outside to take Nigel's call, I don't miss my mom saying, "I really hope I get to meet her."

Dammit, Bram.

"All right," my mother says, and I look up from my spot on the couch in their sun-room to see her standing in the doorway, her petite body wrapped up in a thick winter jacket, a scarf, gloves, and a hat. "I know you're avoiding me."

"I'm not avoiding you."

It takes her all of two seconds to call me out on my lie.

"Yes, you are." She grins, hands me a fresh cup of a coffee, and sits down beside me. "It's thirty degrees out, and you're sitting in the sun-room of all places. This is the coldest spot in the whole house."

"But the view is perfect." I smile at her and make a show of looking through the large windows and out toward their backyard. The sun has set and the sky is dark, but the glow of the moon shimmers and shines off the lake I used to swim in as a kid.

From where Bram and I are in the city, my mom and Neil live about an hour away, in a more suburban part of New Jersey. Every once in a while, the silence and serenity that comes with stepping outside of the hustle and bustle is a much-needed reprieve.

For a long moment, we just sit side by side and drink from our mugs.

Occasionally, my mother reaches out to pat my knee or my hand like only a mother can, but mostly, we just savor the quietness and the companionship of each other.

That is, until her curiosity gets the best of her.

"So, are you going to tell me about her?"

An exasperated sigh leaves my lungs. "I think you're being a little dramatic. There's nothing to tell."

"I don't think I am." She reaches out and takes my hand into hers. "Can I meet her?"

Her question makes me grimace. "It's not that simple, Mom."

"Why?"

"Because she's not mine. She has a boyfriend," I answer, even though it makes my chest hurt. "And we're just friends."

"From what Bram told me, it doesn't seem like you're just friends."

I shake my head. My *fucking* brother. "Bram doesn't know anything."

"Your brother knows a lot more than you think, Ans."

"Are you sure we're talking about the same person?" I ask on a laugh, and she has to fight her smile. "I mean, you're saying *Bram* and *knows a lot* in the same sentence, and it just isn't adding up right now."

"Okay, smartass." She laughs and nudges my arm with her elbow. "Can I just say one thing, and then I'll drop it?"

"I think we both know you're going to tell me no matter what I say."

She snorts and shakes her head. "Can you drop the sarcasm act for one minute?"

"Fine. I'll shut up." I make a show of acting like I'm zipping my mouth shut with my index finger and thumb.

Her responding smile is contagious, but it doesn't take long for her eyes to turn serious.

"Relationships are hard, and marriages are even harder. But I can tell you, whoever this girl is, if she's the one for you, if she's meant to be an important part of your life, there won't be any question. You'll be able to *feel* it." She gently taps the palm of her hand to the center of my chest. "Right here."

The soft seriousness of her tone makes me keep my mouth shut and listen.

"When it came to your father and me, I thought I felt it, but when I look back, I know I never did. It wasn't until Neil that I *really felt it*. That I really *knew*. And when I met Neil, it was awful timing, Ansel. Horrible timing, actually," she says on a quiet laugh. "He had a girlfriend, and I was in the middle of a divorce and had two young boys. It was a total mess."

My eyes go wide with surprise. "Neil had a girlfriend when you two met?"

She nods. "Like I said, horrible, awful timing."

"I didn't know that."

"Well, you and Bram were just kids at the time, and I was trying like hell to keep you guys out of all the drama. And trust me, there was some drama. There were a hundred different reasons why Neil and I shouldn't have been together.

"But I felt it, Ansel. And he felt it. And now, here we are, over twenty years later. Together. Happy. Still feeling it. All I'm saying is, sometimes, it's not black-and-white. Sometimes, things are very, very gray. And all you can do is lead with the best intentions, and then it's up to fate to decide."

"This feels like horrible advice for a mother to give her son about cheating."

She smacks me. "I said to *lead with the best of intentions*. I just know...sometimes, you can't control the rest."

"Why did you tell me all of this?"

"I don't know. I guess I just felt like you needed to hear it."

I let her words soak in, and I stare out through the windows and up at the sky.

I don't know why Indy is the girl in my paintings, the girl inside my mind.

And I sure as fuck don't know why I'm so drawn to her, why I can never seem to stop thinking about her. Why being with her feels like my own personal slice of heaven.

But I guess all I can do right now is what my mother said.

Lead with the best intentions.

Fuck, I hope I'm doing this.

If Indy's in a relationship with Matt, that's her choice. I can't rob her of the one she would have to make to be with me.

And with the way her face crumpled at the idea of being together the other night, it doesn't seem like she's ready to make it.

That's why I kept the truth about the kiss to myself.

"Now, if you don't mind," my mom says and stands up from the couch. "I'd like for you to come inside with me so we can eat some dessert, okay?"

If there's one thing I've learned over the years, it's that one never keeps Della from her dessert.

"Okay." I grin without hesitation and take her outstretched hand. And as we walk into the house, I remind myself of her last piece of advice.

Let fate decide.

chapter twenty-two

Indy

At a little after six, I trudge up the steps inside my building, and even my bones ache with how damn tired I am. The day was a blur of crazy kids excited about Valentine's Day and crazy adults feeling the exact opposite.

Mary, my newly single coworker, is having a Single Girls party tonight, and at least ten percent of the female faculty is going.

She tried to wrangle me into coming to the thing, but I reminded her—*and myself* a little bit—that I have a boyfriend.

And the three music lessons I had after school proved to be just as difficult.

From here on out, I'm going to make it a rule that I call out of work on any and all holidays that don't result in a day off already.

When I reach the front door of my apartment, I find a large bouquet of beautiful flowers sitting on my doorstep. Shades of reds and pinks and whites fill my eyes, and I reach down to run my index finger over the petals of the roses inside the vase. A small white note sticks out from the top, and my heart pounds wildly inside my chest as I pull it into my hand and read the printed text.

Happy Valentine's Day, baby.
Sorry I couldn't be there, but just know I'm thinking about you.
And I hope these flowers put a smile on my pretty valentine's face.
Love, Matt

The rhythm inside my chest skips a beat before returning to a rapid pace—this time, for an entirely different reason.

Sweet, thoughtful, thousands of miles away Matt.

The flowers were a caring gesture, but my heart hurts at the oftentimes long-distance reality of our relationship. We've been together for over a year, and I can count on one finger how many holidays we've spent together—*not this past Christmas, but the previous one.*

This overwhelming feeling of disappointment overcomes me, and I hate my mind for turning something like flowers from my boyfriend into something bad.

Why am I disappointed? Why am I feeling this enduring melancholy?

Because your boyfriend is so far away, I force myself to think. Any other reason I could come up with—any other person I could think about—is unwarranted and inappropriate.

I nod, convinced I have myself under control, and grab the bouquet. I carry the flowers into my apartment and set them on the kitchen island. Once my jacket is off and my keys and purse are on the counter, I grab the takeout menu from the pizzeria up the street and call in an order for delivery.

I'm too damn tired to cook, and pizza seems like the perfect kind of meal to eat when it's Valentine's Day and you have no place to go and no one to see.

After a quick wardrobe change into my favorite flannel pajamas, I send Matt a brief text thanking him for the flowers. Then I grab my laptop, flip on the television, and make myself comfortable on the couch while a rerun of *The Office* plays in the background.

Not even five minutes later, my phone vibrates with a call.

Incoming FaceTime Call Matt

My thumb hovers over the screen before tapping accept. When I finally do, his hazel eyes and jovial smile light up the screen.

"Hey, baby," he greets.

Baby.

I rub at my cheeks and lift my mouth into a smile. "I'm surprised you're awake."

He offers a little shrug, and I force myself to focus on the way the fabric of his shirt forms to his muscled shoulder as he moves—as opposed to the way he would look without it. The image is blurry and half-formed because I can't remember the last time I saw him without a shirt. "I just wanted to make sure I got to wish you a Happy Valentine's Day before I went to bed."

"That's sweet." I point the camera of the phone toward the bouquet of flowers in the kitchen. "Thank you for the pretty flowers."

"I'm glad you got them," he answers, and I put my face back in front of the camera to meet his eyes. "Sorry I'm not there to celebrate with you, but just know I miss you like crazy, baby."

"That's okay," I respond easily. Perhaps too easily.

I'm not sure when I got so okay with him being gone. "I doubt I would've been much fun today anyway. I had one hell of a long day with the kids. I ordered a pizza, and I'm settled in for the night."

"Pizza? That's kind of sad, baby."

"Meh." I shrug. "I think I'll live."

"I would expect someone with your status to be out and about, schmoozing the town," he says.

I tilt my head to the side.

"What do you mean by that?"

"I hear you've been outed as the muse of a certain famous artist."

"W-what?" I stutter, and the hand holding my phone begins to shake of its own accord. Why is he bringing this up?

I've told Matt exactly nothing about Ansel or the time I've spent with him. I haven't told anyone.

And the painting? *Jesus.* I thought the media had moved on.

It takes everything inside me to keep my face neutral.

"What are you talking about?"

"I saw Lily's article." Matt's smile is nothing more than a soft crest of his lips.

What is he talking about?

"What article?"

"You didn't see her article, baby?" he asks, and his eyes crease with incredulity. "It published this morning."

My God. The press did die down. It's my *sister* who didn't.

"I didn't," I answer truthfully. Because, yeah, honestly, I haven't seen or heard a thing about this supposed article. "But I was pretty busy today with classes and music lessons…" I can barely get the lame excuse past my lips because the guilt that's starting to migrate up my throat is almost too much to bear.

The fact that I haven't told Matt anything about the time I've spent with Ansel is starting to feel like a thousand tons on my shoulders. I know I should, but I can't find the words. I don't know what I would say or where I would begin.

I don't understand any of it myself.

It's not like you've cheated on Matt, I try to reassure myself. *You just spent time with him. That's it.*

"You look like you're exhausted," Matt says and pulls me from my scattered, racing thoughts. "I hope you're planning on calling it an early night."

"Pretty sure you should be the exhausted one," I retort, trying to make him feel that way with subliminal nudging at this point. I can't keep my freak-out inside much longer. I *need* to get off the phone. "I mean, it's what, after midnight your time?"

"Yeah." A yawn escapes his lips, and he grins. "And I have to get an early start to prepare for a breakfast meeting. Mind if I let you go now?"

"Of course."

Thank God.

"Well, I'm glad I got to see you today," he says with a sweet smile. "Miss you, baby. And Happy Valentine's Day."

We say our goodbyes, and when I tap end on the call, the very first thing I do is snag my laptop from the couch cushion beside me and go to the *New York Press*'s website.

My sister's article is the first thing to pop up in the arts and leisure section.

Ansel Bray Accidentally Painted My Sister: An Exclusive Interview

Just the fucking title of it makes my heart take a nose dive into my stomach.

Oh. My. God. What was she thinking?

I click the link, and my jaw goes slack when I see side-by-side pictures in the center of the article—*Ansel's painting and a picture of me that was taken for the school website last year.*

I kind of want to vomit, and I can't even get through the whole article before I'm grabbing my phone and calling my sister.

"Hey, buttercup," she greets on the second ring. "Happy Valentine's Day."

"Lily," I ignore her greeting altogether. "What is going on?"

"What do you mean?"

"Why did you write that Ansel Bray article?" I question, and my words come out harsh and rigid around the edges. "I mean, why was I even mentioned, Lil?"

"I told you I was going to write a column on him," she responds without hesitation. "You were at the interview with me. I figured you at least had an idea of what I was going to write about."

"Are you fucking kidding me right now?" I snap. "You really think I had an idea that you were going to include me, *your sister*, in the article? I feel completely blindsided by this!"

"Whoa," Lily mutters, and surprise raises her voice. "You're, like, insanely upset right now."

"Of course, I'm upset!" I shout. "You put my picture in your column and didn't give me any sort of heads-up," I retort and stand up from the couch to start pacing the floor of my living room. "I mean, isn't there some kind of code of ethics where you have to ask for permission to use someone's photo before you publish it in the newspaper?"

"But you're my sister," she says like it's some sort of excuse. "And it's not like I said anything bad about you, Indy. I said all good things. I mean, I compared you to this amazing, gorgeous, stunning painting that people are raving about," she continues, and it only makes me cringe more. "I'm a little confused on why you're so mad about this… If anything, the article debunks the assumption that you're the girl in the painting…"

Why am I mad?

Because…because I am!

You're mad because this is going to make it harder to spend time with him.

Is that why I'm mad? Because Ansel is involved? Because I can't seem to stop spending time with him, and this article is going to get in the way of our friendship?

My subconscious laughs at the use of the last word, but I tell it to fuck off.

I'm confused enough as it is without its two cents.

"Indy?" My sister's voice fills my ear. "Are you still there?"

"Yeah," I mutter and run a hand through my hair. "I'm just… I'm sorry I freaked out… I just… I guess I was just a little surprised."

"It's okay." Lily lets out a deep exhale. "And I'm sorry I didn't give you a heads-up. When I think about it, and hear your side of things, I guess I can understand why it might have upset you a little."

"It's fine, Lil."

"Are you sure you're okay?" she asks with concern.

"I'm fine. Promise."

It's a blatant lie, but I just can't find the strength to pull her into my muddled web of feelings.

"We good, then?"

"Yeah." I nod even though she can't see me. "We're good."

"You're not going to come over here and strangle me in my sleep or anything, right?" she jokes, and my laugh *almost* seems natural.

chapter twenty-three

Ansel

// "The buyer still wants to remain anonymous," Nigel responds, and I roll my eyes. "But they've increased the offer."

This is the third call I've received today about selling one of my paintings from the show in his gallery, and I was done with the conversation before the first call came through.

"I don't really give a shit, Nigel."

The first offer was $200,000.

The second offer was $250,000.

The third offer? Who fucking cares.

His soft chuckles fill my ears. "You don't even want to hear the offer?"

"I'll listen to the offer when this mysterious buyer tells me who they are."

I'm not a fan of this smoke-and-mirrors approach. And, if I'm being honest, I'll probably never sell the painting he's after.

Fuck if I'm going to let some pretentious art collector store a painting I consider priceless in some secret art room where only wealthy friends and fellow investors can stare at it.

I'd rather cut off my dick than do that.

"I liked you a lot better when you were poor and desperate for money." Nigel laughs again. "But I'll let them know."

"I liked you better when we were younger too."

Nye mutters a selection of choice words, and a few moments

later, we end the call.

Fifteen years ago, when I first jumped into the art scene, I *was* desperate. Desperate to make a name for myself and to make a living off my art.

My first big paycheck was for $1500, and you would've thought I'd won the goddamn lottery back then.

Obviously, times have changed. And as my success has grown and my bank account has thrived and my paintings have flourished in popularity and value, I've turned protective of my work.

Money only gets you so far in life.

Sure, it can provide stability and allow you the comforts and luxuries that most could only dream of. But it can never replace the fact that a good life is one lived with meaning. A life lived with passion. A life lived with love and adoration and human connection.

I've had the success.

I've had the emotionless fucks and one-night stands that come from the popularity.

I currently *have* the money.

And none of those are the things that bring me true joy.

It's important people. True connection. Beauty and agony and cherishing the health in my body.

Without thought, I pick up my phone and type out a message to Indy. It's only been a few days since I last saw her, but after avoiding contacting her at all yesterday—Valentine's Day—out of some pseudo-respect for her relationship, I'm jonesing for another fix.

Me: Something has been bothering me, and I want to fix it.

Indy: That's cryptic...

Me: When are you done for the day?

Indy: 2:30ish, why?

I glance at the clock and see it's already nearing one.

Perfect.

Me: I'll meet you at your school at 2:30.

Indy: Um…do I even get a say in this?

Me: Do you want a say in this?

Indy: Bring fresh coffee, and you have a deal.

My responding smile could probably light up my whole fucking studio.

Me: I'll see you at 2:30.

It doesn't take long before I'm shutting off the lights of my studio and walking into Luce's office to let her know I'm leaving for the day.

"It's, like, one," she says and raises an eyebrow in my direction. "I mean, I know it's Friday, but you never leave this early…"

"Well, today, I am."

"Are you feeling okay?" She searches my face. "You don't look like yourself."

"What do you mean? I feel fine."

"You're, like, smiling and shit. It's weird."

I furrow my brow. "What's wrong with that?"

"You never smile."

"I smile."

"Uh, no, you don't," she retorts on a laugh. "Not even on your birthday."

"No one smiles on their fucking birthday once they reach thirty."

"Yeah," she chimes in with a cheeky smile. "And you're thir-ty-four, so…"

"Are you done?"

She shrugs one bony shoulder and rests her chin on her hands. "Are you going to tell me what has you all smiley and shit?"

"No."

"Then, yeah, I'm done."

"I'll see you Monday," I say through yet another smile. "If Nigel calls, let him know I don't want to talk to him."

Now Lucy's mouth curls up at the corners. "Will do."

With the essentials in my pockets, I shrug my leather jacket over my shoulders and head out the door.

First stop, coffee.

Second stop, *Indy*.

I arrive at Indy's school early. Thirty minutes early, to be exact.

Instead of waiting outside in the blistering cold, I decide to hit the buzzer on the front door and let them know I'm a visitor for Ms. Davis.

They let me inside, and I walk in the direction of the front office to get my visitor's pass.

Drawings and artwork line the walls, and I smile at the idea of budding new artists. A few tiny people roam about outside of their classrooms, but mostly, the hallway is silent.

I grin when I see a little boy with curly red hair attempt to get a sip of water from the fountain and miss his mouth entirely.

He swipes one hand down his shirt, soaking the liquid into the cotton material, before giving it another try and managing to hit his mouth bull's-eye on his second attempt.

I walk inside the door marked **Office** and am greeted by a pleasant woman in a turtleneck and sweater vest. The nameplate on her desk says **Mrs. Shirley Williams,** and it suits her. She looks exactly how I'd picture a Shirley to look.

"I'm a friend of Ms. Davis."

"Does she know you're coming?"

"Yep."

"Okay, then," Shirley says. "I need to see your ID, and if you could just sign there for me…" She nods at the clipboard on the edge of the desk. "I'll get you a visitor's pass." I do as she asks, and she smiles as she hands me the pass. "Her classroom is located on the second floor, down toward the end of the hall."

"Thanks."

I press the name tag to my leather jacket and follow Shirley's directions with ease.

The door to Indy's classroom is open, so I stand at the threshold and watch her for a quiet moment while she instructs a class of little boys and girls on how to keep the beat by clapping their hands.

They stare up at her like she's a wonder of the world, and I can one hundred percent relate.

She notices movement out of the corner of her eye as I cross my arms over my chest and lean into the doorjamb. Her eyes widen with surprise, and I offer a little wave in the form of a fresh cup of coffee.

"You're early," she mouths, and I shrug.

"Who are you talking to, Ms. Davis?" a little girl in the front row asks. Her gaze follows Indy's and latches on to me. "Who is he?"

The rest of the class moves their attention toward the door, and Indy lets out an exasperated laugh. "Looks like you've been caught red-handed, and now you need to face the consequences."

A confused smile crosses my lips. "Consequences?"

Indy doesn't respond. Instead, she gestures me inside. "This is my friend," she announces to her class. "Class, everyone say hello to Mr. Bray."

"Hello, Mr. Bray!"

"Hi." I laugh and run a hand through my hair as I walk toward the front of the classroom and set Indy's coffee on her desk. "It's nice to meet you."

"Why are you here?"

"What is your first name?"

"Are you Ms. Davis's boyfriend?"

The questions are thrown rapid-fire toward us, and I now understand what Indy meant by *consequences*.

"All right," Indy says calmly toward her students. "Everyone just settle down for a minute, and if you have a question, you know the rules."

"We have to raise our hands!" they shout back toward her.

Indy nods. "Exactly."

Every hand in the classroom shoots up to form a field of waving arms.

She shoots an amused grin in my direction and whispers, *"Consequences."*

I laugh. "I think I can handle them."

They're just a bunch of kids, right?

"Amy." Indy points toward a little girl with a blond ponytail seated in the back of the classroom. "What is your question for Mr. Bray?"

"Are you one of the guys on my mom's books?"

I tilt my head to the side and look at Indy for a little clarity, but she just shrugs and shakes her head. "Your mom's books?"

"Yeah!" Amy shouts toward me, inside voice be damned. "My mom has all these books with guys with their shirts off! You kind of look like one of 'em!"

Fucking hell. So much for *just a bunch of kids.*

Indy has to cover her mouth with her hand as her shoulders start to vibrate with laughter, and it takes everything inside of me not to laugh. "Um…I'm pretty sure I'm not one of those guys."

"Oh." Amy's disappointment is evident. Her lips turn down into a little frown. "Never mind, then."

The class starts to chatter and argue among themselves, and Indy's big blue eyes meet mine.

"I'm really hoping Amy's mom reads romance novels." The only other option I can think of that would apply would be some type of adult magazine.

"Me too," Indy agrees with a secret smile. "Now, if you don't mind, I need to corral my class back into order, and I don't think it will be possible with you standing up here. Take a seat in the back while we finish up."

I smile at the way she orders me rather than requests. Seeing her as a teacher is like seeing her in another light.

"You got it, Ms. Davis."

chapter twenty-four

Indy

"I can't believe *the big thing* that was bothering you was the Met. You're kind of dramatic, you know that?" I tease Ansel, and he feigns a scowl.

"It was tragic, Indy. You're a New Yorker, for God's sake."

"Well, I've been now." I waggle my brows and look around the vast displays of painting and sculptures encased within one of the most popular art museums in the country, if not the world.

"Yeah, thanks to me."

"Minor semantics." I grin and follow Ansel's path toward a long wall of large, ornately framed paintings.

"By the way, I still think you're dramatic."

"I'm an artist, Indy." He grins at me in my periphery. "We're known to be moody, intolerable, stubborn bastards. Dramatic isn't exactly far removed from that list."

For the past hour, we've explored the Metropolitan Museum of Art's creative and iconic nooks and crannies, and I've yet to grow bored of listening to him tell me about the artists and the sculptors and showing me his favorite works.

His passion for art shines in his words, and I don't think I could ever get tired of that kind of love and adoration.

The more time I spend with him, the more I realize he is infinitely interesting to me. Each encounter, I learn something new—about him, about myself, about life. It's as if he has the ability to open my eyes to worlds I didn't know existed.

"Also, I guess I should admit, I'm glad your art neuroses got the best of you today." I nudge his arm with my elbow. "Thanks for bringing me here."

"You're welcome." He wraps his arm around my shoulders, and the warmth of his body permeates my sweater. "And if you like this, then one day, you need to go to Paris to see the Louvre."

"You've been to Paris?"

"More than a few times," he answers. "It might be my favorite city in the world, and that's saying a lot coming from a homebody like me."

I smile at his playful words, but mostly, my mind flits off into a tiny daydream.

Of Ansel and me in Paris. I imagine myself inside the City of Love, exploring its beauty and charm. The Louvre. The Eiffel Tower. Montmartre. All of the places I've heard about but have never seen up close and personal.

I want to see his favorite places and works of art with that mesmerizing passion shining from his eyes.

He stops in front of a painting titled *The Birth of Venus,* and I blink out of my unrealistic fantasy as Ansel invites me to look at it closely.

We're not in Paris.

Though, I suppose, *I* could be.

A gold plaque sits below the large framed work and names Alexandre Cabanel as the artist.

My gaze moves across the canvas and takes in the soft lines of the female form. The angels hanging above her. The way her hair rests on top of the water and the tender curves of her body.

"I think this is the tenth Venus I've seen today," I joke, and Ansel's responding chuckle causes a smile to kiss my lips.

"In Roman mythology, Venus was the goddess of love, sex, beauty, and fertility," he explains, and I look away from the painting to meet his eyes.

"And what does she mean in art?"

"She's the feminine image of love," he says. "Da Vinci, Picasso, Monet… Every great artist has a Venus."

I quirk a brow.

"Their Venus is their muse," he adds. "The woman who consumes their mind and inspires them to paint or sculpt until they either die or their fucking fingers fall off."

I giggle. "That's a bit extreme, isn't it?"

"Not at all." His brown eyes glaze over with something more, something deep, something poignant.

"That's…*intense*," I respond on a mere whisper, and I don't know if I'm responding to his words or describing his eyes.

God, those eyes. I feel like they can see everything. Like they can see *me*. All of my good and my bad and my ugly. All of my imperfections. All of my hopes and dreams.

I stare into them for a long moment, just letting myself bask in their beauty and mystery and familiarity. *They suit him so well.*

"What color were your eyes before the accident?" I ask without thinking. I've been wondering about it for too long, and I'm unable to ignore my curiosity any longer.

"Brown," he says without hesitation. "I thought it was weird at first…" He shrugs. "That my new eyes are nearly the same color as the old ones."

"It's fate," I declare, and he laughs.

"Fate…or biology. It turns out, over fifty percent of the world's population has brown eyes."

"Maybe," I nod. "But these aren't just brown. These are something special."

Ansel slips his fingers under my chin and leans down to press a soft kiss against my cheek. His next words brush across my skin. "A muse, a true muse, changes you forever. When you find your Venus, she alters your art and your soul in such a way that there is no going back."

My heart flutters and flips inside of my chest, and goose bumps roll up my spine and arms and neck in disquieting waves.

My eyes flick to his lips, and before I know it, without rational thought or reason or anything but letting feelings and fate guide me, I stand up on my tiptoes and press my mouth to his.

Gently, tenderly, softly, at first, but quicker than it started, the moment consumes me, and I lose sight of where we are or what we're doing. My lips turn gluttonous when he slides his tongue into my mouth to dance with mine, and the power of it all has me balling my fists into the leather of his jacket.

When the kiss grows deeper, I moan against his mouth.

He slips his hands into my hair, and everything solid in my body melts into him.

This kiss, this fucking kiss, I don't want it to end.

Suddenly, the sounds of shoes resonate against the tile floor, and I'm yanked back to the present. To the fact that we're not alone. To the reality of our very public display.

Shit.

I pull away from Ansel to find two female employees walking into the room, completely oblivious to us and our activities as they talk quietly about setting up a new display.

My lips tingle, and I lift my hand to touch them with my fingertips. It's like I can still feel his mouth on mine. I can still feel his kiss.

But also, fuck, what was I thinking?

I shouldn't have done that.

I shouldn't have just up and kissed him like that.

"That wasn't supposed to happen," I whisper, and Ansel grabs the flesh of my upper arms to steady me.

"It's okay, Indy."

I shake my head, and he nods.

I stare up at him, trying to find reason in this situation, but the only thing I want to do is taste his lips again, and my heart and mind respond with fervor, racing a mile a minute. But he doesn't give me any more time to get lost in confusion and doubts.

"Now," he says and holds out his hand. "It's time to show you my favorite Monet. Well, my favorite Monet that's at the Met." He winks, and just like that, we're back to simply walking through the museum together.

Casual. Laid-back. No pressure.

I just wish someone would explain that to my tingling lips and racing heart.

chapter
twenty-five

Ansel

S he kissed me. *Again.*

But this time, she was sober.

Strong and intoxicating, the power of her kiss was enough to pull me and my body right into action without any trouble.

I wanted to ask her if she felt it too.

If she is just as high off me as I am her.

I wanted to ask her how she can still be in a relationship with another man when there is this undeniable connection between us. This strong, palpable magnetic pull that seems to vibrate from my body to hers. *From my heart to hers.*

But in a matter of seconds, the spell was broken and her guard was back up, and I had to revert my focus to damage control. Her mind was already off to the races, most likely spinning with uncertainty and guilt and doubt, but I refused to let her fall into a tailspin.

I don't know what this is, but I know it isn't some flimsy attraction that would end after a careless night of sex.

I've had enough of those to last a lifetime.

Whatever this is, it's different. It's special. It's fucking real.

But Indy isn't ready to face all of that.

All I can do right now is avoid doing something that will push her away…and wait. Wait for her to see what I do, for her to realize the magic between us isn't going away.

Luckily, I was able to do just that. After that fucking incredible kiss, instead of saying all of the things I really wanted to say, I started talking about art again and took her to see my favorite Monet.

She thawed out around the edges, and the more I teased and joked with her, the more she smiled and laughed, and eventually, we were back to being us.

When the museum announced it would be closing in ten minutes, I convinced Indy I could feed her the best fucking tacos she's ever tasted from Tacombi, and she didn't hesitate to go along with the plan that led us back to my house. Eating takeout tacos.

"Shit," she mutters, and I glance away from a rerun of *Parks and Rec* to find Indy swiping away a blob of sour cream from her shirt.

A laugh bubbles up from my throat, and she tosses a glare in my direction.

"Don't say a word."

"I didn't say anything." I bite back my smile and lift a taco-less hand in the air, raising my proverbial white flag.

"You want to, though," she retorts with a giggle and a scowl. "You're probably already thinking about what you can use for a make-shift bib."

Bingo. I've already spotted the extra napkins on the coffee table.

I grin, and she nudges my arm with her elbow. "Just forget this happened, okay?"

"Just like that time you spat bacon all over my kitchen?" I tease. "Should I forget it just like that?"

"I'm ignoring you." Another nudge to my arm, only a little harder this time, and Indy grabs one of the napkins on the table and slips it into her shirt like a bib. "There, is that better?"

"Perfect." I grin. "But it might be smart if we invested in actual bibs. I mean, surely, that would prevent a lot of ruined shirts…"

"Shut up." She rolls her eyes on a giggle but focuses back on her tacos.

It doesn't take long before we've finished our takeout and the inevitable food coma has set in. We lounge lazily on the couch, and Indy flips through the television stations in a fruitless search to find something to watch that isn't a reality show or commercials.

I fucking hate television, but when it comes to Indy, I'm finding I'll do just about anything if it means spending more time with her.

"Wait a minute…" Indy pauses, and I glance in her direction to find her pointing toward the bench by the window. "What is that?"

"A painting."

It's her painting. The one she painted for me in my studio and called my rainbow.

She squints her eyes. "Why is that out here?"

"Because I like it."

"Oh my god." Indy groans. "Anyone who walks into your house can see it."

"So?" I don't bother to tell her that she has nothing to worry about. No one but she and Bram come inside my house.

She scowls and stands to her feet, striding right toward the painting. Once the canvas is gripped between her fingers, she turns toward me and raises it into the air. "You need to hide this somewhere."

I chuckle at her ridiculousness. "No, I don't."

"Yes, you do," she refutes. "A closet, under your bed, *the trash*. For the love of God, put this thing away."

"Don't even think about putting that in the trash, Indy."

She raises a challenging brow. "It's my painting, and I'll do whatever I want with it."

"Actually, it's *my* painting."

She sticks out her tongue and starts to make a beeline for the kitchen, and I'm on my feet in a matter of seconds. Indy squeals when she sees I'm right on her tail, and it doesn't take long before I reach her and wrap my arms around her waist to stop her momentum.

"Let me go!" She giggles and holds the painting out of my reach.

"Give me the painting, Indy."

"No!"

"Give it to me." I gently dig my fingers into her sides, and her giggles come rapid-fire.

Fuck, she's adorable.

"No way!" She giggles some more and starts to lose her grip on the canvas. I capitalize on her fading hold and steal it from her fingers.

"Aha!" I cheer, but I have to stop my victory chant when I realize Indy is barreling directly toward me. *Apparently, this battle isn't over yet...*

"Give that back!" She jumps onto my body and wraps her arms and legs around me like a monkey.

"No way." I hold the painting high above my head and grin down at her.

"Ansel!" She giggles some more. "Give that to me so I can hide it!"

"Never."

We're both laughing now, and Indy wraps her hands around my neck and pulls my face toward hers. "Give it to me," she says, and her warm breath brushes across my lips.

It's meant to be playful, but having her so near, her mouth this close to mine, flips something inside of me. And our teasing moment turns into something else. Something that has my gaze locking with hers and my lips parting.

"No," I whisper.

"Yes," she whispers back, but her words don't pack the punch they had before.

She searches my eyes, and my gaze flicks down to her lips and back to her eyes again. I feel so fucking consumed by her that I barely register when the canvas hits the top of the dining room table with a soft thud.

"*Indy.*" I want to ask her for permission. I want to tell her I need to kiss her. I want to make sure it's okay. But when her lips part and her eyes grow needy and dark with desire, I can't hold back.

I push my hands into her hair and press my mouth to hers.

Our kiss is hard and deep and so fucking out of control, I don't know who is leading it. Her fingers dig at my shoulders and her legs tighten around my ass, and when she starts to grind herself against me, I lose it.

"*Fuck,*" I groan against her mouth. "I need you."

"I need you too."

Between her words and the way she's kissing me and pressing her tight little body against mine, I couldn't stop this moment if I fucking wanted to.

Which I don't. Good God, I don't.

I grip the curves of her ass with my hands and carry her up the stairs and into my bedroom. She keeps her delicious little mouth fused to mine and kisses me like her life depends on it.

Indy. Her name is in my mind, a constant chant, a continuous prayer, a fucking thank-you to the heavens above.

We're a chaotic mess of hurried hands and insatiable mouths, and it doesn't take long before our clothes are a distant memory that litter my bedroom floor.

I lay her on my bed and she stares up at me with those big blue eyes of hers, and I'm fucking done for. Her beauty is unmatched. She is everything I've imagined, pictured, *painted.* She is...*breathtaking.*

Her creamy skin is bare, her breasts heave up and down with each erratic breath, and her hips vibrate with need. She is the most perfect thing I've ever seen in my life.

"Ansel," she whispers my name, and I can't wait any longer.

She reaches out for me, and I barely have time to pull a condom from my nightstand and slide it on. But I do. And then I'm hovering over her, locking my gaze with hers, and sliding myself inside of her.

Fuck, it's perfect. *She's* perfect. We fit together *so fucking perfect* it's as if we were always meant to do this, to be *this.* I slide my hand behind Indy's neck, growling into another kiss as she whimpers in pleasure.

I move my hungry mouth to her breasts, sucking and feasting on her skin, and her legs come up around my hips to pull me closer. It doesn't matter that closer is an impossibility.

Her eyes fall closed. Her lips part. She moans again.

Fuck.

I try to take my time, slowing my movements, savoring how good she feels, how good this feels, but when she opens her eyes again and locks that heady blue gaze with mine, it's hard to hold back, to make the moment last. I'm caught between the intoxication of the climax and extending this moment I never want to end.

Indy slides her hands into my hair and pulls my face to hers. She moans as she kisses me, deep and hard and with a passion I've never known before.

We lose ourselves to chasing each other's pleasure, chasing our own pleasure, chasing the high that is us, together.

There is no going back for me after this.

chapter
twenty-six

Indy

nside this room, *Ansel's room*, there is nothing but twilight and shadows. Soft breaths and gentle caresses surround us in a cocoon of warmth and sated limbs.

His strong body supports the weight of my lax one, and a delicious ache pulses between my legs.

And the lingering memories of what we just did fill my head.

I know what Ansel feels like inside of me.

I know what he looks like when desire consumes him.

I know the way his eyes melt and his lips part when he's close.

And I know what he sounds like when he comes.

When I'm truthful with myself, I can admit I wanted to know all of it. Fantasized about it, even.

And now that I've experienced it, I know my fantasies were nothing more than bland placeholders.

Silence spreads across his bedroom, and we both let it linger as we continue touching each other. Never stop caressing each other's skin. Never stop glancing into each other's eyes.

It's magic. *He's* magic.

The guilt will come later; I know it will. But for now, I refuse to let it root itself in a moment I don't want ruined.

I'm loyal by nature. When I make a commitment to someone, I stick by it. I know what I did goes completely against that, I know I let myself play much too closely to the fire, but there *has* to be a reason I'm here.

A reason I'm unable to pull myself from Ansel's arms and leave like I should.

"Are you okay?" His voice is soft, and he tightens his grip on my body, pulling me as close to him as physically possible.

"Yes," I say. For now, it's the only answer I'm willing to explore.

When it comes to this man, it's like something inside of me shifts, and I can't resist him. I can't ignore the way he makes me feel. I can't turn a blind eye to all of the crazy things that have brought us together. The things that I don't understand at all.

I can't do anything but follow my heart.

"What are you thinking about right now, Indy?"

"The girl in the painting."

"What about her?"

"Do you think she's really me?"

"Indy…" He hesitates and averts his gaze.

"Just tell me," I whisper.

"It's hard to tell you something I don't even really understand myself, but deep down, yes, I know she's *you*. The way you move, the way you talk, the things you do. They're all the things I love about her."

All the things I love about her.

"It doesn't make sense." A soft, incredulous laugh leaves his lips. "In fact, it's the most irrational thing that's ever happened to me." He reaches down to brush a few pieces of hair away from my forehead. "I wish I knew why. But, Indy, I don't. All I know is there is some intangible thing that draws me to you, and as hard as I try, I can't avoid it. Can't resist it. Can't do anything but give in."

"I know what you mean," I whisper.

Delicate and haunting, Ansel's knuckles slide against the flesh of my cheek, down my neck, and across the top of my breast.

"Let me paint you, Indy. Just like this."

My heart flips inside my chest, and I can't come up with a single reason to say no.

I can't, and I don't want to.

"Okay."

"Yeah?" he asks, eyes widening in surprise.

"Yeah."

I sit up, but Ansel pulls me back down on the bed.

"What are you doing?" I question. "Don't you want to go to your studio?"

He shakes his head and drags his body to the end of the bed and out of it. "Stay here. I'll be back with the paint."

He leaves the room without a single stitch of clothing, and I collapse into the sheets.

My heart is racing, and I lean into the smell of Ansel all over the bed beneath me.

He has a clear toolbox full of paint and a handful of brushes when he returns, but no canvas.

I sit up, and the sheet falls down to my hips.

"Aren't you forgetting something?"

He raises an eyebrow like he doesn't understand.

"The canvas," I say, even though I feel like it should be obvious.

"You are the canvas, Indigo."

"What?"

"I want to paint *you*. I want to feel the curves of your breasts and the pulse in your chest as I move the brush across you. I want to paint you in a way I've been dreaming about since before I knew you were real."

My teeth dig into my lip, and a new ache, this one needy and consuming, starts up between my legs.

We don't speak anymore as he positions me flat on the bed and gets to work.

The glass-and-gold table in the sitting area becomes his workstation at the side of the bed, and his paints get lined up one by one on the top.

Blues and purples and pinks, it's all the colors I've loved all my life.

My breathing shallows, and I'm not surprised Ansel hears it.

When it comes to me, Ansel seems to hear everything.

"I know. I don't know how, but I just know, Indy. Everything about you, it's right there in the open for me to see."

I nod. It's all I can do.

With a dip of the bristles in the bluest of indigos, he puts paint to my skin.

Each stroke drags me a little deeper into the heaven we've created. He tugs at his lip with his teeth, and his forehead furrows with concentration.

While he explores with the brush in one hand, his other roams the rest of my landscape.

It is, without a doubt, the most beautiful art I've ever experienced.

chapter twenty-seven

Ansel

ndy's chest rises and falls with easy breaths as I move the brush across the hollow below her collarbone. Her face is lax, and her jaw is slack, and her lips are parted in rapture.

I watch in fascination as the feathered strokes I've left on her breasts move with the motion of her breathing.

Her nipples are tight and pink, the perfect complement to the palette I've used around them, but the desire to paint them is too strong to let them be.

I grab a clean brush and dip it into the pink paint before swirling it slowly around the peak of one, and then the other.

Indy's breathing changes from slow and steady to the deep, dragging pulls of arousal, and her legs fall open beside me.

Untainted by paint, the area between her legs taunts me to take a taste.

I lean down and press my mouth to the slick honey, and she gasps.

She tastes perfect and pure and like my life's greatest desire.

Her moans drive me to explore with my tongue, around, to the top, and inside.

In need of my hands, I toss the brush to the side and grip the flesh at the inside of her thighs hard enough to leave the skin mottled from my fingertips.

The wet paint is slick beneath my hand as I reach up to palm the weight of her breast, and she arches into the feel of it.

I move away briefly enough to get a condom from my nightstand and roll it on with my clean hand.

Indy watches with dark, bottomless eyes and palpable want.

When I climb back on the bed, I fit my hips between her legs and slide myself inside to assure that no paint gets where it shouldn't.

Her body feels warm under mine as I lean my chest to hers to let her paint cover me. It swirls and mixes between us, and I don't even have to see it to know that it's the most beautiful, perfect piece I've ever created.

"Ansel," Indy moans as I put my mouth to hers.

"You…are perfect, Indigo Davis."

Our climax happens quickly, but just like with everything else between us, it's completely in sync.

Once I clean up my paints from the table and dispose of the condom, I kneel beside my sleeping angel and brush a few pieces of hair out of her eyes. "Indy," I whisper gently, but she doesn't stir.

The truth is, I want her to stay here. In my house. In my now-dry-paint-covered bed. With me.

So I don't even bother trying to wake her again.

I slide into bed beside her, turn off the light, and pull a perfect, painted Indy into my arms. She wraps her little body around mine like a vine and snuggles her face into my chest. And it takes all of two minutes for her breaths to turn soft and her body to grow heavy and relaxed against mine.

"Good night, Indy," I whisper into the dark room and place a soft kiss to her forehead. "I will never recover from this night. Never recover from *you*."

Once more image break

"Good morning, Ansel."

I blink my eyes open to find bright blue staring back at me and the early morning sun coming in through the windows. "What time is it?" I croak out, and Indy smiles.

"A little before eight, I think."

"Too early," I tease on a groan and make a dramatic show of closing my eyes. "Go away and don't come back until it's at least nine."

"No way." Her giggle brushes against my cheek. "It's time for you to wake up and make me breakfast."

I peek at her through my lashes. "Oh, so that's how it is?"

"Uh huh." She adjusts herself under the blankets until her entire body covers mine. Her naked little body is warm and soft, and I move my hands to her ass and shut my eyes closed again.

Mmm…perfect…

"Hey," she says and presses playful kisses to my cheek. "Wake up."

Eventually, I give in to her demands and work my eyes open until they're face-to-face with bright blue again. The blue of her eyes, the blue of her body, and the blue on my sheets, my life is a perfect shade of indigo.

Pretty sure I could get used to this every morning.

"There," she says with a grin. "That's better."

A soft chuckle jumps from my lips. "Just for the record, you wake up too fucking early."

"I know, right?" she responds on a sigh. "It's a hazard of my job, I guess. During the school year, I usually wake up by six."

I cringe. "Yeah, that's way too early."

"When do you usually get out of bed to start your day?"

"It depends on what I have going on," I say and press a soft kiss to her lips. "But usually no later than nine thirty or ten."

She grins. "By *nine*, I'm usually well into my day."

I run my fingers up and down her back, and when my hand reaches the spot where her hips meet the curve of her ass, I remember something. "I have to admit," I say and tap the right side of her lower back. "I wasn't expecting this."

"Expecting what?"

"This tattoo." A red lotus flower etched into her skin. It's delicate and feminine and yet still big enough to catch your eye.

It's beautiful and completely wrong at the same time.

"Oh." Her lips form a tiny O and then lift into a mischievous smile. "I guess your visions of me don't show you everything." We both laugh. "I got it a few years ago."

"I guess they don't," I agree, rather than go into the details of what made me bring it up. If I bring it up, I'll have to tell her there is more than one painting of her, and I'm not sure if I'm ready to do that. I'm not sure if *she's* ready for me to do that.

I feel like it might be too much for her.

"Lucky for you, seeing my paint all over your beautiful body this morning is satisfying enough to make me give in to your demands." One last kiss to her lips and I push myself out of bed. Once I slide on a pair of sweat pants, I turn around to see she's still lazing it up in my bed. "Are you expecting breakfast in bed, miss?" I tease, and she shakes her head on a laugh.

"No, but I wouldn't mind a shower."

She glances down at the dried paint covering nearly every inch of her body, and I shake my head.

"Oops. Sorry. That's the one request we can't fulfill."

"Ansel."

With a swoop and a bend, I reach into the bed and pluck her out of it, tossing her over my shoulder for good measure.

"Ansel!"

"This way, miss. Your breakfast awaits."

chapter twenty-eight

Indy

"What time does the clock above the door say?" Ansel asks from behind the canvas, and I glance up from my cozy spot on the leather couch to see the hour hand pointed toward the number ten.

"A little past ten."

We were supposed to be on our way to the kitchen when Ansel claimed inspiration struck. We rerouted to the studio, Ansel tossed me a long-sleeved shirt to keep me warm, I settled onto the couch, and we've been here ever since.

"Really?" he says and meets my eyes. "No wonder I'm so hungry. And I'm sure you're probably starved by now too."

I offer a little shrug and grin. "Maybe just a little…"

"Just a little?" He is unconvinced.

"Okay, a lot, actually."

"I figured as much, you little liar." A soft chuckle leaves his lips as he sets his brush down and runs a hand through his hair. "How about you stay put, and I'll run down and toss some cinnamon rolls in the oven?"

My eyes perk up. "You have cinnamon rolls?"

"I do." He waggles his brows. "Sit tight and I'll be back."

A minute later, the handsome artist is out of the room and bounding down the stairs, and I'm left inside his studio, staring out the window and attempting to *sit tight* until he gets back.

It's much easier to be the subject when your eyes are fixed on the gorgeous man holding the brush. It's easy to get lost in watching his every move. The way his eyes change. The way his brow furrows. The way he licks at his bottom lip.

But without Ansel to gawk at, I can only manage to sit tight for all of two minutes.

Eventually, I get a little restless and decide to explore the expansive room.

With bare feet and curious eyes, I tiptoe around the space and take in all of the art supplies and finished paintings. I run my hand over the bottles of paint lined up in a neat row on the counters and let the various brushes tickle my fingertips.

When I notice a small, little room toward the back, I push open the already cracked door and peek inside.

More paintings. I grin and step inside, taking in the brilliance that is Ansel Bray's mind. *God, he's talented.* I let my gaze wander around the room, but when shades of brown and blue and pink catch my eyes, I stop dead in my tracks.

The girl in the painting.

Only, it's not the same one in the gallery; it's a different one.

The painting is a visual of her from behind, the delicate lines of her bare skin being showcased from the back of her head to her neck to the small area where her lower back meets the curves of her hips.

When my eyes make their way down her body, they freeze on the right side of her lower back and latch on to red.

A gasp jumps from my lips, and I cover my mouth with my hand. *How can that be?*

Instantly, my knees buckle, and I have to reach out and grip the wall to prevent myself from falling to the floor.

But my eyes? They're fixated. Stunned. Locked on to a tiny, red heart etched onto the girl in the painting's skin.

And my heart starts to fold in on itself as vivid memories of the day I got my first tattoo show like a movie behind my eyes.

The memories stab like a knife, and the realization of how deep this connection between Ansel and me goes shocks me to my very core.

I *am* the girl in the painting. I don't know why, but I know without a single doubt, that girl is me.

The urge to flee the situation, to try to run away from my own thoughts, is so strong, I find my feet moving of their own accord. I make my way out of the studio and into his bedroom and get myself dressed as fast as humanly possible.

Just calm down, Indy, I tell myself. *Calm down. You can't just go sprinting out of here without saying goodbye.*

Shit. I have to get it together.

But how? How do I get it together after seeing that?

chapter twenty-nine

Ansel

S oft but quick footsteps move across the floor above me, and I smile to myself as I wait for the coffee machine to finish brewing.

I don't know what Indy is up to, but it's obvious she is no longer in my studio.

I open the oven to check the Pillsbury cinnamon rolls and find the dough rising and browning with the heat. One quick check of the timer and I see they have less than ten minutes left to bake.

The coffee machine beeps, and I grab two mugs from the cabinet.

Footsteps move down the stairs and make their way into the kitchen, and just as I'm pouring the fresh brew, I glance over my shoulder to find Indy walking into the room.

"Hey," I greet with a smile before turning back to the coffee-maker. "I was just about to bring these up." But something makes me look again, and when I do, I realize she's fully dressed. My brow furrows in distress. "Are you leaving?"

"Yeah." She nods and averts her gaze to her boots. "I just…uh… remembered I have a music lesson today. In about forty-five minutes, to be exact."

A music lesson? On a Saturday?

"Oh." I look down at her fingers and find them fidgeting against the material of her pants. "Are you sure everything is okay?"

"Yep." She nods again, and the smile that slides across her lips feels all wrong. It's awkward and forced, and I don't like it. "But can I get a rain check on the cinnamon rolls?"

"Of course," I respond with a hesitant smile. "Let me call Hank to give you a lift."

"That's okay." She looks away from me. "I'm going to take the subway."

My stomach roils with unease when I take in her shielded eyes and recount the strained, hesitant tone of her voice.

Something is wrong.

"Are you planning on stopping home first?"

"Yeah," she answers. "I can't exactly go to my lesson in yesterday's clothes and covered in paint."

Instantly, I know that the story she's telling me is filled with lies. Not even the savviest New Yorker can make that kind of round-trip commute in forty-five minutes, let alone change and shower in between.

Is it guilt? Is she confused? Is she doubting what happened between us last night?

"You sure everything is okay?" I ask again, knowing the more I push for an answer, the further and faster she'll run away.

"Positive," she answers.

I hate that she's leaving like this.

I hate that I don't know what the fuck is happening.

This, whatever is going on, feels like it's completely out of my control.

And all I can do is let her go.

But I refuse to let her go on some awkward, uncomfortable moment where she is lying to me through her teeth.

That is one thing I *won't* let occur.

Between one breath and the next, I cut off the distance between us and pull Indy into my arms and press my lips to hers. A tiny gasp escapes her mouth, but then her lips willingly participate.

It's deep and emotional, and with my lips, with this kiss, I try to understand what is going on and I try to tell her all of the things I can't say, but mostly, I show her how much she means to me.

She means everything

This, *us*, it means *everything*.

Before Indy, I was the grumpy bastard who didn't even entertain the idea of a relationship or love.

After her, I am a man who can't live without it.

chapter thirty

Indy

Time stands still, and the rest of the world is mere background noise.

Paint streaks the skin just below my thumb on the back of my hand, and I stare at it, mesmerized.

The subway car jockeys back and forth, light flashing through the window like a strobe, and my mind takes the opportunity to mirror it.

Intense and all-consuming, scenes and stills of Ansel and me together, paint smearing between our bodies, take my mind hostage and clog my throat.

His hands on me, my hands on him. I can still taste his tongue on the inside of my lips, and a memory of him running it along the vein in my neck draws my hand there.

The woman across from me notices the paint on it and smiles.

"Fun day?"

Sweet merciful Jesus, she has no idea.

The corner of my mouth hitches involuntarily, and she goes back to her sudoku.

And then I remember what made me leave.

My stomach turns, and the train screeches to a halt just in time.

When the doors open, I'm off in a dash, shoving people out of my way carelessly and fighting the stairs until I can get to fresh air.

Big, heaping gulps burn my lungs and steady my stomach, but I know it won't be long before I take another turn.

If I can just make it to my apartment, maybe I'll be able to think rationally enough to figure out something concrete. An actual *fact* I can latch on to to regain control.

With giant steps I imagine are better suited to someone twice my size, I see about doing just that.

People and buildings around me blur together as I traverse the few blocks between the subway and my apartment and climb the stairs inside until I'm standing in front of my place.

Salvation lies on the other side of this door, I'm sure of it, and answers are inside the memory box in my closet.

They have to be.

"Surprise!" Matt greets as I swing the door open, armed with a bouquet and a smile. Returned from his trip much earlier than expected—waiting for me to come home to my apartment from my lover's studio.

Air freezes in my lungs, refusing to move out so the new can come in. Before I know it, he's wrapping me up in his arms and pulling me inside. "God, I missed you," he whispers and leans forward to press his lips to mine.

Rigid and unyielding, my lips take their cue from my lungs and cease to function as I know them.

He doesn't notice.

Instantly, guilt and shame curl inside my gut.

His kiss feels all wrong, foreign and, ironically, like betrayal. The cynical part of me wants to laugh. I'm *actually* worried about what the man I'm cheating with will think if he finds out I'm kissing my boyfriend.

My hands shake and my stomach hollows with the realization of how low I've sunk and what it means I have to do now.

I'm shocked by how easily I lost myself in the actions of a morally devoid woman I swore I would never become.

Just before Matt attempts to take it deeper, to slip his tongue inside my mouth, I pull away and disentangle myself from his arms.

I'm the worst. And I'm only going to get more awful as the minutes tick by.

"You're home early," I say, and even though I don't mean it to, it comes out like an accusation.

His eyebrows pull together, but he doesn't make too much of it.

I guess he doesn't automatically suspect that the reason for my upset is his interruption of my affair.

God, Indy. Affair.

How did I get so off course?

He nods, the pinch in his eyebrows smoothing out as he tries to explain himself. Like he's the one who's done something wrong. "I cut the meeting short. For once, I paid attention to how you sounded instead of what you said."

Tugging at the scarf around my neck, I look to the carpet and question, "What do you mean? How did I sound?"

"Like you weren't okay with the fact that I'm always gone."

That's just the thing, though. I was okay with it. Never disappointed or lonely, I didn't mind Matt's trips. I didn't mind at all.

I should have realized what that meant earlier.

When Matt steps forward to help me take my coat off, I take two steps away from him and wrap myself in it. It feels like a barrier against everything I know is coming.

"Indy?" His brow furrows again, and this time, it sticks. "Are you okay?"

"Yes… No… I don't know…" I pause and shake my head. "I just…I have something to tell you, and it's not easy."

I hate myself for the awful way I've strung him along.

I hate the fact that throughout our entire relationship—before that, even—I've basically been sleepwalking through my life.

And I really fucking hate the fact that it was another man who woke me up.

But all the hate in the world for what is doesn't change that it *is*. And Matt deserves to know the truth, even if it makes me feel ugly.

"Okay," he says slowly, trying to get his bearings in a storm he had no warning was on the horizon. "Let's talk about it."

It's the last thing I want to do—to admit so many faults in myself—but I refuse to allow myself cowardice any longer.

I follow his lead into the living room, and when he sits down on my sectional, I have a hard time forcing myself to sit beside him.

Fuck, this is awful.

"What's going on, sweetheart?"

Just tell him, Indy. It's not going to go well, no matter how you word it.

I look into the depths of his hazel eyes, and my heart aches. So much time with one man that I gave so little effort. I mean, we've been together for a while, and I never once even considered moving in together.

"I..." I have to swallow hard just to open a path through my throat for the words. "I don't think we should be together anymore."

"What? Why?" he asks, his head jerking back with the blow. "I know I've been gone a lot, but I'm willing to change that."

I'm shaking my head already, and the motion gets a little bit harder with every word he speaks.

"I know you haven't been happy—"

"Matt," I interrupt softly. "That's just the thing. I haven't been happy or unhappy or angry or sad or any other blessed thing. I've just been going through the motions for a long, long time."

"Indy," Matt starts, reaching to my leg to squeeze it. I pull it away, but he pushes forward anyway. "We can work on this. We can—"

The pressure of each word he speaks builds and builds inside my chest until I can't take it anymore, and my emotions explode all over the room.

"I haven't been faithful to you while you've been gone!" I nearly shout, unable to contain my sins any longer. It's a far more aggressive delivery than I would have liked, but at least I don't feel trapped inside my own body anymore.

His brow furrows, and his hazel eyes search mine, almost as if he's not sure he's actually understood the language I've used. "You... you've been with another man?"

"Yes," I whisper.

"I can't fucking believe this!"

All I can do is nod. Because honestly? Neither can I.

One day, I was just kind of muddling through each day.

And the next, I met Ansel, and my life was changed forever.

"What the fuck? Is that why you look like this?" he questions, and anger raises his voice as he takes in my less than stellar appearance. "Like you're wearing yesterday's fucking clothes? Because you were just with him?"

I don't know how to respond to that.

But he takes my lack of response as answer enough. He runs his hands through his hair erratically and looks toward the window. It takes a good thirty seconds before he can look at me again. "Who?" he asks. "Who is he?"

I shake my head because I can't bring myself to even say Ansel's name. There's too much at work here, and despite the fact that I want to be honest with Matt, I won't tell him this.

"Fine," he says. "Don't tell me. It doesn't matter anyway. You've already made up your mind, right? I mean, that is how you started the conversation. You and I are done?"

"Yes." I don't think I've ever seen Matt angry like this, and that only makes me feel worse. I've driven him to a place inside himself he's not even familiar with. I know it doesn't help with the shock or the hurt, but giving concise, truthful answers will at least shorten the experience for both of us.

"I'm sorry, Matt," I say, but I know an apology given like this seems empty. Still, I try. "It wasn't supposed to happen like this. This isn't what I intended."

"Oh, so you accidentally fucked him?"

I cringe at his poisonous, potent words, but I know I deserve it.

Matt grabs his coat and stands, and the effort it takes to follow him with my eyes feels Herculean. But I breathe through the anxiety and discomfort. It's the least I can do after everything I've just done to him.

"I'm sorry," I say again.

"Me too," he says, and the silence stretches between us like a rubber band. It's tight and constricting, and I feel like a bird locked inside a fucking cage.

He lets out a heavy breath and, with a sudden start, walks to the door without looking back.

It shuts behind him with a click, and just like that, an entire chapter of my life is over.

chapter
thirty-one

Indy

An hour has passed with me on my couch, unmoving from the spot where Matt left me. My thoughts are scattered and my brain is fried, and the paint from making love with Ansel feels dry and brittle now.

I don't know what to do, I don't know what to think, and I don't know where to go from here.

I'm single. Free to do as I please, and yet now, it somehow feels more wrong than ever.

I'm shaken by my actions, by the choices that got me here and the truths I've yet to face, and I'm not even sure I know myself anymore.

Another hour of reckless soul-searching passes, and at last, I pick up the phone and call Lily.

But when she answers, the enormity of the situation consumes me, and I lose control of my emotions. I sob into my hands, and the tears drip between my fingers, raining down onto my socks and the floor beneath me.

"Indy." My sister's voice is in my ear, and the concern and worry only make me cry harder, deeper.

"Indy, what's wrong? Where are you?"

"H-home," I stutter through my gasping breaths.

"Are you hurt? Are you okay?"

"N-no…I don't know…" I can barely get the words out, and it only freaks her out more.

"Fuck you're scaring me, Indy," she says, and in a rush, she adds, "Just stay there. Stay right there. I'm coming over."

And I don't try to stop her.

Instead, I whisper, "Thank you."

Not even an hour later, four frantic knocks pound against my front door.

When I open it, Lily's eyes are wide and worried, and she scrutinizes my face. She takes in the remnants of my tears and my red eyes and my trembling lip and the paint still on my arms.

"*Oh my god.* Are you hurt? What's going on?" she asks. I just throw myself into her arms.

She grunts her surprise but doesn't push me away.

Instead, she lets me cry into her shoulder while she eases us into my apartment, shuts the door, and leads us toward the couch.

She sits me down, takes off her jacket, and then sits down beside me, wrapping her arm around my shoulders and pulling me closer to her. "What's going on, Indy?" she asks. "You need to tell me something because I am freaking out over here."

"God, Lily…" My voice shakes, and my lips turn down into a frown. "I don't even know where to begin…"

"Well…" She offers a soft smile and gently rubs my back. "The beginning is generally a good place to start."

I look into my sister's still-worried gaze, and I inhale a deep, rickety breath into my lungs. And once I get myself together, once I can breathe and talk at the same time, I tell her everything.

I tell her about Ansel. I tell her how I first tracked him down at the gallery.

I tell her how I've been spending time with him. I tell her that we made love.

I tell her how he makes me feel. That I'm so drawn to him.

That I'm falling for him.

And then I tell her about Matt.

How he came home early, and I ended things. That I admitted to cheating, and that he, understandably, reacted angrily.

I'm about to tell her about the other painting I found in Ansel's studio when she sucks me back into the topic before it.

Matt.

"That sanctimonious bastard!" she yells, jumping up from the couch and pacing.

"Lily?" I question, wiping a lingering tear from my face as I flash to emotionally sober. That's usually all it takes to snap me out of it—someone else going crazy.

"I can't believe him!"

"He wasn't that bad, Lil." She shakes her head like a lunatic. "Seriously," I emphasize.

Suddenly, she drops to the couch next to me and takes my hand in hers. "Okay. Okay," she pep-talks herself. "Just tell her."

"Just tell me what?"

"Indy…Matt…*the rat bastard*…has absolutely no high hill to stand on. He cheated on you too."

"What?" I whisper, searching my sister's eyes. "How…when?" I shake my head. "You knew?"

Lily nods guiltily and squeezes my hands to keep me from pulling them away.

"A while ago, seven or so months, I think…"

"This happened seven months ago?" My eyes pop wide open. "What the fuck, Lil?"

And she's just telling me this now?

"I know. God, I know how it seems, Indy. But…" She pauses and grips my hands tighter. "As far as I know, it only happened once. I saw them in Chinatown together. He swore up and down it was the biggest mistake of his life and that he regretted it. I don't know, Indy, I really believed him, so I didn't tell you."

I'm shaking head to toe, and I have absolutely no idea what I'm supposed to feel. Lily keeps talking to try to soothe it.

"I felt like I had finally gotten my sister back," she whispers, and tears well in her eyes. "You seemed happy for the first time since... I didn't want to ruin it."

"Since Adam," I finish for her, and she nods.

"I see now that you weren't happy..." She pauses and her voice shakes. "That you haven't been happy. God, I'm so sorry. I should've told you."

I shake my head because that's all I can do. I should be mad at her. Incredibly pissed, even. I should feel betrayed that she didn't tell me the truth.

I felt like I had finally gotten my sister back. Her words repeat inside of my mind over and over again, and once the initial shock wears off, it's impossible for me to be mad at her.

And I don't feel betrayed. I mostly just understand.

Before Matt, I was a bit of a mess. Actually, I was a real fucking mess. A shell of myself. I barely spent time with my family, and doing simple tasks like taking a shower and going to work felt like the world's biggest feats. And just before I started dating Matt, I made a point to change my miserable, hermit ways. I didn't want to be the sad girl who was letting her life pass her by.

Beneath all the wreckage, I wanted to find myself again.

So, eventually, I started to open myself up to my family, my friends, *life*.

I started going out and doing things. Drinks with friends. Family dinners. Outings with Lil.

By the time I was in a relationship with Matt, I was at least *trying* to be me again. I was trying not to be so isolated. I was simply *trying*. And I think it's safe to say my sister misconstrued Matt as being the reason for the positive change.

Of course, she should have told me the truth. But deep down, I know her fear was what held back the truth.

Fear that I would crawl back into my pathetic shell again.

Fear that I'd go right back to the sad, mostly absentee sister.

"You should go visit him," she says, pulling me from my thoughts. "Adam, I mean. Matt can go fuck himself."

I laugh despite the fucking mess that is my life right now, and Lily smiles her sweetest smile through the apologetic emotion that still rests beneath her eyelids.

"You need to get some sort of closure," she adds on a soft whisper, and I know she's right.

Before I can move on to Ansel, to any of the things I want from him—with him—or to the painting I saw in his studio, I have to go back.

To the day that changed me forever.

chapter thirty-two

Indy

The soles of my boots sink into the snow-covered ground and leave a path of my footsteps behind me. It's cold, frigid, even, but I hardly notice as I walk across the grounds of the cemetery.

Just beyond the big oak tree and past the tragic section of grave-stones in memoriam of an entire family with the last name Conroy, I stop at my intended destination.

In Memory of Adam Thomas Lane.

His gravestone is as white as the crystalline snow. It stands here, before me, with its youthful glow, strong, erect, and ready to last a hundred years. Yet I'll never see Adam's golden skin, his tall frame, or his brown eyes. I'll never see him behind the lens of his camera or flashing that handsome smile.

There's such cruel irony in that.

I reach out with a gloved hand to touch the marble and run my fingers over the engraved black lettering, but quickly, I remove the glove. My bare fingers blanch in the wintry wind, but I don't care.

Somehow, the feel of the stone on my skin brings me some peace. It's beautiful, polished and smooth. It was the most expensive option in the catalogue, and Adam's mom and I chose it without hesitation. He will never see it, of course; he will never know, but we will. *I* will.

I bend down to read the lettering at eye level.

Loving fiancé, son, grandson, nephew, and friend.

My heart clenches, and I run my whole hand over the stone.

Died January 31st.

The day that changed my life forever.

For the longest time, I used to come to this cemetery, to Adam's grave, when I felt like my foundation would crumble if I didn't speak to him again, like an unsteady Jenga tower with someone tugging at a crucial brick.

I would spend hours upon hours here, just talking to him. I know it sounds ridiculous, but somehow, for the first year, this slice of stone steadied me enough that I could go back to my life, go back to trying to move on.

As time went on, my visits became less frequent.

Until they became pretty much nonexistent.

I don't know why I stopped coming here, but I think I'd reached a point where I was simply trying to live my life. It wasn't that I was forgetting Adam, I could never forget him, but I just didn't need to come here to remember him, to talk to him.

"I still miss you," I whisper into the frigid breeze. "I still think about you, and I often wonder what life would be like if you were still around, if you were still here."

Rationally, I know I'm just talking to bones. But inside my heart, I hope Adam can hear me. I hope God is carrying my voice to the heavens so Adam knows I'm thinking of him.

"Four years is a long time, but simultaneously, it feels like no time at all. I'm sorry it's been a while since I've come to see you. But, just know, you're always in my heart. No matter what."

I stare across the vast rows of gravestones before finally moving my gaze back to his.

"I feel bad I haven't responded to your mom. She's reached out to me so many times, yet I haven't answered her," I whisper, and a soft sigh leaves my lungs and billows into the air in a white puff. "Sometimes, it's just easier not to think about you, you know? Sometimes it's just easier to be distracted by my everyday life and not think about the wonderful memories of you that hurt my heart. But I promise, I'll call her. I'll go see her."

A bird crows in the distance, and I look up toward the sky to see it flying from the big oak tree and across the cemetery. I follow his path until he's just a blip in the sky, a tiny black dot my eyes can hardly see.

"I'm still at Great Elm," I whisper and look back at Adam's name. "I'm still teaching music, but I'm not…" I pause and realize just how sad it is that I can't even admit the truth—*that I'm still not playing the violin.* That the day Adam died was the last day it was in my hands.

And when I open my mouth to tell him something else, I can't get those words out either.

God, my life is a fucking mess right now.

I'm a fucking mess right now.

Instead of saying all of the things racing through my mind, I find myself rambling inside my own head.

I've met someone, Adam. I've met someone, and he's an artist like you, a painter, actually, and his paintings remind me of the silly photographs you used to take of me.

Do you remember when we got the heart tattoos and you forced me into taking that ridiculous picture to commemorate it? As if a tattoo wasn't commemoration enough.

Well, one of the paintings…it looks exactly like that photograph, and I don't understand why.

He seems to understand everything I'm feeling and thinking just by looking into my eyes.

It terrifies me. He terrifies me.

I inhale a deep breath and run one gloved hand across the top of his gravestone.

Who I am when I'm with him terrifies me. I cheated, Adam. Had an actual affair.

I shake my head in the cool wind.

I went against everything I thought I stood for. But I didn't feel like there was an option. It felt inevitable. Like some kind of otherworldly force was pulling me toward Ansel, and I was powerless to fight it.

And the worst part of all? The hardest part to admit to myself? I don't want to take it back. Not for a million years.

I don't regret what I did. And if I could do it all over again, I would. Because the way Ansel makes me feel, the way he made me feel when he was making love to me, it was...it was everything.

I never thought I'd fall in love again, Adam, but...

The frigid wind taps at my bones and my ungloved fingers burn, and I realize, unless I want to go back home with fewer limbs, I need to start heading back to the car sooner rather than later.

With my hand on Adam's gravestone, I shut my eyes for a long moment, taking in cold breaths of air, until I find the strength to say goodbye.

"Forever sweet dreams and until we meet again," I whisper and stand to my feet. I blow him a kiss and turn on my heels to trudge back through the grass-covered snow.

When I reach the Zipcar I rented to come out here for the day, I slip inside and click the engine on. Cold air blows out from the vents, and I turn up the thermostat and rub my palms together.

Shit. It's cold.

I don't know how long I was out there, but my body feels like a thick block of ice, trying to thaw itself out.

While I wait for the engine to warm up enough to head back home, my phone vibrates inside my purse, and I grab it to check the screen. A text.

Ansel: How was the music lesson yesterday? Did you make it there and home okay?

I shut my eyes and swallow back the fresh tears threatening to flow from my lids.

This is the second text he's sent me since I left his house yesterday, and I know I need to respond. It would be completely cruel if I didn't respond.

Before I can second-guess myself, I open the message box, type out a simple response, and hit send.

Me: *I did and it was good.*

There was no music lesson, but I just didn't know what else to tell him when I left yesterday morning. Seeing the painting with the tattoo, *my old tattoo*, it was too much to bear, too much to process.

Ansel: *Good. I'm glad. Everything else okay?*

Me: *Yep. I'm just a little busy running errands. Talk later?*

More lies.

Ansel: *Of course.*

God, I hate that I'm lying to him.

And my reasoning is shit, I know that, but I can't seem to do anything else but put some distance between us until I can wrap my mind around what I saw.

I just need a little more time. Just a little more time to understand why.

Before I put my phone to sleep, I catch sight of the name Sally in my text message inbox *again*, and maybe it's because of the visit to Adam, but this time, I open up the text conversation.

Sally: *Hey, sweetie. I'd love to see you. Call me soon.*

Sally: *Hi, Indy. Just wanted to let you know I thought of you today. Would love to hear from you.*

And there are another four or so messages just like those.

Always kind, Adam's mom has been reaching out to me with a

consistent sweetness despite going unanswered by me.

She deserves better than this.

Before I second-guess it, before I can stop myself, I find her name in my contacts and hit call.

This is one promise that I need to keep.

Sally answers on the second ring.

"Indy," she greets, and the way she says my name is equal parts heartwarming and painful. She is the sweetest, kindest soul. A woman who always puts everyone else's needs before her own. A woman who loved her son more than anyone in the world, and somehow, even after she lost him, she still kept her thoughtful, unjaded heart.

"Hi, Sally."

"Wow," she says, and I can practically hear the smile in her voice. "It's so good to hear from you."

"I'm so sorry I haven't reached out for a while."

"That's okay, sweetie," she says in her familiar, motherly tone. "I know you're busy, and I also know sometimes…it's hard."

"It is." My voice quivers, and I have to swallow back the emotion that threatens to take up residence in my throat.

"Why don't you come over to the house for a bit, Indy? I know Bill would love to see you, and I'd really like to give you something. Something Adam would want you to have."

I squeeze my eyes shut against the impulse to pull away and force myself outside of numb comfort. I've been frozen there long enough. "I'd really like that."

After I drop off my Zipcar at the pickup location near my apartment, I hop on the subway and take a ride across town to Adam's parents' house.

The instant I arrive—*before I even ring the doorbell, actually*—Sally steps out onto the small porch and wraps me up in her arms, pulling me inside and demanding I make myself at home.

Bill and Sally's house is just as I remembered. Warm and cozy with a *Southern Living* vibe and enough quilts and hand-sewn inspirational quotes to give TED Talks a run for their money.

Adam hated those quotes. He cringed whenever he spotted a new one on the wall. But I think he'd be proud to know that between all the country rustic items of décor are more than a few of his architectural photographs that had been published in popular magazines across the country.

The thought of that, *the thought of him*, makes me smile.

Sally sets a fresh plate of oatmeal-raisin cookies onto the kitchen table, and Adam's dad is the first to reach out and snag one in his hand.

"Bill," she chastises her husband, and I grin. "You don't have to be such a hooligan about it."

He just chuckles and takes a big ol' bite in spite of her.

Adam's mom rolls her eyes and turns her attention back to me. "When I talked to your mom a few months ago, she said you were still at Great Elm and giving music lessons after school. That still going well for you?"

Ever since I stepped through the door, she's kept up a steady stream of questions, asking me about anything and everything she can think of. I don't mind, though. If anything, it's nice to see Adam's parents again.

"It is," I answer. "The kids are wild some days, but mostly, I enjoy it."

"You teach all grades?" Bill asks through a mouthful of cookie, and his wife groans in annoyance at his lack of manners.

"I do."

"That's good, Indy. That's really good."

Bill, while a happy-go-lucky kind of guy, is generally a man of few words. It reminds me a lot of his son. Adam was never one to ramble on or carry on long conversations. It was like he never wanted to waste his words and saved them up like coins in a rainy-day jar.

"I'm really glad you stopped by today." Sally reaches out and places her hand over mine. "It's good to see you."

"You too."

"Just having you here brings back so many memories. So many good memories."

A wistful smile consumes my face. "For me too."

Her eyes glaze over with emotion. "It makes me feel like Adam is here, smiling down at us."

I squeeze her hand. "Because he is."

A quiet moment spreads throughout the kitchen, and we all let it linger, relishing in the happy and the melancholy and trying to bask in all of the good moments we shared together, we shared with Adam.

It makes me realize how far I've come. How much of my grief I've actually managed to work through. How much easier it is now to talk about Adam without feeling like my heart is breaking. How, while I miss him, I'm not consumed by it.

I probably still have a million miles to go, but at least I've gotten here. To this place.

"Do you want to stay for dinner?" Sally offers, and I shake my head.

"I'd love to, but I should probably be going soon."

"Okay." She nods, but I don't miss the disappointment in her eyes. "But before you go, I want you to take the letter with you this time."

The letter. She's been trying to give it to me for the past year and a half, and every time, I say no.

"I don't know—"

"You need to read it, Indy," she insists and gets up from the kitchen table and levels me with a stare. "In fact, you need to read them both."

"Both?" I ask around a knot in my throat. This is the first I've heard of a second letter.

"Both. Another came a few months ago, all beat-up and taped back up. Apparently, it'd gotten lodged in the sorting machine or something. Lost in the mail for years, but finally found again."

My heart picks up speed as Sally leaves the room to get them without giving me a chance to come up with another reason to refuse.

"You do realize you're not leaving without those letters, right?" Bill asks and lightens the mood a little bit.

"Yeah." An incredulous laugh spills from my lips. "It appears that way."

Adam's mom is insistent, and before I know it, she's stuffing two envelopes into my purse and giving me no choice.

"Just read them, sweetie. Not to make you sad, but to give your heart some peace and closure."

Closure. It's the word I need to hear and the place I need to find.

It might take a bottle of wine to convince myself to go through with it, but I decide right then, come hell or high water, I will give myself this.

I will give myself the chance to accept the things I can't change, and I will give myself the chance to move on.

The chance at having something special again. *With Ansel.*

chapter thirty-three

Indy

By the time I leave Bill and Sally's, it's getting close to dinnertime. I grab a burger and fries from a fast-food joint, and when I step inside my apartment, only silence fills my ears.

What a fucking day.

I kick off my boots and head into my bedroom to slip on a pair of flannel pajama pants, and I toss my long locks up into a messy bun.

Emotionally, I'm drained. Between yesterday with Ansel and Matt and Lily, and going to see Adam this morning and the long visit with his parents this afternoon, I just need to sit down and watch some mindless TV while I stuff greasy food into my mouth.

Once I grab the bag of takeout from the kitchen counter, I plop my ass down on the couch and shove a few fries into my mouth while I flip through the stations.

But it doesn't take long before my gaze is glancing toward my purse. Toward the envelopes inside of it.

Those damn things have been taunting me ever since Sally put them there.

She says they'll give me peace. Closure, even. But I have a hard time understanding how two letters from people I've never met before will have that much impact.

Just read the letters, my mind mocks. *Don't be such a coward.*

Two minutes pass.

I eat all of my burger and fries.

An entire episode of *Friends* plays through on the television.

And still, my mind is fixated on those letters.

Just read them.

On a sigh, I get up from the couch and pull them from the front pocket of my purse.

What's the use of fighting it?

And what's the worst reading these letters can do anyway?

With my index finger, I slide my nail underneath the flap of one of the envelopes and open it.

Inside is a piece of pink paper, and when I unfold it, my eyes are greeted with soft and flowing cursive. The handwriting is neat and pretty, and the words written across the page match.

It's from a woman. And she is thanking Adam and thanking his family and thanking his fiancée—*me*. Because of him, her life was changed. Because of him, she is able to keep living, she's able to see her children grow up and she's able to kiss her husband good night. Because of Adam, the heart inside of her chest is no longer sick with disease. Because of Adam, the heart inside of her chest is healthy and strong and beating.

Her words make my own heart feel full, and I'm starting to understand why Sally was so damn persistent.

Without hesitation, I open the second envelope and start reading the messy and sort of all over the place scrawl on the crinkled white paper.

I know my words could never be enough to ease the pain of your tragic loss, but I figured some words, even if they're not the right ones, are better than no words at all.

Because of your loved one, I am a man who has received an incredible gift.

The gift of a chance at something other than the eternal solitude of never-ending darkness.

A chance that, when I open my eyes, the world around me is no longer empty and black, but is instead vivid and bright.

The eyes are the windows to the soul, and once those windows are closed, evil and loathing spread their roots like ivy. Without your loved one's generous, miraculous gift, my windows would be forever shut, and I would never feel the beauty of painting again.

Thank you for finding it inside yourself to give something born of a situation in which you had no choice.

I stop and reread the sentence. *I would never feel the beauty of painting again.*

My jaw goes slack and my lips part, but I keep reading.

Until I reach the end, and I can't seem to draw enough oxygen into my lungs.

My eternal gratitude.
AB.

chapter thirty-four

Indy

Time is so much like water. It can pass slowly, a drop at a time, or rush by in a blink. The clock says it is measured and constant, *tick-tock, tick-tock,* part of an orderly world, but the clock lies.

The last two hours have passed like thousands of camera images shown slowly, one single tiny frame at a time. My brain is fixated on each paragraph, each sentence, every single fucking word inside the letter that's still gripped between my fingertips and the photos I dug out of the box in my closet to join it.

Over and over again, I read it and glance to the photos that look so much like Ansel's paintings.

And the acute shock of it all eventually turns into something else, something deeper, something unsettling, something *devastating*.

First, I feel sick. Stomach-curling nausea that incites my skin to break out in a sheen of sweat and forces me to run to the bathroom and empty everything I ate for dinner into the toilet.

Then, I pace my living room. Back and forth. Back and forth. No destination, just a circuit leading me from my kitchen to my bedroom. And I do that what feels like a thousand times, but all the while, I don't even feel like I'm inside my body. I am Casper, hovering above the hardwood.

Tears drip down my cheeks in steady waves, and I decide to hop into the shower to wash off the emotion. But after ten minutes of sobbing into the hot water and billowing steam, I realize it's a shit idea.

A pathetic and unsuccessful attempt at getting myself together.

Once I dry myself off and wrap my robe firmly around my body, I check my phone to find another missed call from Ansel.

I wonder if he knows I'm avoiding him?

It hasn't been long since we've spoken, but the distance and chain of events between us make it feel like an eternity.

I don't want to ignore him—every cell inside my body is revolting against it—but fuck, I don't know what to say.

How do I even begin to tell him the truth of our connection?

I grab the letter, *his* letter, from my nightstand and read the words he wrote to Adam's family again. The words he wrote to me.

God, how could this be?

I've read this letter what feels like a thousand times, and still, I've yet to wrap my mind around it.

I trace my index finger over his initials.

And I cry. I cry a lot, actually.

By the time I've pored over his words a hundred more times, I feel my heart beating inside my chest, but it doesn't feel like my heart. I look down at my hands and wiggle my fingers, but they don't feel like my hands, my fingers. And when I inhale air into my lungs, I might as well be watching someone else breathe.

I'm just...*numb.* And my body is so fucking tired. My bones ache and my muscles throb and I should probably sleep, but I know it's an impossibility. Not with the way my mind races. Like a sprinter jumping out of the blocks at the sound of the gun—only, there is no finish line. There is no destination. Only this never-ending path of uncertainty and disbelief and utter confusion.

I slide the letter into the pocket of my robe and head back into the living room.

To the box I pulled from the very top shelf of my closet. Its contents spill across the coffee table like liquid from an overturned glass.

Wedding invitations.

My engagement ring—the one Adam gave to me while we were

on a weekend trip to Los Angeles for his shoot with a popular architecture magazine. The night before we flew back home, he drove us to Santa Monica and proposed to me on the beach.

It was magical. One of the happiest days of my life.

I slide the ring onto my finger and watch the way the glow from the recessed lights in my living room bounces off the center diamond. When Adam put this ring on my finger, I thought it would stay there forever.

But our forever was short-lived.

I slide it off again and place it back inside the box before picking up the stack of photographs.

Adam's photographs.

With shaky hands, I rifle through them all before settling back on the one that set the last couple of days into motion. My hair is down, and I'm grinning a small, over-the-shoulder smile, the tiny red heart etched into the skin of my lower back.

It is identical to Ansel's painting, and now…now, I have some understanding of why.

When this photo was taken, I thought Adam and I would grow old together. I thought we'd get married and have kids and, years later, grandkids. When he died, I lost all hope. I lost hope for the future. Hope for love. A robot girl just bee-booping through the motions.

Until hope came crashing back in again.

Until Ansel.

God, it feels so good to be near him. So good to come alive again.

I fear once I tell him the truth, once I show him the letter, *his letter*, he'll walk out of my life and take all of that hope with him.

Will he ever be able to stop wondering how I really feel about him? Will he know how he really feels about me?

Four years ago, Adam died. And four years ago, Ansel regained his sight.

Ansel's eyes are Adam's eyes.

chapter thirty-five

Ansel

walk up the stairs of her apartment building and rap my knuckles against Indy's front door.

Once. Twice. Three times. And I wait.

She hasn't answered my texts or calls and rather than waiting—rather than denying the almost instinctual feeling that all is not well—I decided to take things into my own hands. To come to her. To see if she's okay. To just…see her.

This feeling of impending doom sits on my chest, and my heart twists and turns beneath my ribs as I wait for her to answer the door. When footsteps filter out from inside her apartment, a large breath of air escapes my lungs on a whoosh.

And then, she's there, opening the door in nothing but a robe.

She's beautiful. *God, she's beautiful.* But, in my eyes, Indy is always beautiful.

But something doesn't feel right. Not in the way she discreetly averts her eyes from mine. Not in the way her teeth bite into her bottom lip. Not in the way she's yet to say a single word.

"Hey," I say through a smile, but her responding smile feels foreign and forced. "Everything okay?"

"Yeah." Indy nods. "What are you doing here?"

She shivers from the coolness of the hallway and gestures me inside before closing her door with a squeak and a click.

Why am I here? Because I feel like something is terribly wrong.

Because I have this nagging anxiety that's crept inside my veins, and it's making me feel like, any second, the world is going to end.

I'm here because the night I made love to you, the night we made love, my heart was forever changed. And now, it feels like you've just taken it all away and left me floundering for no fucking reason.

"I haven't heard from you in a while…" I pause and run a hand through my hair. "And I just wanted to check on you, make sure you're okay."

"Sorry about that," she says and moves her gaze to the floor. "Things have been a little busy."

It's like she can't even look at me. Like it's causing her physical pain.

"Are you sure everything's okay?" I ask and reach down to slip my fingers under her chin so she has to meet my gaze.

It's then I realize I've shown up unannounced.

What if her boyfriend is here?

Internally, I cringe.

Indy in her robe. Her boyfriend waiting down the hall in her bed.

Fuck. I can't let my mind get lost in something like that unless I want to drive myself crazy.

"Is this a bad time?"

She shakes her head.

"Have I…" I pause, but I force myself to continue. Force myself to ask the questions that might help me understand why she's been so distant. "Have I done something to upset you, Indy?"

She scrunches up her nose. "Of course not."

"Well, I guess that's good news, huh?" I try to lighten the mood a bit, but the air around us is too heavy and thick with tension and unsaid words.

"Yeah." Indy forces another smile. "Do you…uh…do you want some coffee?" she asks over her shoulder as she turns on her bare feet and heads into her kitchen.

"Coffee would be great." *Even though it feels like an excuse. A way for you to avoid telling me what's really going on.*

Fuck, this is uncomfortable. We're basically walking on eggshells around each other, and I don't understand why.

I want to go back in time. Back to that night. Back to the Indy who was playful and looked at me with her heart in her eyes. But all I can do is follow her lead into the kitchen, where, apparently, avoidance and diversion are being brewed.

I lean my hip against the kitchen island as she fills the coffee machine with water and taps the button to start. But when she's done, she just stares at the coffeepot and doesn't turn around to look at me.

It's a knife to my heart.

"You know you can tell me anything, right?" I say quietly. "You can tell me anything, Indy, and I won't judge or get mad or any of that bullshit. I'll just listen."

But, fuck, don't tell me you regret that night.

Don't tell me you're done with me.

Don't tell me you want to be with him instead of me.

With her back still to me, she stays silent for a long moment, still staring at the coffeepot on the kitchen counter. Or maybe she's not staring at anything at all. I can't be sure.

My fingers itch to touch her, my lips crave the taste of her mouth, and my arms vibrate with need to wrap her up in my embrace and fix whatever it is that's bothering her. But I don't push. Instead, I just wait. Patiently. Silently. Giving her time.

At least I'm here. With her.

The coffee machine beeps, and she fixes us up two mugs and turns around to meet my eyes, handing me a warm mug. Her eyes search mine for the longest time, and I watch as she forces a deep, heavy breath in and out of her lungs.

"I have something I need to show you," she whispers so softly, so quietly, that I barely hear the words leave her lips.

"Okay."

"Just give a minute." Indy sets down her coffee on the kitchen counter and heads into the living room.

Four, five, six, I don't know how many minutes go by before she comes back into the kitchen holding something in her hands, but I'm too busy to notice because I'm searching her eyes, her face, her mouth for some kind of answer.

"Here." She holds out her hand. "Just...here."

My brow furrows. "What is it?" I ask, but she doesn't answer. So, I glance down to see a photograph in her hand and take it into mine.

My eyes scan the picture, and instantly, déjà vu and familiarity lift their hands and slap me in the face. *Hard.*

This photograph is identical to my painting.

And this is her, *Indy*, with the tiny red heart engraved into her skin. The very tattoo I've pictured so many times.

The tattoo is real.

She is real.

"Indy," I say through a throat full of disbelief and look up to meet her eyes. They are wet with unshed emotion, and her lip quivers. "W-what is this?"

"My fiancé took that photograph of me several years ago," she whispers. "That was my first tattoo. I covered it with the lotus two years ago."

"Your fiancé?" I ask, somehow mining the uncomfortable words from the deep recesses of my throat.

"His name was Adam Lane, and he died four years ago," she says, her voice scratchy with irritation.

"Four years ago?" I ask softly, and she nods.

Indy reaches into the pocket of her robe, and with a shaky hand, she holds out a wrinkled white envelope toward me. "You should read this," she says quietly, and I watch as one small tear slips past her lid and down her cheek.

Fuck, she's crying. I want to comfort her. I want to wrap her up in my arms and tell her it's going to be okay.

"Indy," I whisper and start to step toward her, but she gently pushes the envelope into my chest. My brow furrows as I watch her step back and put distance between us.

"Please…" She pauses and swallows hard. "Just read it."

I peel it open and pull out a folded piece of paper.

I look at her as I unfold it, but her eyes never leave the sheet of paper.

When I move my gaze down to the letter, to the words written on the paper, to the signature at the bottom, my heart clenches inside my chest. "H-how did you get this?"

Tears are in her eyes, and I'm so fucking confused.

These are *my* words. The very personal, heartfelt words I wrote right before my surgery. The words I wrote to my donor's family. The very words that didn't feel good enough. This is the first time I'm actually seeing them with my own eyes, but these words are ones I can never forget. They are forever engraved inside of my mind.

"Indy?" I ask. "Why do you have this?"

"I went to see Adam's family."

"Okay…"

I look down at the letter again, and my eyes latch on to my signature.

My Eternal Gratitude.
AB

"His mother wanted to show me the two letters she'd received from the recipients of Adam's organ donations," she whispers and her voice cracks. "One letter from a thirty-year-old woman who received his heart and…this."

This. *Mine.*

I glance down at the letter and then back at Indy.

Tears stream down her cheeks in steady waves, and I'm too fucking shocked to react to anything.

Her fiancé was my donor.

Her fiancé was my donor.

Her fiancé *was my* donor.

Over and over again, my mind gets stuck on that one reality.

Oh my god.

Because of her fiancé dying four years ago, I gained my sight back.

His death, his eyes, they gave me my life back.

And, in an instant, everything makes sense.

Why I couldn't stop seeing her.

Why I painted her.

"God, Indy," I whisper her name like a prayer. "I don't know what to say."

Because I don't. It's too much to wrap my head around. It feels like some kind of cosmic joke. Like the stars aligned just to fuck with me.

I am in love with her, so damn deep in love with this woman, yet I can't shake this feeling that I am a part of her pain. I know I didn't have a role in Adam's death, but I feel accountable for the agony that's sliding down her cheeks right now.

"I'm so sorry, Ansel," she says through another onslaught of tears. "I'm so sorry. I had no idea."

Sorry? Why is she sorry?

I try to stare deep into her eyes and search for answers, search for what she is thinking and feeling, but she keeps averting her eyes from mine.

Fuck, can she even look at me now without thinking of him? Without it causing her pain?

I see her drawn, defeated shoulders painting a picture of her heart. And in her blue eyes, I see her mind has built new walls with her so lonely, so sad on the other side.

I want to remove those walls, brick by fucking brick, but I know I can't.

Not when I'm the cause.

"This is so hard," she whispers. Tears flow unchecked down her cheeks and drip from her chin. She's too sad to cry out or wail, and she just stands there, still as a statue, while the magnitude of her hurt sweeps over her.

This is so hard. She is in pain right now, and it's because of me.

My heart feels like it falls out of my fucking chest and onto the floor. I look away, and then I look at her again.

"I'm so sorry, Ansel." A sob spills from her throat, and she lifts up her hand and swipes the tears away from her cheeks. "I don't know what to say. It's just too overwhelming. Too hard. I can't…"

Too overwhelming. Too hard.

The walls of her apartment are closing in around me, and my heart is pounding so loud in my ears, I can't hear anything else.

It doesn't matter how much I love her. Knowing I'm carrying a part of her dead fiancé with me is too hard.

I have to get away from here.

Her tears, her pain, the photograph, the fucking letter… It's all too much.

I can't, she said.

"I'm sorry, Indy," I whisper and set the letter and the photograph on the kitchen counter. "I'm just…so fucking sorry."

Next thing I know, my feet are moving toward her door.

And I'm opening her door and moving down the hall and to the stairs.

Then, I'm outside. And my feet are pounding against the pavement and my heart is beating so loud it might have actually invaded my skull, and I can't do anything but keep walking.

When my phone starts ringing in my pocket, I turn the fucker off.

And instead of taking the subway, I hail a cab because I just need to get out of here.

Away from Brooklyn.

Away from the girl who can't look at me anymore without it causing her pain.

chapter thirty-six

Indy

Before I know it, before I can process what's happening, the letter and photograph are back on my kitchen counter and my front door is closing.

I call out for him, but Ansel is already gone.

When I open my front door, the cold air of the hallway permeates my bones, and he is already disappearing down the stairs.

I yell for him again, but he doesn't stop.

My stomach is in my damn feet. My heart is in my throat. Endless tears stream down my face. I rush upstairs to throw on some clothes, any fucking clothes I can find, and I run back downstairs in a panic.

I grab my phone and I call him.

It rings once, twice, three times, then it goes to his voice mail.

I try again, but this time, it just goes *straight* to voice mail.

Fuck.

I'm out the door again and walking as fast as I can toward the subway station I know he'd have to take to get to the Village.

The wind is so cold, it's damn near blistering, but I hardly register my pathetic attire of a flimsy sweatshirt and a pair of yoga pants.

Time is going too slowly, and I pick up my pace until I'm pretty much sprinting as fast as my legs will take me.

One block. Two blocks. Three blocks.

My lungs burn and my heart is banging against my rib cage, but I just keep going.

When I reach the station, I frantically search for him.

Left. Right. Every-fucking-where.

But he's nowhere. Just...*nowhere.*

And when I reach the platform he would take, there is no Ansel to be found.

I try to call him, but it goes straight to voice mail...*again.*

He doesn't want to talk to me.

He doesn't want to be anywhere near me.

A sob escapes my lungs, and I lift my hand to cover my mouth, to try to stop the emotional hurricane threatening to make landfall.

But it doesn't work.

It's too much for him. The letter. Adam. It's all too much for him.

One tiny sob turns into two which turns into three, and then it doesn't stop.

And within those wretched sobs is the sound of my heart breaking.

Hearts don't snap like hard pretzels or burst like an overfilled balloon.

No. A heart breaks in the heaving waves of a new reality. A tragic reality that has arrived uninvited. A heart breaks when you're forced to face the possibility of a life you can't bear to fathom.

A life without Ansel.

chapter thirty-seven

Indy

Seven days have passed, and each day I greet the sun like a climber greets their rope, fingers holding on as tight as fucking possible despite the pain.

But it's no use.

I'm just a shell of a woman.

I can't eat. I can't be awake without thinking of Ansel. And I can't think about Ansel without crying. It's a vicious and what feels like infinite cycle of hell.

It's Friday, and I've called off work every day this week.

Canceled all of my after-school music lessons.

Claimed I have the flu.

But, in reality, I have something much worse than the flu.

The flu is awful, but it goes away. Each day, you begin to feel better until, eventually, you're back to your old self.

But heartbreak does no such thing. It is a never-ending, boundless sadness.

God, the word sad sounds so childish, like something flimsy. Something I should be able to change with a happy thought or a smile. But sad is nothing of the sort. It sits inside your soul like a seed of depression, and with the right conditions, it spreads its roots and chokes the hope out of your heart.

In this sadness, this heartbreak, I can't see a past or a future. I'm merely living by the moment. And every day is measured from the second I wake up into this new reality and until my body can no longer take it and sleep lets my weary mind and aching heart rest.

Several knocks to my door and I turn up the television.

What's on the TV? I don't have a fucking clue. But whoever is on the other side of the door needs to go away.

Unfortunately for me, whoever it is has a key.

A minute later, my sister's voice is bellowing from the entryway, and the front door is closing with a resounding click.

"Indy!" she calls again. "Where are you?"

I don't answer. Instead, I pull a pillow from the couch and put it over my head.

Maybe if she doesn't see me, she'll go away.

Her footsteps get closer, and I hold my breath.

But it's no use.

"Indy, what in the hell are you doing?" she asks, and the pillow is yanked from my hands.

I groan. "Go away, Lil."

"Good God, this place is a mess."

I ignore her. Even though I know she's right. My kitchen and living room are a shrine to barely eaten takeout containers, dirty laundry, and unread mail.

"Fucking hell," she mutters and starts walking around my apartment, picking up garbage.

"Just go home, Lil," I say, and she tosses a glare my way.

"Yeah, right," she retorts. "Like I'm going to leave you like this."

"It's fine."

"It's fine?" Her eyes go wide, and she pointedly looks around my apartment and holds up an old pizza box in her hands. "You sure about that?"

I sigh and avert my gaze back to the television, and Lily continues to clean up my apartment until she appears happy enough to sit down beside me on the couch.

"Have you gone to work this week?"

"No. I haven't been feeling well. I think I have the flu."

She snorts. "This isn't the flu, honey."

I glare. "It's the flu."

"Pretty sure when you say the flu, you really mean heartbreak."

I roll my eyes. "Why are you here?"

"Because I haven't heard from you all week, and I was worried."

"Well, as you can see, I'm fine."

Lies, it's all lies coming out of my mouth, but my lies and pretending I'm fine are all I have right now.

"Indy," she says quietly and wraps her arm around my shoulders until I have no choice but to go into the hug she's started. I rest my head on her shoulder, and she brushes her fingers gently through my hair. "You're not fine."

She's right. But I don't have the words to explain just how much I'm not. Wordlessly, I hand her the letter.

Her brow furrows as I hand it to her, and tears are already pricking my eyes thinking about the words, *the signature,* inside that letter.

"Just read it," I whisper, and she does.

I'm left to watch her eyes consume the words, moving *down, down, down* the page, until she reaches the end.

"Oh my god," she gasps. "That's…" She pauses and meets my gaze.

"Ansel Bray."

"Oh my god, Indy." Tears fill her eyes, and she glances between the letter and me. "I don't even know what to say. I mean, I thought the first part of this story was a lot to take in. I was even starting to feel like your life was a bit of a fucking mess, but *this*—" she holds up the letter "—this is nearly unbelievable."

"Four years ago, Adam dies. And four years ago, Ansel regained his sight," I whisper for the sole purpose of trying to make myself come to terms with it. "Ansel's eyes are Adam's eyes."

"Ansel's eyes are Adam's eyes," Lily repeats my words. And like a bullet to my gut, it spurs another wave of nausea to hit, and I have to lie back on the couch just to gain my bearings.

Tears fill my eyes, but I blink them away. I'm so fucking tired of crying.

"Have you talked to him?" she asks, and I shake my head.

"He doesn't want anything to do with me now."

I silently pray she won't say his name out loud again. I don't think I could take it.

"I don't think that's true, sweetie."

"It is," I retort. "It's too much for him. And honestly, I can't even be mad at him. I understand why. But it still doesn't stop the pain, Lil. And fuck, it hurts so much."

"I know it does." She rubs her hand gently on my back. "You know what I think?"

"What?"

"I think you need to get out of this apartment."

"I'm not going anywhere tonight, Lil."

"Not tonight," she says. "Tomorrow night."

"What's tomorrow night?"

"Shawn Messi is having a party at Ultra for his fortieth birthday."

Shawn is a popular nightclub owner in NYC and someone my sister has grown to be friends with over the years. Their friendship is merely based off personal gain, though. Where Shawn loves the publicity Lil's column gives his clubs, my sister loves the VIP access to some of the city's most popular hot spots.

"That sounds like the exact opposite of what I want to do tomorrow night."

"Indy," she whines. "Come on. It'll be good for you to get out of this apartment for a few hours."

"Not interested."

"There will be dancing."

"No thanks."

"There will be free alcohol."

"I'll think about it."

chapter thirty-eight

Ansel

The music is so loud it makes my skin tingle and my lungs feel like mush. The bass forces my heart to thump in time with its rhythm, and I tip my fourth—*or is it fifth?*—glass of whiskey back and let the amber liquid flow down my throat.

Over the roar of music, a distant, hazy chatter can be heard, but I can't make out what's being said. I look over to see Bram and two of his bandmates—Nix and Lee—standing in the corner of our VIP booth, schmoozing it up with three women. Bram grins, says something, and the women laugh, acting like he's the most entertaining bastard they've ever met.

Fucking groupies.

Fucking Bram.

The bastard barreled into my house this evening on a goddamn mission, asking a hundred questions about why I haven't been answering my phone for over a week.

Because I don't fucking want to.

Because I can't stand to be around anyone or anything.

Because I can't stop thinking about Indy, and just the thought of her damn near chokes me.

I told him it was because I didn't feel like talking to him, but he called bullshit and let me know Luce and Nigel have also been trying to reach me.

And my mom too.

Ever since I left Indy's apartment, since I walked away from her, since I removed myself from her presence so I wouldn't cause her any more fucking pain, I've been a real pathetic asshole.

Instead of forcing my misery on other people, I've stayed holed up in my brownstone, alternating my time between my bed and my studio.

Although, even when I'm in my studio, all my fingers seem to want to paint is her.

But my sheets are still covered in her paint, and all my studio does is remind me of her. It's a fucking disaster.

And now, because of Bram's fucking insistence, I'm sitting in some nightclub called Until or Ulta, fuck, I can't remember. All I know is that it's for some rich guy's birthday. Apparently, said rich guy owns the joint and wants to spend the whole night flaunting how great he is and how much money he has.

One of the cocktail waitresses sets a fresh glass of whiskey on the table beside my chair, and I don't hesitate to lift it to my mouth.

Happy birthday to the owner of this club. Cheers to you, you pretentious douchebag. I hope you go bankrupt.

I laugh at my own joke.

"What are you laughing about?" someone purrs into my ear, and I look up to see a blonde with big, fake tits and plastic lips smiling down at me. Her hand is on my shoulder, and she's rubbing at my skin.

"Nothing," I respond.

"What?" she asks and flutters her eyelashes. "You don't want to tell me?"

"Nope."

She pouts. I look away.

Fucking Bram. I should've stayed home.

The only reason he got me out of the house was because he mentioned whiskey.

I figured, what the hell. I'd drink a few and then head home.

Little did I know he was bringing me to the land of annoying music, pretentious assholes, and aggressive-fucking-women who either don't realize I'm not interested or they don't care.

"What's your name?" the woman asks.

"Chuck."

"I'm pretty sure that's not your name." She slaps my shoulder on a high-pitched giggle. "You're Ansel Bray, right?"

"Nope."

She giggles again. "You're so funny."

Funny? This chick has a weird fucking sense of humor.

She takes it upon herself to sit down *right beside* me on the black pleather couch. If she gets any closer, she'll be in my fucking lap.

"What are you drinking?" she asks and puts her hand on my thigh.

"Whiskey."

"Mmmm," she says through a little moan. "I love whiskey."

Liar. Only alcoholics or people trying to escape their fucking misery—*people like me*—like whiskey.

"Good for you."

She giggles again and reaches across my body, brushing her hand over my chest, and takes my glass from the table. She lifts it to her lips in a dramatic display, takes a drink, and licks her lips.

Immediately, I wave down the cocktail waitress and ask her to bring me another glass.

"Aren't you going to ask my name?"

"No."

More giggles.

"It's Serena, by the way."

I don't respond. And, hopefully, in about thirty seconds, I won't even remember her name.

The cocktail waitress brings me a fresh drink, and I make damn sure it's out of what's her name's reach. I prefer my alcohol devoid of lipstick, desperation, and collagen, thank you very much.

"You're not much of a talker, are you?" she asks. "Don't worry, I don't mind." She rubs her hand up and down my chest. "I love the broody, mysterious type."

Broody artist.

I think about Indy, and I think about the very first time she said those words to me.

We were on the subway, playing music for each other, and fuck, she took my breath away. Her smile. The way her blue eyes lit up when she was amused. The way those eyes slow-danced with emotion when the music in her ears was affecting her.

What's her name's voice fills my ears, and I outright ignore her and just let myself fall headfirst into thoughts of Indy.

Fuck, I miss her.

I miss her smile and her laugh and the way she bites on her bottom lip when she's nervous. I miss her kiss and her touch and the way it felt to make love to her.

I feel like she's mine, like she belongs with me, but I also feel like she was never mine to begin with.

She can't even fucking look at me anymore.

When she looks at me, when she looks into my eyes, all she sees is him.

Adam. My donor. His eyes are my eyes, and because of that, because Indy knows that, she will never be able to look at me without pain. Without heartache.

When I went blind, I thought painting gave me life. I thought it was my life.

But I was wrong.

Painting gave me purpose. Indy gave me life.

Fuck, I just want to hold her again. Touch her again. Kiss her again. Show her how much I love her.

Because I do. I love Indy.

chapter
thirty-nine

Indy

"C an we just go?" I ask on a huff, and Lily looks down at me, makeup brush in her hand and glares.

"Just chill out," she mutters. "And close your eyes. Just a few more finishing touches to your eye makeup and we'll be all set."

I groan. "Why did I let you talk me into this?"

"Because you love me, and you know I'm right."

"Right about what?"

"That you need to get out of this fucking apartment."

I'm tempted to back out, to tell her I'm not going to this stupid club for Shawn Messi's big birthday bash, but I know she won't let me off the hook that easy.

Especially after she showed up to my apartment with a little black dress, stilettos, and enough makeup to fill one of the Kardashians' glam rooms. All for me.

"There." She grins at me. "All set, buttercup."

I look at my reflection in the mirror, taking in the rare occurrence of sparkle and shine and stiletto heels, and I can't deny my sister worked some magic. Somehow, she turned a disheveled hermit into a girl who looks like she has her shit together.

"You like?"

"Yeah." Hesitantly, I nod. "You did good, Lil."

Her responding smile is victorious. "Let's go have some fun tonight!"

Fun? Fuck. I don't know about fun.

Tonight, in this sexy dress and far-too-high heels, I will try not to fall on my face.

I will try not to think about Ansel.

I will try not to cry if I do think about Ansel.

I will simply try to make it through.

Before I know it, we're flashing our IDs to the bouncer manning the entrance at Ultra.

He glances between my photo and my face, and with a curt nod, he unclicks the velvet rope and lets me inside behind my sister.

One foot through the tinted glass doors and my senses are assaulted by pounding music and people. So many people. And they're dancing and laughing and drinking, and everyone around us looks like they're having the time of their lives.

Celebrating.

Partying.

Living.

Everyone but me.

I shut my eyes for a brief moment and breathe through the pressure that settles itself on my chest, pushing down on my lungs like a vise.

What am I doing here? I shouldn't be here.

"Come on!" Lily calls over the music and grabs my hand. "Let's go get a drink!"

God, I wish I wouldn't have agreed to this.

I swallow past the building anxiety inside my chest, and we shuffle through the crowd until we reach the bar.

But before we even get a chance to order, Lily gets sidetracked when she spots Shawn Messi near the DJ booth.

"Happy birthday!" she shouts toward him.

"Lily! Get your ass over here!" He yells back, and immediately, her excited gaze darts to mine.

"Go say hi," I encourage and offer a friendly wave to Shawn. "I'll stay here and get a drink."

"Are you sure?"

"Positive," I say. "Tell him I said happy birthday."

I don't have to tell her twice. A minute later, I spot her standing in the DJ booth with Shawn, smiling and laughing and just being my outgoing, extrovert sister that I know and love so much.

One of the bartenders makes eye contact with me, and his eyes offer up his assistance with a little grin. *Yes. Alcohol.* The club is too loud to shout my order across the bar, so instead, I point toward the bottle of tequila on the back wall and the container of limes near his hip.

He nods his understanding and holds up one finger. "One shot?" he asks, and I shake my head.

I'm not much of a drinker, but fuck, one shot of tequila isn't going to be enough to quell this earthquake of emotion threatening to shake itself out of my body.

I hold up two fingers, and his lips pop wide with a smile and what I can assume is an amused laugh.

He makes quick work of my order, and before I know it, he's sliding two shot glasses of tequila, limes, and salt in front of me.

"Trying to catch up?" he asks and I shrug.

I feel like I've been playing catch up ever since I met Ansel Bray.

"Something like that."

The alcohol floods my bloodstream, and the weight of my unease lifts from my chest and my shoulders. And for the first time since I stepped into this club, my knees aren't shaking and my palms aren't sweating.

I look toward the DJ booth to find my sister, but she's not there anymore.

I search the crowd for her, but the damn place is too packed.

Fuck it.

I order another shot of tequila from the friendly bartender, and it goes down even smoother than the first two.

When Camila Cabello's voice starts to bounce off the walls of the club, I can't stop myself from sliding into the center of the room and letting the music wash over me.

Maybe it's the alcohol.

Maybe it's the song.

I don't know.

But I dance. By myself. In the middle of the club.

Camila sings about never being the same, and the lyrics glide over my skin and leave goose bumps in their wake.

I'm not the same. Haven't been the same.

Not since Ansel Bray barreled into my life.

I raise my hands in the air and I look up at the ceiling, and I let my head fall back and my eyes close as my body moves to the music.

It feels good.

I feel good. Despite all the shit that's going down inside my head and inside my heart, I just feel good for once. A smile crests my lips and I open my eyes, but in an instant, a mere second, the room stops.

Just...*stops.*

The music.

The people dancing around me.

My heart.

Ansel is here. In a roped-off VIP section, and he's not alone.

A blond woman is sitting right beside him, and she's laughing and lifting a glass to her lips and taking a drink. He leans his head back against the couch, and the blonde takes it upon herself to get more comfortable. *In his lap.*

I should look away, but I can't.

Ansel is in the corner of the room, with another woman in his lap, and all I can do is stand here and watch like some sort of brokenhearted voyeur.

I am bumped from behind, and like someone pushed play, the room comes to life again. I hear the music and the crowd and I feel the throng of dancers around me, but I'm frozen. My eyes still locked on

Ansel and the blonde.

"I almost couldn't find you!" Lily's voice fills my ears, and I look to my left to find her holding two glasses of champagne in her hands. "Don't be mad, but Shawn happened to mention that New Rules is here. And Ansel is here too. I think you should go talk to him."

"I know," I say, but I can barely get the words out of my mouth.

"How do you know?"

Instead of answering, I move my gaze toward the VIP section.

But this time, instead of the woman just sitting in his lap, I have to witness her lean forward and press her mouth to his.

"What the fuck?" Lily questions, but I can barely hear her over the erratic, pounding rhythm of my heart.

I know I shouldn't feel angry or jealous or sad.

He has a right to try to move on. And for the entire duration of the time we'd spent together, I had a boyfriend.

I know the nausea that fills my gut is unwarranted, and I know there shouldn't be tears in my eyes.

But just because I know it doesn't make it not real.

This moment is so real, so palpable, so in-my-fucking-face, that it's choking me.

I need to leave.

I need to get out of this club.

Just as I turn on my heels, my eyes lock with brown.

He sees me, and I don't miss the instant recognition that covers his face.

Shit.

"Excuse me," I mutter as I push through the crowd. "Please, I need to leave!"

"Indy! Wait!" Lily yells toward me, but I don't stop.

I can't stop. And before she can reach me, I'm out of the club and I'm hailing a cab, and I'm gone.

Away from the club. Away from the pain. Away from the man who still holds my heart in his hands.

chapter forty

Ansel

The lips touching my mouth are foreign and unwelcome, and I open my eyes to find that stupid fucking woman in my lap and her plastic lips pressed to mine.

What the fuck?

I yank my face away, but when my eyes glance to the dance floor, to the sea of people in the center of the club, a potent, familiar, breathtaking pair of blue eyes locks with mine.

Indy. Her face is broken, and her eyes look so sad. So fucking sad that I feel my heart break all over again.

In an instant, she goes from standing in the center of the dance floor to pushing through the crowd.

"Indy!" I call out toward her and jump to standing.

The blonde tumbles off of my lap and onto the floor. She gasps and yells profanities at me, but I don't give a fuck. I'm on my feet and running out of the VIP area and following Indy.

But the club is so packed, and there're too many fucking people.

"Move! Fucking move!"

I push my way through the dancing fools and the drunken idiots, and it feels like it takes me years just to get to the front of the club. Once I reach the entrance doors, I shove them open and nearly knock the bouncers over, but I don't even stop to apologize.

My feet pound on the pavement, and I'm frantic. Looking left and right and just anywhere and everywhere to try to find her.

"Indy!" I shout, and the line of people waiting to get inside the club looks at me like I've lost my fucking mind. "Indy!"

But the second time I shout her name, someone else's voice joins mine.

I glance over my shoulder to find her sister walking out onto the sidewalk, and when she meets my eyes, she strides toward me and shoves two hands into my chest.

"What were you thinking?" Lily screams. "Why are you doing this to her?"

"Doing this to her?" I ask, but my question goes on deaf ears, and Lily's gaze turns to fire.

"You're just out here kissing other women! What the fucking fuck!"

Her insinuation pisses me off.

"Kissing other women?" I spit back. "That's the exact opposite of what I'm doing! That woman in the club wasn't anything but an annoyance. I mean, fuck, my goddamn eyes were closed when she moved in and pushed her plastic lips to mine!"

Seething anger vibrates the space between us.

"You are—" Lily starts to say something, but I cut her off.

"Other women might as well not fucking exist because these days, all I do is think of Indy. Dream of her. Lose my mind over her. I'm fucking miserable over here!"

"What the hell?" Lily screeches and shoves at my chest again. "She broke up with her boyfriend because of you. She's in love with you, you idiot!"

She broke up with her boyfriend?

"What?" My jaw goes slack. "She doesn't love me. She can't even look at me. All I do is cause her pain."

"She doesn't hate you, you dumbfuck! She's in love with you! She's been a goddamn mess over you! She can't sleep. She can't eat. She can't even go to work. She's devastated!"

In that moment, I feel what's left of my pathetic heart break and crumble into dust and ashes.

I don't even know how to respond.

"I didn't know," I say, but my voice is a whisper. "I didn't know. I thought she was done with me. I thought it was too much for her. I thought whenever she looked at me now, I just reminded her of Adam."

"No." Lily shakes her head. "Whenever she looks at you now, she sees what she lost, Ansel. She sees *you*."

I'm crushed. Confounded. And if I could go fetal on the sidewalk without someone calling the cops, I probably would.

"God, Lily," I mutter and swallow hard against the emotion that threatens to creep up my throat. "I didn't know. Fuck, I didn't know."

"Well, now you do." She's still pissed, and I don't blame her.

I'm pissed too.

Pissed at myself.

Pissed at that stupid blonde.

Pissed at the universe for fucking with me so hard.

I scramble to pull my phone out of my pocket. "Where do you think she went?"

"I don't know."

I try to call Indy, but it goes straight to voice mail.

And I call her again and again and again, only to be left with the same result.

"Call her, Lily!" I demand. "Call her from your phone!"

Her eyes go wide, and she searches my face. I don't know what she finds, but whatever it is, it has her reaching into her purse to call her sister.

"Is she answering?" I ask, my voice panicked.

Lily shakes her head. "It's just going straight to voice mail."

"Fuck! Try again," I urge, but I can't even wait for her to do it. Instead, I yank the phone from her hands and try to call Indy myself.

Lily startles but doesn't say anything. Instead, she just stares at me with wide eyes, watching me fall apart outside of this goddamn club.

It rings and rings and fucking rings until Indy's sweet angel voice is in my ears and telling me to leave a message.

"Fuck!"

"It's okay," Lily whispers and gently places her hand on my arm. "Just calm down, okay?"

Calm down. How can I stay calm when I've just watched my whole fucking world run in the opposite direction from me?

How can I calm down when I feel like I've lost her for a second time?

Lost her for good.

chapter forty-one

Indy

Even though I tossed and turned all night, I don't find the strength to push myself out of bed until ten. The sun is well on its way to being the center of the sky, and I'm running on fumes.

There's a kind of a tired that simply needs a good night's sleep, and another that needs so much more. A kind that is a bone-deep wearing of emotions that leaves you restless and fatigued and the equivalent of a five percent battery life on an iPhone.

After last night at the club, I'm the other.

I left in a rush of devastation and hopelessness and a desperate need for self-preservation.

Although I don't feel like I preserved anything. If anything, the thin shell I've been pretending is me has been left cracked and corroded.

And I've been ignoring the outside world ever since.

Ansel.

Even my sister.

She called me no less than fifteen times last night, and I sent her a text message, telling her I made it home safely and I didn't want to be bothered and I would call her when I was ready to talk.

And then I turned off my phone.

Am I being a coward? Probably.

But it's all I can manage right now.

When I shuffle my way into the kitchen to brew up some coffee, pounding knocks to my front door stop my path.

"Delivery!" a female voice shouts from the other side.

"Just a minute," I mutter and drag myself to the front of my apartment.

The instant I open the door, a pretty woman with full lips, an ample amount of cleavage, and wearing sky-high stilettos greets me on the other side.

She doesn't look like someone who delivers packages for a living…

"This is for you," she says, and I scrunch up my nose.

"What is it?"

She looks down at the wrapped package in her hands and back at me, and her eyes seem to be questioning my intelligence. "Pretty sure it's obvious."

I blink and she sighs.

"It's a painting."

"A painting?"

I blink again.

"You know, like a painting. It's something artists create." She huffs an annoyed breath. "I'm pretty sure this isn't that hard to understand."

"Who are you again?"

"I'm Lucy. Ansel's assistant," she answers like I'm the biggest moron on the planet, and before I can even wrap my brain around that revelation, she adds, "So…are you going to take it or not?"

Holy shit. Why is Ansel's assistant here?

She blows a pink bubble from her lips, and I try to regain my ability for speech.

"Oh…uh…" I mutter and reach out to take the package from her hand. "Of course. Sorry."

But she doesn't leave right away.

Instead, she stands there, scrutinizing my face.

"He's a mess, you know," she says matter-of-factly.

I don't know what to say to that. But it doesn't matter because she appears content to hold a one-sided conversation.

"And whenever Ansel is a real fucking mess, he becomes an intolerable bastard," she continues. "So, thanks for that."

"Thanks?"

"I'm assuming you're the reason."

"I...I..." I stutter and shake my head.

"Well, enjoy the painting, I guess." She shrugs, flips her hair over her shoulder, and leaves. Just up and walks away without a goodbye or anything.

I stand in my doorway for a long moment, just watching her stilettos eat up the walkway while I grip the package in my hands.

I'm not sure what urges me to go back inside, but eventually, I do. And I stride straight to my kitchen and set the package on the center of the island.

I stare down at it, unsure of what to do with it.

Do I open it?

Do I ignore it?

Do I try to forget it exists?

Curiosity gets the best of me, and I take the small white card off the top of the package and work to see what lies beneath the brown wrapping.

I slide my fingers under the rigid paper and tear. One, two, three, four, I tear until it's revealed to me in its entirety.

A hand goes to my mouth and tears fill my eyes, and I gaze down at the painting, *Ansel's painting*. I don't know how long I stand there, still as a statue, trying to make sense of it.

It's me, but in this painting, there is a violin in my hands.

And I'm playing it.

My face is so serene, so calm, so at peace.

And there is a soft, tiny smile on my lips.

And my eyes are so bright and burning and just...*happy*.

I don't even know I'm crying, but I am. Tears drip down my cheeks in steady waves, and when I read the small gold plaque at the bottom of the frame, a sob jumps from my throat.

Venus and the Violin.

Memories flood my mind.

Ansel and me. The Met. His words.

"She's the feminine image of love," he'd said. *"Da Vinci, Picasso, Monet... Every great artist has a Venus. Their Venus is their muse. The woman who consumes their mind and inspires them to paint or sculpt until they either die or their fucking fingers fall off."*

My hands shake. Tears drip onto my kitchen counter. And I look down to see that the small white card is now on the floor.

I pick it up, and I see my name is written on top. **Indy.**

I open it, and my eyes latch on to Ansel's familiar and messy but beautiful scrawl.

I don't know why I feel like I need to tell you to play again, but I do.
Play again, Indy.
I don't know why I know that music—the violin—makes you thrive. That music brings you inner peace. But I do.
Let music inside of your soul again.
But one thing I do know.
One thing that is an infinite certainty.
I love you, Indy.
More than I have ever loved anyone or anything.
I painted this over a year ago, and it belongs with you.
This is you, my Venus, with your violin.
-Ansel

This is the most painfully beautiful gift anyone has ever sent me, and so many emotions flood my veins that I don't even know what or how I'm feeling.

And questions, so many questions race through my brain.

How does he know about the violin?

How does he know what music really means to me?

And how does he always seem to get me? Know me?

He loves me, but he can't stand to look at me? Be with me?

At first, I just stand there, in a puddle of my own tears with my thoughts scattered across the kitchen. But before I even know what I'm doing, I pick up my cell phone and call the one person I need right now.

And an hour later, my dad is opening the front door, and I kind of push myself into his arms and hug him tightly.

"Indigo?" he asks, but he doesn't let me go. "What's going on, honey?"

I don't say anything at first. I can't.

I savor the comfort of home. Of my dad's hug.

One minute turns to two and two turns to three, and when the urge to sob has been swallowed down enough for words to be a possibility, I inhale a deep breath. "Do you still have my violin?" I ask on a whisper. "Or did you end up getting rid of it?"

"Of course, I have it, Indigo."

We're in my dad's music room, and it hasn't changed one bit since I was last in here. The walls are still covered with music memorabilia and instruments, and stacks of sheet music litter the corners and fill the shelves.

It's both a vision of peace and turmoil to my eyes.

I used to spend hours upon hours in this room. Learning how to play every instrument I could get my fingers on. But it didn't take long for me to realize the violin was what I loved most.

"What do you want to play?" my dad asks quietly from his spot behind the piano.

I don't even have to think about it.

"The Four Seasons," I whisper.

"The whole concerto?"

I nod.

I know I'm going to be rusty as hell and both my dad and I will miss a bunch of notes, but it doesn't matter. It was the last composition I played. For a crowd of thousands. And in order to do this right, in order to play the violin again, it needs to be this, it needs to be Vivaldi.

Somehow, my dad manages to find the sheet music beneath the stacks and sits down at the piano.

And I pick up the violin. Its slender strings caress my fingers, and I tenderly trace its curves under my palm and inhale a deep and shaky breath. It's been so long since I've held it in my fingertips. So long since I've felt its weight in my hands.

"You ready?" he asks and I nod.

I adjust the violin beneath my chin, and I grip the bow in my hand.

My dad waits for my cue.

With a deep, nervous inhale, I pull oxygen into my lungs, and then I strum the bow across the strings and begin.

Not even two beats later, the piano accompanies me.

Instantly, there is something about the vibrations that feel so heavenly, as if they are liquid energy seeping right through my skin. There's something about the way the violin sings in my hands that makes my heart race. And God, it's both harrowing and euphoric the way it encompasses my body.

It's heaven and hell all at once.

It's everything I've dreamed of, everything I love, but it's painful, releasing all of the tragic memories I've been trying to avoid.

But I keep playing.

First, Spring.

Then, Summer.

Then, Autumn.

By the time we fall into winter, I'm lost to the harrowing notes. The haunting rhythm. Liquid emotion spills from my eyes, and I watch the drops fall onto the hollow body of my violin.

But I keep playing.

Music—this violin in my hands—it is the rhythm of my soul. It flows through my veins and swirls in my head. To me, music is life and life is music. It's in everything I see. It's in the air I breathe. It's in my DNA. And the violin is *my* instrument, and I never should have gone a day without playing it.

I shouldn't have let over four years pass by without picking it up in my hands.

When we reach the end, I sob. Not out of sadness or fear or uncertainty, just...this cathartic kind of sob that feels like it's been buried inside of my bones for a decade.

My dad doesn't say anything.

He gets up from the piano and pulls me into a tight hug and lets me cry for a long moment.

"Are you okay?" he asks, and I nod into his shoulder.

"I'm incredibly sad and incredibly happy at the same time. It's overwhelming."

"Hearing you play again, seeing you play again," he says and inhales an unsteady breath. "It filled my heart, Indigo. It was...beautiful." He hugs me tighter. "Whatever brought you back to this, back to the violin, don't let it go."

chapter
forty-two

Indy

I hardly remember the walk back from my parents' house.

I don't remember how I got there or how long it took me.

But I do remember standing in front of my door, key in my hand and heart racing inside my chest. I remember lifting the key to the knob but being unable to insert it.

And I remember walking back outside and heading toward the subway station.

I got on. Stood in the center of the car with my hands gripping the silver pole and my mind a million miles away, yet steady and focused at the same time.

One transfer, several stops, and even more rain-soaked blocks later and I stand in front of Ansel's brownstone. The lights are on. And the moisture falling from the sky pelts against the glass of the windows.

The temperature is ice-cold, and the drops freeze against my exposed skin on contact. To feel it is the opposite of enjoyable. Not like a warm summer rain that cools everything down and urges steam to billow from the pavement.

But oddly enough, I want to feel it all the same.

I want to experience each drop, together and apart, same and different. I want to see the droplets soaking my eyelashes before they hit the ground like saltless tears. I need to be in this, chaotic and wild. It's as if nature looked inside my soul and pulled this weather from it.

My pea coat grows heavy, and the rain falls, crazy and hectic, while gusts of wind swirl in all different directions.

And yet, I'm just standing here, taking this beating from Mother Nature.

Standing here and trying to find the courage to knock on his door. Trying to find the strength to face him again.

I force my feet to move until I reach his door. My hands shake. Rain and tears mingle on my face, the salty, emotion-filled tracks blending with the fresh sky-fallen trickles.

Somehow, I find the strength to lift my hand and knock.

Ansel opens the door, and my breath is stolen from my lungs.

He's beautiful, so fucking beautiful, and his eyes are wild as they take in my wet and downtrodden appearance.

"Shit, Indy," he mutters and opens the door wide, trying to coax me inside. "You're soaked."

I shake my head and take two steps back.

He furrows his brow, and more tears start to flow down my face.

"Indy?" he asks, and the way my name falls tenderly from his lips makes my chest ache.

"Why?" I ask, and my voice comes out louder, harsher than I planned.

"I swear to you, Indy, I didn't kiss that woman. I didn't want to—"

"No," I interrupt him. "I don't care about that stupid kiss."

Because I don't. That kiss is inconsequential to me. It's barely a blip on my radar, and it wasn't what made me run out of the club. His mere presence made me run. Being that close to someone you love so much but can't be with is soul-crushing.

His brow furrows deeper in confusion, and I oblige with another response.

"Why did you paint that, Ansel?"

He looks at me, but he doesn't say anything. His full lips pinch into a thin line as his eyes search mine.

"Why?" I scream at the top of my lungs and step toward him.

My emotions are too potent, too strong to control myself. With two hands, I shove right into his chest. My fingers scrape against the zipper of his sweater hard enough to break the skin, but it doesn't matter. Superficial pain is nothing compared to the agony that trembles beneath my skin.

"Why, Ansel?" My voice drops and quivers, and a painful shriek escapes my throat as I shove my hands into his chest again, but this time, I don't let go. I grip his sweater so tightly, I can feel the material wrinkling beneath my fingertips.

I sob. Big, fat tears tripping from my lids like a waterfall and I bury my face into his chest.

His strong arms wrap around me like a vise, and I can't do anything but cry into the solace of his embrace. And the rain doesn't quit. It pelts down on us, soaking our hair, our clothes and dripping between our bodies.

I'm wrecked.

Shattered.

But I'm also comforted. So fucking relieved.

It's all so confusing.

"I don't know, Indy," Ansel whispers into my hair. "I just saw it. I still see it," he says, and then his voice shakes as he adds, "And for some reason, I just know. I just know you. My soul knows your soul. It's crazy and insane, but it's the only way I can explain it."

His words unleash something inside of me.

Something I've been keeping locked tight inside my heart.

Something I need to say out loud, if only for the sake of letting myself hear it.

"Over four years ago, I played the biggest concert of my life," I whisper through my tears, but my face, it stays buried against his chest. "My music always seemed to be the one sore spot in my relationship with Adam. He was always too busy with photo shoots to see me play. Not once did he see me play at Julliard. And when I gained a spot with the New York Orchestra, he didn't make it to a single concert. And it hurt, you know. It hurt that he was never there. I wanted him there. I *needed* him there."

I inhale a shaky breath as visuals of that night flash behind my eyes.

But I can't stop now. I have to keep going. I have to tell someone. I have to tell him.

"We had a pretty big fight over it, and that night, he was trying to make it. He was trying to be there, at Lincoln Center, to see me play. But like always, his photo shoot had him running late. And I was mad at him, Ansel," I say, and a sob wrenches itself from my throat. "I was so mad at him for not being there. It was the biggest night of my career, and he missed it. He missed the entire thing."

Ansel's fingers grip me tighter to his chest.

"He was trying to be there. Riding his motorcycle through New York traffic. That stupid bike I hated so much because he would never wear a helmet and rode like a maniac through the busy streets of the city… And he never made it, Ansel. He never made it to my concert."

Another sob and three more shaky breaths.

"He died trying to get there. All because I gave him such a hard time about it. All because of me, he died." The last six words are painful, like knives scraping against my tongue as they leave my lips.

All of the guilt I've held on to for so long boils to the surface and releases itself through more tears, more sobs. My body shakes with grief, and Ansel grips me tighter.

"God, Indy," he whispers into my wet hair. "I didn't know."

"The last time I saw him, I was mad and pissed and upset, and I never once said I love you. Those are his last memories of me," I cry. "Not happy. Not loving. Not how they should have been. But angry and mad and just…awful. When I found out what happened, I couldn't even touch a violin anymore without getting sick."

"It wasn't your fault, Indy," Ansel says quietly, but his words are firm. "There was no way for you to know."

"I should've known," I reply. "But I should've known."

"Indy," he says, and his voice turns soft and soothing. "His death wasn't your fault. There is no doubt in my mind that he was rushing to your concert because he wanted to be there. Not because you guys had a fight the night before, but because you were important to him."

It wasn't your fault, Indy.

Somewhere, deep inside of me, I've always held deep-rooted guilt that I'd let Adam down. That I'd played a role in his death. But Ansel's words permeate my bones, and I feel a small part of that weight slowly lift from my heart.

I find the strength to lift my eyes to his, and I search his face for some kind of sign, some kind of answer to all of these crazy circumstances that have brought us together, some kind of explanation for the electric connection that pulled us toward each other.

Still pulls us.

"What are you doing to me?" I ask on a whisper. "What are you doing to me, Ansel? It's like you've reached inside my chest and wrapped your hands around my heart and soul. Today was the first day I've picked up the violin in four years," I whisper in a rush. "Because of the painting. Because of you. You affect me in ways no one ever has, and I know this is insane for you. I know this is terrifying, but my heart has already made her choice. And she wants you, Ansel."

The words fall from my lips before I can stop them, and still, I can't stop them.

It's like the faucet has been opened, and I'm just letting everything I'm thinking and feeling flow out.

"God, I'm sorry. I'm so sorry I'm saying all of this to you. I'm not trying to make you feel bad for walking away. I just…I just…" *I just want you. Only you.*

chapter forty-three

Ansel

place both of my hands on the wet skin of her cheeks and bring her gaze back to mine. She is tear-stained and rain-stained and so fucking lovely, it makes my chest ache with need for her. In my eyes, no one will ever compare to Indy.

"Three years ago, I picked up my brush again," I say and stare deep into her eyes. "Because of you. You saved me, Indy. And yeah, this connection of ours and the situation that has brought us together are scary. Insane, even. But I don't care about the why or the how. I don't care about anything but *you*."

"Ansel," she whispers my name like a prayer.

"I love you, Indy," I tell her even though those three little words don't even come close to how I feel about her. "Not because of my eyes, but because of what's inside of your heart and how your soul matches mine. I'm so deep in love with you, Indy, there is no going back for me. There is no moving on from this." I press my lips to hers, softly, tenderly, and I lift her hand to cover my chest. "This is real love. And fuck, I feel like I've been waiting my whole life for this, for you."

Her heart is in her eyes, and tears are now in mine.

"I love you too," she says in a rush. "I love *you*."

The girl in the paintings.

The girl in my mind.

The girl who owns my heart.

She steps up on her tippy-toes, pressing her lips to mine, and I respond with fervor. Tasting her lips and tongue and savoring how good it feels to finally be kissing her again.

The rain runs down our faces to where our lips meet, each of us tasting the cold drops and each other's skin. But instead of detracting from the intensity of the moment, it brings us to new heights. I press my lips to hers more firmly, and the wave that runs through me is intoxicating, making my head swim as I pull back to take in her beautiful face.

But it's only seconds before we're kissing again.

Pouring everything we have into this kiss.

Our love. Our hope. Our everything.

There is something so heavenly about a kiss in the rain, a tender moment that just won't wait. And this kiss, our kiss, it is a burst of love being expressed and not caring about the fucking rain or anything around us. A connection that shows the strength of our feelings, the mutual need for each other. It is a rebellion against the elements. Nature can bring the rain, but we are telling her to fuck off.

I slide my hands under Indy's ass and lift her up, and she wraps her legs around my waist.

We don't break the kiss when I walk us inside my house.

Or when I shut the door.

Not even when I walk us up the steps and into my bedroom.

I lay her on the bed and remove her wet clothes. She smiles up at me and giggles when I toss her jeans and they hit the hardwood with a slop, and my fucking heart is bursting inside my chest.

My clothes are gone next, and I climb into the bed, moving my body over hers.

I kiss remnants of tears and rain from her cheeks and her mouth, and her lips smile against mine. I sweep the drenched locks of her hair away from her creamy skin and kiss along her collarbone and neck.

She wraps her hands around my back, and her fingers flex with need into my skin.

And when our vibrating desire for one other becomes too strong, too powerful to resist, I slide inside of her.

She moans into my mouth, but her eyes never leave mine.

I breathe in deep. In and out. And I just stare down at her, taking in the way her breasts move up and down with each pant. The way her eyes glow with desire. And the way her hands can't stop touching me. My face. My shoulders. My back. Anywhere they can reach, they touch.

Fuck, I feel like I have waited so long for this. I have craved her skin and her warmth and her moans and her tongue tasting my breath and the way it feels to have her clenching around me tightly.

She wraps her legs around my waist, and time is forgotten.

The only thing I'm aware of is her.

Her eyes.

Her skin.

Her moans.

And how much I love her.

In the dim light of my bedroom, Indy is cuddled up to my body, her arms wrapped around my waist and her head on my chest. Music plays softly through the speakers in my bedroom and my heart is ablaze with nothing but love.

This, us entwined together, is a little slice of heaven, warm and cozy perfection.

I lazily stroke her still-damp hair with my fingertips, and the warmth of her petite hands against my skin makes me grin.

If I could spend the rest of my life doing this, lying in bed with Indy, I'd do it in a heartbeat. She brings me a peace I've never known. A calming of the storms inside my heart.

With Indy inside my embrace, I feel like there is nothing to fear or doubt. Hope for the future cocoons the room, filling the silence with solace and contentment and...love. It feels like all the love in the world is inside my bedroom.

"*Comptine d'un autre été*" begins to play, and Indy smiles up at me, her big blue eyes glowing.

"This is our song,"

Without hesitation, I shake my head. "No, it's not."

There is only one song that could possibly encompass what Indy means to me. And although this composition is beautiful, it's not beautiful enough.

I found our song a long time ago. Years ago, in fact. Before I met her. And the instant I heard it, I thought that kind of love was impossible. I thought I'd never feel like that about anyone.

I was convinced of that very fact.

Until Indy.

"What are you talking about?" she questions and scrunches up her nose at me. "This is definitely our song, Ansel."

It's my turn to smile. "We have a song, but you just haven't heard it yet."

"You realize that makes no sense, right?"

Her adorable incredulity urges a soft chuckle from my lips. "Yeah, but once you hear the song, you'll understand."

"Okay…" she singsongs the lone word and pauses just long enough to search my eyes dramatically. "Are you going to tell me, or are you trying your hand at telepathy?"

"Oh… You want to hear it?"

She rolls her eyes and I laugh.

"Give me a second," I say and sit up. "I need to grab my phone."

A minute later and I'm climbing back into bed with a gloriously naked Indy. "Come here," I say and rest my back against the headboard, and she snuggles back into my body.

"Are you going to tell me the name of the song?"

I shake my head. "Just listen."

With the help of my phone and the Bluetooth speakers throughout my house, I turn the volume way up and hit play. The opening of Ghinzu's "Sweet Love" begins to fill the space around us, enveloping

261

us in the soft, subtle piano notes.

And then the lyrics come.

Slow. Steady.

But it only takes two lines, and Indy is climbing into my lap, her thighs straddling my legs and her hands on my face. Tears are in her eyes, and a smile is on her lips. She locks her gaze with mine but never stops listening to the song.

The music grows in power. Stronger. Deeper. Until it reaches out and touches Indy's skin in the form of emotional eyes and goose bumps making a path up her arms.

In an instant, she leans forward and kisses me, a moan on the tip of her tongue. And I wrap my arms around her body and savor the taste of her mouth.

It doesn't take long for our kiss to turn passionate.

Panting breaths.

Greedy hands.

Erratic lips.

She lifts her hips up, and I slide inside of her.

Our eyes are locked and our lips are just barely touching, and I move inside of her. Slow at first, but as the music speeds up and the lyrics say everything I want to tell her, everything inside my heart, the urgency and need for her become too strong to deny. And I can't hold back.

I can't go slow.

I need to feel her wrapped around me, taste her lips, touch her skin, kiss her breasts.

I need it all. I need *her.*

My sweet love.

My once-in-a-lifetime, written-in-the-stars, forever-starts-right-now kind of love.

epilogue

Two years later
Indy

My shoulders are back. My spine is straight. The fingers of my left hand engage the strings of my violin, and my right hand drags and pushes the bow back and forth, bringing the music to life.

The notes start out clean and clear, but they morph into an airy, almost magical harmony. And the divine vibrations travel from the violin to my fingers to my chin to my chest *to my heart*. It feels so heavenly and my body melts into the moment.

Occasionally, my eyes drift to the sheet music, but it's more out of habit than needing to follow along. Mostly, though, I just lose myself inside the music and play.

God, it doesn't get any better than this.

The sounds remind me of sunrises and sweet dreams. And there is this intangible quality to it. Like you can sense the beauty, but you can't quite grasp what it is that makes it so beautiful. What makes it so special.

As I hit the final notes, I shut my eyes and savor how good it feels to play.

How satisfying it feels to move the bow across the strings.

How amazing it is to feel the music pulsating inside of me.

Yeah, this is my happy place.

Eventually, though, reality pulls me out of my trance in the form of a familiar voice coming through the sound booth speakers.

"Great job, Indy," Don, the producer, says. "I think we're all set here."

I open my eyes and offer him a nod through the glass before setting down my violin and taking off my headphones. And just as I walk out of the sound booth, Bram is there to greet me with a big, friendly smile.

"Looking as beautiful as ever."

That's definitely sweet, but it's a flat-out lie. I'm thirty-eight weeks pregnant and ready to pop. Beautiful left the building about two months ago when tired, uncomfortable, and puffy showed up without an invitation.

"Yeah, right." I huff out an annoyed sigh. "I'm as big as a house."

"You're gorgeous. My favorite and most gorgeous sister-in-law," he says with a grin, and an amused laugh leaves my lips.

"I'm your only sister-in-law."

"But my favorite and most gorgeous one, nonetheless." He winks and reaches out to gently rub my belly. "How's my little niece doing?"

"Good." I glance down at my stomach and offer up a silent prayer that my ever-growing belly has reached its peak. "Hopefully, she's ready to come out soon."

He looks up to meet my eyes. "I thought you still had another two weeks to go…"

Two weeks. Sheesh. Why is pregnancy exactly ten years long?

"Are you trying to ruin my day?" I glare, and Bram has to fight his smile by biting down on his bottom lip.

"Ansel mentioned you were on a bit of a rampage today."

My glare only gets stronger. "I'm sorry, Ansel said what?"

"Nothing," he mutters, but the smile he fought so hard against is now present and shining on his face. "He said nothing."

"You're a terrible liar."

"Maybe." He shrugs. "But you know what you are?"

"What am I?"

Grumpy? Sweaty? Miserable? All three would be apt descriptions of my current state.

"Fucking brilliant." I quirk a brow, and he continues. "I heard the last half of your recording session, and it was perfect, Indy."

Holy hell, a real, genuine compliment that has nothing to do with trying to make me feel better about not being able to see my feet and days away from pushing a baby out of my body...

It's the unicorn of compliments and, instantly, I soften around the edges. "You really liked it?"

"Loved it," he says and sits down beside Don, the producer of New Rules's next album. He pats him on the back and grins. "Tell her, Donnie. It was perfect, yeah?"

"That it was," he agrees with a quick glance and smile in my direction. "You and Mac brought your A game."

Even in my cranky, uncomfortable, far-too-sweaty for doing nothing but standing here pregnancy state, I can't not smile at that.

Six months ago, Bram came to me with an idea.

One that involved adding a small violin composition to the beginning of one of the tracks on New Rules's next album. At first, I outright said no. But then, once good ol' Mac Davis jumped on the bandwagon, I had to agree. *Seriously.* The only answer my stubborn, music-loving dad would take was yes.

And two months later, my dad and I composed something we were really proud of, and thankfully, New Rules loved.

Despite my initial resistance, I'm so thankful I ended up doing it. The whole process, working with my dad, creating music with my dad, has been a dream. An incredibly special and unforgettable experience.

Just over two years ago, I was a music teacher at a small private school in the Bronx, and I couldn't even look at the violin. And now, I'm playing the violin every day and composing music for one of the most popular bands in the country.

Life is crazy, I tell you. Just crazy.

But life is also really draining when you're carrying around a full-term baby inside your body. My feet ache inside my sandals, and I glance down to see the familiar puffy and swollen appearance that has become a staple of my life for the past few months.

"All right," I announce and snag my purse from the closet. "I'm going to head home and relax a bit."

Bram stands up to give me a big hug. "Love ya, sis."

"Love you too."

"And tell your sister I say hello." He winks and flashes a little grin in my direction, and a laugh escapes my throat.

"Yeah, I'll be sure to forget that."

"C'mon, Indy," he teases. "Just tell your beautiful sister I said hello."

The *last* thing my sister Lily needs is Bram Bray.

He's good-looking, of course, and charming, most definitely, but he is trouble with a capital T. And my sister gets into enough trouble as it is.

I'm just thankful Ansel and I didn't end up having the big wedding we'd originally planned. Who knows what would have happened if Bram had a whole week of wedding activities to work his magic on Lil.

"Yeah, okay," I say with a roll of my eyes. "I'll be sure to tell her."

"Promise?"

"Goodbye, Don!" I call over my shoulder as I turn for the door and promptly ignore my brother-in-law.

"Indy!" Bram shouts toward me on a laugh. "You better promise!"

"Bye, Bram!"

I open the door, and his responding chuckles follow me until I'm in the hallway and heading for the elevator.

When I spot Hank waiting for me outside, I sigh with relief.

Thank God.

The last thing this big preggo body wants to do is stand around and wait, or worse, walk several blocks because he can't find a spot near the doors.

I swear I'm not usually such a diva, but I'm nine-and-half months pregnant. Surely, that provides me with some kind of free pass to be intolerable.

"Afternoon, Indy." Hank greets me with his familiar friendly smile and helps me into the car with a gentle hand. Once he ensures I'm safely inside, he starts the engine and pulls out into the road, heading for home in Greenwich Village.

New York passes me by in a blur of skyscrapers and taxi cabs and people hurrying in various directions, and eventually, my mind slowly drifts off to one very special day that ended in "I do."

It was less than a year ago, and Ansel had pretty much had it with our moms' meddling and trying to plan our wedding. Between the flowers and invitations and all the people they wanted to invite, he was done with all of it. Not to mention the whole part about the press latching on to the idea that Ansel Bray was marrying *the girl in the painting*.

Once we had to start talking about having security on our wedding day, my soon-to-be husband needed an escape.

A weekend getaway, he said.

I agreed, even though I didn't really have a choice. Once Ansel sets his mind to something, he's determined and nearly impossible to budge.

So, I gave him free rein, thinking he'd pick somewhere like the Bahamas or Hawaii, somewhere tropical where we could just lounge around on the beach all day and drink piña coladas. Someplace where we could wrap ourselves inside a warm, cozy, picturesque bubble and forget about the rest of the world for a little while.

But I should've known. Bahamas, Hawaii, those aren't destinations for handsome, broody artists. Not even close.

A seven-hour flight later, we were in Paris.

And not even twenty-fours after we landed, Ansel was getting down on one knee in the Louvre, right in front of *Venus de Milo*, one of the most famous sculptures in the world.

He proposed to me...*again.*

I cried...*again.*

And of course, I said yes...*again.*

By the next day, we were married in this secret little garden in the center of the City of Love by an officiant named Luc.

Sure, our moms were pissed when we got back home and they found out we'd rained on their wedding-planning parade, but it didn't matter. Nothing could change the fact that the day I said "I do" to my handsome, broody husband was the very best day of my life.

It was just the two of us.

Unexpected and quiet and intimate.

Simply put, it was us. It was *perfect.* So perfect, in fact, it's the exact day the little bundle of joy inside my belly was created.

Yeah, life is definitely crazy. Insane and messy, even. But when you find the person you're meant to spend the rest of your life with, it's beautiful.

A beautiful mess of hope and kisses and smiles and just...*love.*

So much love.

Ansel

"Ansel?" Indy's voice filters up from the first floor of our house. "Where are you?"

"Upstairs! In the bathroom!" I call back and step out of the shower, grabbing a towel from the rack and starting the process of drying myself off.

Slow but sure, her footsteps make their way up the stairs and into our bedroom.

"I thought you were going to be in the Upper East Side studio all day?" she asks, and I hear the sounds of sandals being flipped off her feet.

Hell, I'm pretty sure they even hit the wall.

This grouchy demeanor of hers has become a staple over the past few weeks. It's pretty adorable and the idea of it makes me grin, but wisely, I keep my mouth shut about her mood *and* the wall. "I did, but I didn't end up staying as late as I thought I would."

If I'm being honest, I left earlier than I probably should've so I could be home with Indy. My beautiful wife has reached a point in her pregnancy where she is over being pregnant. Needless to say, she's ready for our daughter to make her big debut, and I just want to be here to support her, even if that means being her grouchy-remarks punching bag.

Our daughter.

God, sometimes, I still can't believe that this is my life.

That Indy is my wife.

That my days are filled with her smiles and her laughs and I can kiss her, touch her, hold her whenever I want to.

She is my own personal Cindy Lou Who. She brightens this Grinch's life and fills his heart with nothing but love. Hell, she has the power to turn this normally jaded, broody artist into a fucking heart-eyes emoji.

And fuck, I wouldn't change it for the world.

I peek out from the bathroom and watch as my wife flops herself onto our bed on a sigh.

"Tired?" I ask, and my ears are graced with another sigh.

"You have no idea."

"How did it go today?"

"Really good," she answers and grabs her pregnancy pillow from the edge of the bed. Once she's content with her position—on her side with the pillow beneath her belly and between her legs—she closes her eyes and snuggles further into the bed. "But I'm exhausted and ready for a nap."

"Did you eat lunch already?"

"No." She groans but doesn't even bother opening her eyes. "I need to, but hells bells, the idea of getting out of the bed and walking back downstairs sounds miserable."

"How about I bring you something up?" I grin and finish drying my hair with the towel in my hands. "A little lunch in bed."

"That would be amazing," she says on a relieved sigh. "Although, I should be bitching at you right now."

"Bitching at me?" I question with a furrowed brow *and* an amused grin. "For what, exactly?"

"For telling Bram I was on a rampage today."

Fucking Bram. Of course, he said that. The bastard.

"I didn't tell him that."

Well, not those words exactly. I might've mentioned Indy was in a "mood" today. But, in my defense, the morning hadn't gone all that smoothly. Her favorite sandals broke, and when she tried to get dressed, she found out her belly had officially outgrown most of her shirts.

She sobbed for a good five minutes in our walk-in closet, and I did my best to console her, but she wasn't having any of my complimentary words.

I told her she was beautiful, and she told me I was lying.

I told her I wasn't lying, and she told me I was annoying.

It was a bit of a rough start, but when it comes to Indy, I'm the most patient man in the world.

And I wasn't lying. Indy is beautiful.

And a pregnant Indy? Well, she's fucking breathtaking. All glowing skin and full curves and just...her round belly is carrying our baby. There is nothing more beautiful than that.

I toss on a pair of boxer briefs, a T-shirt, and jeans and crawl into bed beside my wife.

Her eyes are still closed, and I reach out to brush her hair behind her ear. "What sounds good for lunch?" I ask on a whisper, and she peeks her eyes open at me.

"Pancakes?"

I grin. "You want pancakes for lunch?"

She nods. "And some bacon."

"Okay."

"You'll make it for me?" Her voice is full of so much hope, I couldn't say no if I wanted to.

"Of course."

"And bring it up here?"

I grin. "Definitely."

"And feed it to me?"

I laugh at that. "You're wanting the five-star treatment, yeah?"

She smiles and shrugs. "Okay, so I'll feed myself, but you making it and bringing it up here would be a dream."

I reach out to place my hand over her belly. "Well, you know I'm a fan of making your dreams come true."

"If that's the case, then please tell our daughter to come out soon."

I pull up Indy's shirt, revealing her belly, and put my lips to her skin. "Hey there, little miss. Don't you think it's time to make your big debut? Even though we don't know what we're going to name you, we're ready to meet you."

Indy giggles. "But we *do* know what we're going to name her."

"We do?" My eyes perk up, and I rest my chin on Indy's belly to meet her gaze. "You've decided on a name?"

Indy nods. "I've decided."

Since I knew whatever my gorgeous wife decided to name our daughter would be perfect, I'd given her free rein on choosing. And for what feels like months and months, she's searched no less than a thousand names.

But as far as I knew, she'd yet to find *the one.*

"You've decided?" I ask and press a soft kiss to the bare skin of her belly. "Like, you're certain this is the name?"

"I'm certain." She nods, and a secret little smile kisses her pretty lips. "Our daughter's name will be Venus Lane Bray."

My heart skips a beat inside my chest, and I search Indy's eyes. "Why that name?"

"Well, Bray because it's our last name," she teases and I smirk.

"Yeah, I kind of figured that one."

"And Lane because of Adam," she says, soft as a whisper. "Fate brought us together, but I know he had a hand in it. In a crazy, unbelievable kind of way, if it weren't for him, I never would've found this kind of happiness. This kind of love."

Fuck. Any second, I'll be the heart-eyes emoji.

"And Venus?"

"Because not too long ago, someone told me Venus is the image of love. And this little baby inside of me," she says and places her hand over mine, "is the purest image of our love."

Venus Lane Bray.

A little girl who was created from love.

A little girl who will hopefully have her mother's big blue eyes and beautiful smile.

A little girl who already owns my heart.

"It's perfect, Indy," I whisper back and lean forward to press a soft kiss to my wife's lips. "I love it, and I love you."

Venus Lane Bray—a perfect name for our daughter.

Perfect like Indy is for me.

She found parts of me I didn't know existed, and in her, I've found a love I didn't know was possible.

THE END

Surely, after reading Ansel and Indy's story, you're ready for another love story that will steal your heart.
Don't worry, we have just what you need!
Prepare yourselves, things are about to get swoony, hilarious, and downright addictive!

Grab THE DAY I STOPPED FALLING FOR JERKS today and find out why readers are swooning all over the place for Oliver Arsen.

2019 has started off with a bang, and we are more than ready to keep the Max Monroe train moving. More characters for you to love.
More books for you to devour.
More laughs. More smiles. More swoons.
More hilarious starts to your Monday morning.
Wait…you don't know about our Monday Morning Distraction?
Find out why everyone is laughing their ass off every Monday morning with us.
Max Monroe's Monday Morning Distraction.
It's hilarity and entertainment in newsletter form.
Trust us, you don't want to miss it.
Stay up-to-date with our characters, us, and get your own copy of Monday Morning Distraction by signing up for our newsletter:
www.authormaxmonroe.com/#!contact/c1kcz

You may live to regret much, but we promise it won't be this.
If you're already signed up, consider sending us a message to tell us how much you love us. We really like that. ;)

Follow us online:

Website: www.authormaxmonroe.com

Facebook: www.facebook.com/authormaxmonroe

Reader Group: www.facebook.com/groups/1561640154166388

Twitter: www.twitter.com/authormaxmonroe

Instagram: www.instagram.com/authormaxmonroe

Goodreads: https://goo.gl/8VUIz2

Bookbub: www.bookbub.com/authors/max-monroe

Amazon: bit.ly/MMAmazonAuthor

acknowledgments

First of all, THANK YOU for reading. That goes for anyone who's bought a copy, read an ARC, helped us beta, edited, or found time in their busy schedule to help us out in any way.

Thank you for supporting us, for talking about our books, and for just being so unbelievably loving and supportive of our characters. You've made this our MOST favorite adventure thus far.

THANK YOU to Basil and Banana.

THANK YOU to our amazing readers.

THANK YOU to all of you awesome and supportive bloggers.

THANK YOU to our editor, Lisa.

THANK YOU to our beautiful formatter with beautiful formats, Stacey.

THANK YOU to Jenn and Sarah and Brooke and everyone else at Social Butterfly PR.

THANK YOU to our Camp Love Yourself Members.

THANK YOU to Ansel and Indy for inspiring us so much during the process of writing this book.

And last, but certainly not least, THANK YOU to our family.

Basically, thank you to everyone we love and adore! Our readers, our bloggers, our fellow authors, our entire team, just everyone!

We love you tons and tons and tons!

Max: Like a lot.

Monroe: Yes. Like *so* much.

Max: *Sooooo* much.

Monroe: Exactly. We love you *soooooooo* much.

Max: An insane amount of love.

Monroe: A crazy, insane, unbelievable amount of love for you guys.

Max: It's like if you could fit all of the love in the world into a bottle, we'd need at least five of those bottles.

Monroe: Probably more like twelve.

Max: You're right, we'd need twelve of those love bottles even to come close to how much love we have for you guys.

Monroe: A twelve-pack. Of love bottles. [looks at Max] I think we nailed it.

Max: [grins] And that's a wrap, ladies and gentlemen!

Seriously, thank you for letting us do what we love every single day. Our forever gratitude *and* a twelve-pack of love bottles,
Max Monroe

Printed in Great Britain
by Amazon

26029009R00159